A GLIMPSE BEYOND

J.D. SULLIVAN

aethonbooks.com

CHAPTER 1
NEW BEGINNINGS

DILLON HAD NEVER REALLY THOUGHT about it, but as it turned out, proving you're a time-traveler is a lot tougher than it sounds.

It hadn't been much easier to convince himself, honestly. He and Sherisza had arrived some seventy years before the time they'd left, but if it wasn't for Daevol tapping into newsfeeds, Dillon wouldn't have known. The crushing weight of the time shift had left him unconscious, as massive usages of the Chrono Drive often did, but in the vast expanse of space, there wasn't anything that stood out to say they'd gone back in time. Only the digital clock–the one that let Dillon know what time it was back home on Earth–going haywire said anything was amiss.

For her part, Sherisza had seemed unperturbed about the entire ordeal. Dillon had no idea how many times she had gone forward or back through history. By her words, this was the first time she had gone back, and she had only gone forward the once, jumping those six years ahead to avoid the plague that had wiped out her people and planet. He'd expected going back to her home world in the past and seeing it repopulated might be too much for her to take, but she hadn't hesitated at all.

Mostly, it had to do with them being so far back in the past. She and her sibling hadn't even been born yet, so there was little to anchor her in this different time. She had brought them down to Kiandar with Daevol's help, the ship's AI guiding her past sentries and trackers and anything else that might've led to them having to answer a lot of uncomfortable questions. From there, she had begun the work of finding those people history had said disappeared without a trace, to see if they had, in fact, come forward to the "present" aboard her ship.

It was a lot for Dillon to wrap his mind around. Sherisza had spent months going through records and history, trying to identify people who might have disappeared *because she'd gone back in time and rescued them.* Per her twin brother's theories, history had to account for any changes made by time travelers, and so that had given Sherisza a place to start looking. Now, she was trying to convince those people to come "back" to her and Dillon's present time, beyond the ravages of the plague, to repopulate Kiandar and its people.

It hadn't been easy, though. The first groups, not surprisingly, hadn't believed she was a time traveler until Sherisza risked bringing them aboard her ship, the *Malshekt*, where the proof lay in digital records. Even still, it had taken a great deal of convincing to get them to agree to abandon their lives and go forward in time. Only the gravity of what had happened to Kiandar and the afterimages of the near-total annihilation of the Kiandarian people had done it.

And reliving the finding of her dead family had torn Sherisza's heart out. Dillon was angry that she'd had to and yet proud that she was willing to do so to save her people. She was an exceptional woman, and he was proud to be her mate, different species though they were.

The lioness woman of Kiandar had a holodisplay in front of her now, working through the schematics of their phase-cloaking device. It would be necessary for future rescues; if anyone saw the *Malshekt*, it could get them captured or destroyed or asked a lot of questions about time travel. Secrecy would be the lifeblood of these rescue missions, and Dillon knew Sherisza wanted to complete her project rather than buy cloaking technology from someone else.

"How's that warp inverter looking?" he asked.

Sherisza glanced at him, those golden eyes shining. "I have a good feeling about this, Dillon. As off-the-cuff as your suggestion may have felt, you were on the right track. Daevol and I are working through turning the theory into reality. I suspect we may have a design for the prototype in a few days, and then we can fine-tune things from there."

"Well, we've got time before we get back to Kiandar," he said.

They did have that, at least. They were cruising along at standard warp speed, letting the Chrono Drive take a break from bending or folding time. The slower speed accomplished several other ends as well. It allowed the two families they'd rescued to try to catch up on where they were in the future; it helped avoid suspicion from the governments of the known galaxy over where they were rescuing those Kiandarians from; and it further gave Dillon's parents time to quell the uproar over his having killed the president of the Quarran Dominion.

Dillon was still working through that himself. He didn't feel bad about it, though he was sure he never wanted to shoot someone in the head again. President MacNault had been behind the biological weapon that had nearly exterminated the entire Kiandarian race, and all over some religious belief that they were a lesser creation and somehow evil for being able to crossbreed with humans. When the man had threatened and, indirectly, tried to kill Sherisza, the last of her kind, Dillon had to do something.

And do something he had.

He'd saved her life and her race, and she had in turn saved his life before anyone had been able to take him–or them–into custody. After that, they had cast their inhibitions aside, no longer denying their feelings for each other. Now, she considered Dillon her mate, and though he was still sorting through the details in his mind, he was thinking of marrying her and having children. It was incredible how much his life had changed in just a few months. And it all went back to this brilliant Kiandarian woman picking him out of half a million or more applicants to be her apprentice.

<Captain, two Kwaagi fighters are on an intercept course.>

Dillon instinctively looked up at the sound of the AI's voice, but the message didn't make him nervous at all. The Kwaagi were a reptilian race, like upright, bipedal dinosaur folk, but they were friendly to Sherisza and Dillon. They had agreed to defend Kiandar from any sort of intrusions, whether by thieves, scavengers, or vengeful members of the Quarran Dominion. And so, Dillon flicked a switch on his front console three times, flashing the *Malshekt*'s lights in greeting to the approaching escorts.

The Kwaagi fighter pilots executed a stunning rollover maneuver in salute before taking places on either side of the *Malshekt*. Whatever most people thought of reptilian races, the Kwaagi military was second to none and its fighter pilots were incredible. Thanks to the work Dillon and Sherisza had done on two of their twenty-one-ship wings and to the rescue of one of their emperor's distant nieces, the Kwaagi were quite protective of Sherisza, her ship, and her planet. And, of course, her mate.

"Captain Rousilarru, we have been dispatched to escort you to Outer Dock Seventeen orbiting your world of Kiandar," came the message over the hailing frequency. The Kwaagi spoke with some hisses, drawn-out S sounds, clacking of their teeth, and clucking of the tongue against the roof of the mouth. To the translator chip Dillon had installed behind his left ear, though, they may as well have been speaking perfect Terran English.

"Acknowledged. Thank you for your protection, gentlemen," Sherisza said.

"You guys want to come over for dinner? We're grilling some steaks tonight," Dillon joked. He was answered only by uncharacteristic hissing laughter from the fighter pilots.

"Our galley is already quite crowded these days," Sherisza commented.

"Could be worse, we could be eating and sleeping on the flight deck for days like those guys do," he said with a nod toward the Kwaagi fighter off the starboard side.

Still, what she'd said was true. With two Kiandarian families, each comprised of four, it was a tight squeeze to get everyone into the galley to share a meal. But that was something Sherisza insisted on. Just as she enjoyed cooking for herself and Dillon, she did so for their passengers as well. It was a tradition among their people, one the guest families obviously appreciated, though they remained a bit stiff around Dillon. None of them had ever met a human before, and they didn't speak or understand a word of Terran English, so it was strange to them to share a meal with him.

The fact that Sherisza considered Dillon her mate did little to alleviate the awkwardness, but no one was rude about it, at least. Dillon was glad the families got time to come out of their cabins, as two adults and two children per cabin was easily as cramped as the galley. At the least, the children were allowed to play together in Dillon's old cabin, the one he'd stopped using once Sherisza had invited him to stay in hers. What the other Kiandarians thought of that, Dillon preferred not to think about, because ultimately it didn't matter.

"Are they going to settle in your old hometown?" Dillon asked at length.

Sherisza blew out a sigh. "Yes, because that is where the cleanup began. Our friends in the Kystar Alliance have already gotten the essential utilities online again, so the town will have all the amenities it needs for them to begin subsistence programs. Once we have enough of my people to populate the town, it should be able to farm and keep its water and power supplies going. From there, it will be a matter of growing the population, but that will take time."

"I don't doubt it. Your people didn't often have more than one set of twins, did they?"

"Not typically, unless one or both children perished for whatever reason. Our population was slow to build compared to your own," she said. "With such a limited genetic pool and our predisposition to have only one pair of children, repopulating Kiandar will not be easy. But we have hope, and a future, and that... that is in part thanks to you, Dillon."

He smiled but looked around the side of his chair. The corridor of the *Malshekt* was quiet, the other couples and their children tucked in their cabins. "How many children did you want to have with me?" he asked when he turned back to her.

Sherisza let a little sigh out of her leonine nose, reaching across her console to run her clawed fingers down the photo clipped to its front. It was a picture of her twin brother, Daevol—after whom the ship's AI was named—riding on a rope swing with Sherisza's children. She was still rattled by their deaths, along with those of all her people, but she was healing now. Having gone back to Kiandar to properly memorialize them had helped her a lot.

Not to mention finally seeing the man responsible dead.

When she turned back to Dillon, her face was downturned a bit in her blushing pose. "As many as we can," she said quietly.

The answer put a warmth in Dillon's already hot-blooded, nineteen-year-old heart. Never in a million years would he have guessed he'd end up in love with a Kiandarian, or that he'd be thinking about having children before he was technically legal to drink alcohol back home. But as he thought of the children already on board, the echo of the sound of little feet padding up and down the corridor of the ship played through his mind and his heart, and it felt right. Their relationship may have only been a few months old, but everything about it felt right.

"So, a pair every year?" he asked.

Her ears perked up at that. "Oh, no. Every third year at the most. As I told you, Dillon, my people only go into season in the autumn, and not while we are nursing children. So, it would likely be only every third year."

"And we could start a couple of months from now?"

Sherisza shrugged. "If you like. I know you and, more pointedly, your parents wanted to see you finish your law degree before we did so. I can be patient, especially now that my dream of rescuing my people from the past has become reality."

"I'm sure you've noticed, but teenaged humans aren't exactly known for patience," he said, and she chuckled. "I think we should let God... or your goddess... decide."

"I am agreeable to that."

Dillon released the harness of his co-pilot's seat. "Daevol, you mind flying us for a while? I think it's time we got dinner started."

<As you wish, Commander.>

Sherisza got up, too, and while they had the flight deck and corridor to themselves, she and Dillon shared a long, passionate kiss.

———

Dillon had only had his translation chip for a few months, but it already felt like a lifetime ago that he couldn't understand others. It made meals a little tedious, as Sherisza had to interpret his words to their guests, but he was glad to at least be able to chat, however slowly, with the Kiandarians. They were immensely curious about humans, doubly so because they knew he was sleeping with Sherisza, and Dillon tried to tell them as much as he could without painting either too bright or too dark a picture.

The Enarrii Conflict was a constant focus of their chatter, these Kiandarians having come from before that war had even happened. They didn't know the Enarrii any more than they knew humankind, so to find their world had technically gone to war against both required Sherisza to do a lot of explaining. It was just as well to Dillon, since he knew little about that war himself, and he got to see how the Kiandarians had viewed it and, as a result, humanity. There was still much he didn't know, but he had learned quite a bit. Not surprisingly, he found Kiandarians had learned to treat humans with the same suspicion humans often treated each other.

In the end, he could sense their guests were pleased that the conflict had ended and there had been peace between Kiandar and Earth. They certainly seemed to take Dillon's and Sherisza's relationship in a new light after that, though their customs were different. They were courteous enough to say nothing, probably because they knew he could understand them. Had they been able to hide their words behind Sherisza's interpreting, they may have said far more. Dillon tried not to worry about it either way.

When the meal was finished, Dillon took the children to his old cabin and introduced them to *Galactic Command*. They were old enough to appreciate a good starship battle game, yet young enough that they didn't care that the game was human-centric. It also helped that humanity was fighting some bug creatures from the reaches rather than any of the races they shared the known galaxy with. The children did get rowdy at times, though. Much like the lion cubs they resembled to a degree, they were playful and energetic, and none of them wanted to leave when their parents came to get them. Only Dillon's promise to play with them again the following day earned their parents a reprieve, and he sighed wistfully as they left.

His children by Sherisza probably wouldn't look like him, he knew. How much of his cocoa skin and startling green eyes would bleed through to them was a mystery. But the more time he spent with the Kiandarian youngsters, the less it mattered—and it hadn't mattered all that much to begin with. Even if they looked fully leonine like their mother, they'd be beautiful, and he knew his own mother's heart would melt the first time she held them. That made him think of his grandmothers, Malinda and Ruth, and how excited they'd be to have great-grandchildren. It might take a bit of explaining why the children were lion cubs, but they'd love them, Dillon had no doubts.

He must've had a hell of a smile on his face when he emerged from his cabin, because Sherisza's mirrored it when she saw him. She held her hand out toward him and Dillon took it before he leaned down and shared a deep but short kiss with her. It was still a tad awkward to kiss a lioness, but it felt more and more natural every time, and Dillon could feel the love in her kisses. He scratched behind one of her ears playfully, and she chuckled before she leaned in and rubbed her muzzle along his cheek.

He took his seat beside her, though when cruising at warp speed on a designated course, there wasn't much flying for them to do. It was too early to think of going to bed, though, and he was happy to spend some time beside her outside their room.

Dillon glanced at the two Kwaagi fighters flying escort beside them, and he felt bad that they were stuck on their ships alone for a multi-day journey. As much as Dillon loved flying the stars and seeing the galaxy, he couldn't imagine doing it alone.

"Are we dropping them off at Outer Dock Seventeen?" he asked, then cursed himself for interrupting. He hadn't realized she'd brought up her schematics for the phase-cloaking device and was already making minute changes.

She smiled but didn't stop her work. "Yes, they will be briefed there on what to expect from the Kwaagi and Kystar who are still at work on the planet below. The Kwaagi emperor was not content to merely have an airborne presence; he has insisted on keeping soldiers on the ground as unobtrusively as possible to safeguard the new settlers."

"He's really going all-in to help you," Dillon said.

Sherisza showed a little bit of fang. "Yes, enough so that he is irritating the heads of the Quarran Dominion. While the Kystar archaeologists and anthropologists have been allowed consistent access to chronicle history and save as much of my people's records as they can, the Kwaagi have not allowed any Dominion presence at all. And, obviously, the Dominion are not happy that we will be returning to Kiandar without being apprehended to answer inquiries about killing President MacNault."

"There's gonna be a reckoning over that at some point," he agreed. "I'm pretty sure it'll happen on Earth, though, and my parents—or at least my father—will represent us. I hate to say we'll *get away with it*, because that's not accurate, but we shouldn't be in any trouble."

"I am more worried about retaliation against my people than myself," she said.

"Well, good thing we have the Kwaagi watching over them," Dillon said. "But you know, a while back, Daevol said you had been inoculated against the plague... do you still have whatever you used as a vaccine?"

"Its formula is stored in the replicator logs," she answered. "I am not certain of its efficacy, but I suppose it would be prudent to give it to our guests, no?"

"Exactly what I was thinking. We can give it to them in the morning."

"Good. Here, let me show you what I am working on."

Dillon squinted at the schematics, his mind going in every different direction as surely as the designs on the screen. "That's going to be well beyond me."

"Not for long. Come closer and listen."

CHAPTER 2

RUMBLINGS

IT WAS hard to leave the families behind on Outer Dock Seventeen. Though they knew of the Kwaagi, they were as unfamiliar with the reptilian folk as Dillon had been. They'd be staying aboard the mobile defense station in orbit of Kiandar for a few days, getting brought up to speed on what to expect, just as Sherisza had said. Soon enough, though, their trepidation would turn to excitement as they went down to colonize this new version of their world.

We'd just better not leave them alone for too long, Dillon thought.

As much as everyone liked to pretend they'd love to be the last person in the world as long as there were books to read, it wasn't true. People needed people, they needed friendships and interactions and even a good argument or fight now and then. It would take some time, but before too long, Dillon and Sherisza would deliver enough people to form a community. And for whatever differences they had on account of being from various times, they would all be Kiandarian, and hopefully, the future of their people would be their primary concern.

"Outer Dock Seventeen to *Malshekt*," came the voice of the

Kwaagi flight director, piercing through Dillon's thoughts.

"Go ahead," Sherisza said.

"Captain Rousilarru, there are Dominion warships in the area. They are keeping their distance from the planet, but you should engage the Daevol Drive from minimum safe distance to evade any trouble."

"Acknowledged, thank you," she answered.

Everyone else still called it the Daevol Drive, unaware that it was a time-travel device in any capacity. Aboard the ship, Dillon and Sherisza had begun calling it the Chrono Drive to soothe the apparent "feelings" of the AI. It was dangerous to use it too close to heavenly bodies or other ships and stations, but Sherisza was more than familiar with its range and limitations. She brought them a little way from the station and then engaged it, their course laid out for the reaches beyond Kwaagi space again.

No one knew where Sherisza and Dillon were rescuing Kiandarians from, but as far as the two could tell, everyone had the good grace not to ask. Sherisza had resolved to go to the reaches beyond Kwaagi space before each trip back through time, to return there a few days later and leave little trail for anyone to follow. Even the bravest of explorers avoided the reaches, and that allowed them to keep up the pretense and mystery, at least for the time being.

Thankfully, for the trip out to the reaches, Sherisza could put the Chrono Drive to its typical use. Whereas they'd traveled at standard warp speed when escorted by the two Kwaagi fighters, now they traveled at roughly five times that speed—and that barely put any strain on the drive. Rather than a more than three-day trip across Kwaagi space, they would arrive in the reaches in roughly sixteen hours. Enough time to have a bite, explore some intimacy, and get a good night's rest before they started their next mission through time.

Sherisza made no mystery about her expectations. She had hardly risen from her seat before she began getting undressed, and she walked to their cabin door, flashing Dillon that little smile over her shoulder. They had refrained from any love-making while they had guests aboard, wary of making things any more awkward for the refugees than they already were. On that note, Dillon let Sherisza decide when and where they would be intimate. Kiandarians were different in their family structure, with twin siblings raising children that the females had by other men. Sherisza was mindful of their guests, so she and Dillon slept together, but that was it.

Now, though, she clearly signaled she wanted to explore their intimacy for the second time. Lord knew they'd waited long enough by Dillon's reckoning. "You're in control, Daevol," he said as he released the harnesses of his seat.

<Acknowledged. Have fun, you two.>

"And turn off your connection to her chip," Dillon added. He could appreciate that the AI was always monitoring Sherisza, but not when they were making love. Not only was Daevol able to monitor her life signs, but he could also see and hear everything she could and record it. That wasn't something Dillon was interested in at all, whether he trusted the AI or not.

The AI issued a dramatic sigh. <If you insist.>

Dillon snickered and entered his and Sherisza's cabin. She was already undressed, sitting on her heels up in their bed. Dillon tried to strut in all cool and nonchalant, but Sherisza began to laugh into her hand, so he dropped the act and chuckled at himself. He got undressed and appreciated every second of her ogling him before he climbed up and sat beside her in their bed. He leaned in toward her as she rubbed her muzzle along his cheek, all the way to her ear.

Dillon cupped the side of her head and kissed her. Her tongue was larger than his and her fangs were still a curiosity, but he savored these little moments with her. He rubbed his cheek against the side of her face like she usually did to him, taking in the scents of her fur, her hair, her breath. She had such a myriad of smells about her, but all of them were pleasant, warm, and inviting even to his weak human sniffer.

It already felt like a lifetime ago that they had been together, but it came back to Dillon in no time. He let her lead him, intent on making sure she drew the line where she wanted it. This was all still so new to him, and he was almost desperate not to make any mistakes. She was cautious and patient, too, as though afraid she might upset him. When their eyes finally met again, there was naught in hers but trust and love.

They made love slowly, each moving in perfect time with the other, his hands wandering her body just as hers caressed his back. She dragged her claws along his skin, but just enough to tease, not scratch, and Dillon caressed her in turn, trying to make sure she was satisfied completely. He spent much of the time looking into those golden eyes of hers, still entranced and bewildered by the love that shone in them. He and Sherisza seemed an unlikely pair, but despite what his being a teenage human said, he didn't feel like this was just lust. The look in her eyes said the same was true for her part.

By the time their intimate dance was complete, she had her arms around his neck, and she was panting and purring in alternating rhythms. Then she whispered his name again, and he lay his head on her breasts, closed his eyes, and fell asleep to the rumbling of her happiness.

———

Dillon wasn't sure how long they'd slept when something rocked the ship. Alarms began to blare, and Sherisza slipped out from under Dillon and rushed from their cabin without bothering to dress. Dillon might've done the same, but he was mindful of one of her first rules when he had become her apprentice, so he at least put on his underpants before he followed her.

Something struck the ship and rocked it violently, and Dillon smacked his face on the back of his chair as he tried to get to it. He tried to shake off the stars, which didn't help, but he got himself seated and buckled in.

"Who's attacking? Dominion?"

<Negative. We are still traveling under the Chrono Drive. My apologies, Captain. I did not expect to have to scan for enemies while in the time stream.>

The *Malshekt* took another hit before Sherisza grabbed the controls and began evasive maneuvers. Daevol brought up the HUD and several holodisplays, and Dillon scanned them all, trying to get a glimpse of their assailant. He finally spotted some odd black ship, nearly invisible against the backdrop of space. It wasn't Kwaagi or Dominion based on the first look, but whose it was didn't much matter. The fact that it kept firing on the *Malshekt* was the first concern.

Thankfully, the *Malshekt*'s shields were able to absorb much of the power of the enemy's weapons, though some of it was getting through. The HUD was indicating damage to the rear of the ship, close enough to the conventional thruster engines to be an issue. More importantly than that, the HUD now had a targeting reticle around the enemy ship. It was still orange as Daevol tried to establish a lock, but Dillon didn't wait.

He flipped the little switch that allowed their Kwaagi disruptor cannons to fire backwards and began taking pot shots at their pursuer without a target lock. The enemy ship evaded all of his shots, though only until Sherisza anticipated one of its dodges and she jolted the *Malshekt* in time with the enemy movement. The Kwaagi disruptors hit the enemy ship head on, and Dillon waited for it to come apart and send its pilot screaming through space at beyond warp speed.

But nothing appeared to happen. The enemy ship broke off pursuit, but as Dillon enhanced the rear-view holodisplay, he could see its lights were still on and it was still moving under its pilot's control. Whatever that ship was, its shielding was strong enough to deflect or at least dampen the damage of a Kwaagi disruptor, and that didn't bode well for anyone.

Sherisza apparently felt the same way, because she brought the *Malshekt* about and took over control of the guns. She flew right at the enemy ship, and Dillon watched as the targeting reticle turned green and began to spin. The ion cannon wasn't charged enough for its disabling blast, but the way Sherisza's finger hovered over the trigger of the disruptors, Dillon knew she had no interest in taking prisoners. She had just started to depress the trigger when the enemy ship disappeared entirely.

"*Maqua!*" she cursed.

"Language, Sherisza," Dillon teased, though he wasn't feeling as humorous as the instinctive reply suggested. "Why don't we slip out of the time stream and see if we can chase him down?"

Sherisza shook her head. "We have no idea where in time he came out, and we could be ambushed by even more such ships. I am going to change our course to the reaches."

"Did either of you recognize that ship?"

<Negative. It did not fit any class or designation in my catalogue.>

"And you know what this means?" Sherisza prompted. Dillon could only shake his head. "It means it came from the reaches somewhere... or some*when*."

"So, someone out in the reaches has similar technology," Dillon mused.

"I have never so much as seen another ship in the time

stream, much less fought within it. We are fortunate that their weapons are not as advanced as their drive technology, or we might not be having this conversation. But why would they just attack?"

<Logic would suggest they did not like coming across an unidentified ship that has the same technology they did.>

"So, they shoot first and ask questions later? That's pretty asinine," Dillon said.

"Agreed. Daevol, extend sensors to maximum range even while in the time stream. Let us know if anything else appears," Sherisza said.

<Affirmative, Captain.>

"You heading to the shower?" Dillon asked.

Sherisza sighed and shook her head, exasperated. "I think I am going to hit the heavy bag for a while before I take a shower. You are welcome to join me for both, of course."

The thought of hitting something had plenty of appeal. "I think I will. Let's just get dressed first," he said, drawing a short huff of amusement from her.

———

Sherisza was still hitting the heavy bag an hour later, and though he had long since worked out any frustration of his own, Dillon alternated turns with her. She had a mean punch, and he noted her gloves had thick padding on the inside to mitigate her claws. It was possible she was just getting in some exercise now, but whatever the case, he didn't see fit to interrupt her flow of thought with questions or suggestions. He let her work out what was bothering her but stayed nearby in case she needed to talk.

Eventually, she punched herself out. After giving herself a vigorous shake, she hopped up and down a couple of times before stretching. "That feels better," she said. "We have been cramped in our quarters or the flight deck far too much these last few days."

"I guess we have, haven't we? At least we got that time together before that dumbass started taking shots at us," Dillon said.

"When we return to the normal time stream, I will contact the Kwaagi and send them the data we have on that ship. It may be something they are familiar with due to their proximity to the reaches. In the meantime, I had best redouble my efforts on the phase-cloaking device, and you and I can work at further amplifying our shields."

"Sure. I guess it's a good thing that guy didn't have Kwaagi weapons."

"Not much more than standard blasters, like the *Malshekt* had before the Kwaagi upgraded our weaponry," she agreed. "While fortunate, I also cannot help but think it points to someone having copied my design. But who?"

"That ship didn't look like the *Malshekt*, though. Not enough to make me think they were made by the same designer or just based on the same design," Dillon said.

"No, but then, it probably did not have amenities such as guest cabins, a full lavatory, or a kitchen, among other things," she countered. "That may have been a copy of my design, but one intended solely for attack."

"You know, it really sucks not being popular out here."

She let a bit of fang show in amusement but didn't laugh. "Daevol, are you able to compare that enemy ship to our own with the data you gathered?"

<To an extent, Captain. It was of similar enough design to the *Malshekt*; however, I was unable to gather data on how it entered the time stream. I cannot say for certain whether it uses the same type of Chrono Drive as the *Malshekt* does.>

"We have a mystery on our hands," she commented.

"Well, we haven't been attacked again, so that's a positive," Dillon said. "If nothing else happens, we check with the Kwaagi like you said. And if they don't know anything, then maybe we just use the reaches in a different direction as our jumping-off point."

"Yes, that would make the most sense. I am nervous, though... what if someone went to Kiandar and stole the design of the Chrono Drive from my home while I was avoiding it? There could already be some other malefactor with my technology seeking to continue MacNault's goal of wiping my people out. All of Kiandar could be in danger again if they can bring the plague forward in the same manner we bring my people forward! Someone could even–"

"Hey, hey," Dillon said, approaching to wrap her up in a hug. "Don't go getting yourself all worked up yet. You've got friends and allies now, Sherisza, and we're not going to let that sort of thing happen ever again, got it? Like you're always telling me... be patient. We'll figure it out, and we'll have plenty of help."

She nodded and let forth a breath, then stroked the side of his face. "Yes, thank you."

"On the other hand, if we don't stop getting attacked, my parents may take us hostage and lock us in a bomb shelter somewhere." She laughed at that, and Dillon pulled her close and kissed her again. "Do you want to get straight to work or have a shower and dinner first?"

Sherisza shook her head. "No, we should see to our needs first. I feel we are exposed now, though, and it is not a feeling I appreciate."

"I don't know, I certainly appreciate seeing you exposed."

She gave him a love tap to the sternum. "Well, come on then."

CHAPTER 3
THE UNKNOWN

THEY ENJOYED a meal and then a shower, the latter being romantic despite a lack of physical intimacy. Soon enough, though, Sherisza was back in her seat on the flight deck, a holodisplay before her so she could work on the design of the phase-cloaking device. Dillon sat beside her, listening to her preoccupied chatter that was mostly aimed at herself. They hadn't gotten much sleep after their lovemaking, but she was still too worked up, even after a workout and a shower, to go back to bed just yet.

Dillon tried to pick up as much as he could about the device and its workings, but as usual, the theories were all beyond him. She was working with focusing crystals and compounds he didn't have the foggiest idea about, but he did recognize many of the other components. Any machine, no matter how complex and how technologically advanced, had to have some of the same base components, and he concentrated on that. If nothing else, he'd be able to build the shell and the acting parts for her while she concocted the part that made it all work.

He had to laugh at himself, as he found it sexy to watch her at work. She was beautiful, athletic, and sensual, but she was also astonishingly brilliant, and he found that just as attractive, if not more so. His amusement multiplied as he considered she was beautiful, intelligent, *and* rich, ticking off all the boxes that would please his parents except the one that said *human*. But even then, his parents liked her, they at least pretended to be satisfied that the two of them were happy, and whatever they thought, Dillon didn't care one bit that she was Kiandarian. She was his, and he was in love with her, he was sure of it.

She looked over at him as if sensing his thoughts and smiled. "I am not keeping you awake, am I? Feel free to go get some rest. I will not be at this much longer, I think," she said despite what he'd been thinking.

"I like watching you work almost as much as I like working with you," he told her. He thought it sounded corny once he'd said it, and he hoped she didn't feel the same way.

"You are very sweet," she said with her little smile.

"How smart was Daevol?" he asked, drawing a curious gaze from her. "I mean, you're brilliant, Sherisza, but you talk about him like he was a genius compared to you."

"He was."

"Sherisza..."

She shook her head. "As I have explained, Dillon, I build things, but Daevol was the one who figured out how to make any of it work. He discovered how to rend the very veil of *time*, and that is something I still, to this day, cannot make any sense out of. I know what the Chrono Drive is built from and how to put it together, but I do not understand why it works at all."

He gestured toward the schematic before them. "You're building this without him."

"True," she conceded with a little half-shrug. "Yet even this is partially based on theories he and others have discovered and distilled."

"Daevol, a little help here?" Dillon prompted the AI. "How smart was the guy you're named after? And how many degrees did he have?"

<Daevol Rousilarru was graduated from the Grand Royal Academy of Sciences with the equivalent of Terran Doctorate Degrees in Theoretical Physics, Astrophysics, Astronomy, Physics, Chemistry, and Mathematics. In human terms, he would have had an IQ of nearly one hundred and eighty.>

"Holy crap," Dillon blurted, almost tempted to ask if he'd misheard the AI. Instead, he prompted, "What about Sherisza?"

She flashed Dillon a sour look, but the AI answered anyway. <As I told you before, she was graduated from the Grand Royal Academy of Sciences with Mastery Degrees in Engineering, Mechanical Sciences, and Astronavigation. Her IQ is roughly one hundred and fifty-five by the same standard.>

"Damn, girl!" Dillon said, turning to look at her, and her sour look melted away into a blush. "I knew you were brilliant. That's got to be a lot higher than mine, I expect. What's mine, Daevol, about a buck twenty?"

<Roughly one hundred and thirty per your academic records.>

Dillon blinked, shocked.

"Quite a bit higher than average," Sherisza commented. "This, too, was a consideration when I chose you as my apprentice. You are adaptable and learn quickly, two important traits where teaching you my craft was concerned. Yet you have more than exceeded my expectations thus far. Do not set my brother on too high a pedestal, Dillon. Though we may not see the universe the way he did, we can use his research to bring his ideas to life."

"Yeah, and we have a bag of it in the back," he said, Sherisza's brow rising. "Did I forget to mention that? Things were hectic after that first visit to Kiandar and everything that happened with MacNault. But when we visited your old home, I grabbed Daevol's notebooks, pads, laptop units, and computer cores. I put them in a storage locker in the back."

Sherisza's mouth dropped open a little. "Right, how could I have forgotten? We should begin uploading all of it into Daevol's memory banks. That would unlock a lot of potential with an AI assisting us with his considerable computing power. It would also make it far less likely that any of it will fall into the wrong hands."

"I assume there's some way we can scan the notebooks in?" Dillon asked.

"Yes, Daevol will be able to optically scan in written notes. The cores and laptop units can be plugged directly into the terminal in engineering. But that can wait until after we have gotten some rest, I think. I am losing my concentration and do not want to make mistakes in these schematics."

"Well, let's clean up and get some sleep, then. Hopefully, nothing else takes shots at us while we're in the time stream."

"Indeed."

They went to the lavatory and got ready for bed, and Dillon found it was even fun to share the time with her just brushing their teeth and her mane. When they returned to their cabin, they curled up together in bed. With Sherisza's head on his chest, purring softly, Dillon didn't stay awake too long despite the tumultuous thoughts swirling through his mind. And yet despite what had happened, it wasn't the violence of the day that fought for dominance.

One hundred and fifty-five and one hundred and eighty? Damn...

———

After breakfast, Dillon spent a while helping Daevol scan in his namesake's notebooks from the terminal in engineering. It was a bit tedious, but it didn't take long for the AI to scan each page, at least. There was so much to do, though, Daevol Rousilarru having filled numerous books with everything from theoretical math to quick sketches of designs to questions about whether he was really alive or just a part of his Goddess' imagination.

Dillon laughed at the last of those. He couldn't help but think even a deity would be a bit confused by the things that had run through Sherisza's brother's head. He was of a brilliance that could sometimes lead people to go mad, their brains going in too many different directions at all times, unable to sit still and appreciate life for what it was. Based on the pictures and videos Dillon had seen, though, the man had enjoyed life with his twin sister and their children. And he had sired a pair of his own with another woman, so he'd lived a complete life, even though it had been cut well short by the bio-engineered plague.

I can only imagine how smart his children had been before they were murdered...

Most curious to Dillon were notes about a region of the galaxy that Daevol had referred to as the Doorstep of the Goddess. It reminded him of what the man had said when he told Sherisza he'd figured out how to build the Chrono Drive. He had mused about taking his people to the very doorstep of the Goddess' realm, though Sherisza had insisted "not without invitation." Had the man been talking purely theology, or was there a place in the galaxy that was so uniquely beautiful and impossible to figure out that Daevol had thought it might be Heaven?

"Daevol, see if you can figure out what your namesake was talking about here with all this stuff about the Doorstep of the

Goddess," Dillon said while he continued flipping pages to scan.

<Affirmative.>

"Seems like he may have been on to something interesting, if not divine," he said. "I don't suppose there's already some things in your memory that he might've been talking about?"

<Daevol Rousilarru was a consummate lover of astronomy, and often theorized about the formation of the universe, whether by natural forces or specific placement by the hand of what the Kiandarians called the All-Father. However, his research into these topics, while extensive, often were interrupted by his theoretical musings on the Chrono Drive, among other things. Though he was brilliant, as you say, much of his work fell by the wayside as he was distracted by each new thing he thought of.>

"Yeah, that's kind of typical of geniuses, though, I think," Dillon said. "Sherisza seems to be a lot harder to distract from her work."

<Indeed. She prefers to see a task through once she has started.>

"Is she still talking to the Kwaagi?"

<Affirmative. We have transmitted all the data we collected on the rogue ship, and they are comparing it to their databases for any similar incidents. Without being able to tell them we can enter the time stream, though, it is difficult to make this incident seem as serious as it was.>

"That's true," Dillon said, flipping a page absently. "We really don't know much of anything about the reaches beyond their space, do we?"

<Nothing they have shared to date, though that may change with how perturbed Sherisza is about the attack.>

"Not just her." Dillon tossed the notebook back in the duffel bag as they finished scanning it. "How's the damage to the rear of the ship? Anything that needs immediate attention?"

<There does not appear to be any structural damage. The conventional thrusters are in normal operating condition so far as diagnostics can tell. They will need touchup repairs, but I do not sense they will require more than that.>

"Hopefully, it can wait 'til we return to Outer Dock Seventeen again with the next group of Kiandarians," Dillon said. "Anything else I should look at?"

<Relay A-316 is due for replacement soon.>

"All right, I'll do that now."

Dillon got a replacement part from the storage cabinet and grabbed the toolbox. He left the engineering section and made for the ship's main corridor, where the indicated relay was located. He had just set the toolbox down when Sherisza looked at him from around the edge of her seat. She motioned for him to come over, so he left the box and replacement part and went to stand behind her seat. She smiled softly when he wrapped his arms around her.

"The Kwaagi do not have an exact match, but they have been skirmishing with an unknown species from the reaches for weeks," she said. "They are offering us a lucrative contract to go farther into their space and modify another of their wings to join in the fight. This would cause a substantial delay in our plans to bring others to Kiandar, though..."

"Can we go help them, then retrieve the next group of Kiandarians and just come back into our time stream a month earlier?"

"I do not know how any of this works, whether there would be issues with us being in two places at once in the same time frame, but I suspect it would, at the least, alert many others that we have a time-travel device of some sort. My instinct is to keep the time stream *pure* by only going to and from places where we do not already exist."

"I think I understand," he said, scratching the back of his neck. "If we want to help the Kwaagi, though, we should do that first. A little delay in bringing settlers is only going to be an inconvenience, not life-threatening, right?"

She let out a leonine sigh. "Agreed. Daevol, send a message to the Kwaagi, let them know we are heading to Outer Dock Five and will be there as soon as possible."

<Confirmed. Transmitting message.>

"Strap in so we can get underway, Dillon," Sherisza said.

"Hang on," he said, rushing back to secure the toolbox and supplies first. Engaging the Chrono Drive didn't seem to put any undue G-forces on them or their belongings, but it just seemed the prudent thing to not have anything loose that could project toward the flight deck in the event of a fight or sudden stop.

Soon enough, he returned and got buckled in, and after laying in their course, Sherisza engaged the Chrono Drive. She must have set it for quite some speed because Dillon nearly lost consciousness after the echoes and the shivering of the universe about them subsided. He held onto wakefulness, though, and shook his head to clear it. And thus, he had a perfect view of the HUD as it came up and indicated that black ship was behind them again.

A voice crackled across the hailing frequency, garbled and not in any language Dillon's translator chip could make sense of. A quick glance at Sherisza said hers couldn't, either. Dillon couldn't even tell if it was a warning, some type of request, or what. The inflection, tone, and words themselves were all impossible to make out, but their intent seemed clear a moment later. The enemy ship fired two blaster bolts at the *Malshekt*, and though they were absorbed by the shields, Sherisza growled.

She brought the *Malshekt* about and headed straight for the enemy ship. She didn't even hesitate this time, firing the Kwaagi disruptors the moment she had a target lock. The enemy began evasive maneuvers, but it did take several hits. Like the first time they'd encountered it, the disruptors didn't disintegrate the ship, but the enemy did flee. Sherisza gave chase, her face set in a fang-showing grimace, and she opened the hailing frequencies herself.

"Whoever in the six hells you are, if you attack this ship again, I will destroy you," she said, firing a burst warning shot, all four of the disruptor blasts hitting the rear of the retreating bogey.

And then the enemy ship spun about the way Sherisza had so brilliantly done in some of their dogfights. Dillon could only watch in slack-jawed fascination as the enemy ship fired its own ion cannon, taking the *Malshekt* right in the nose. Everything in the ship went dark, and Dillon and Sherisza both grunted and clutched behind their left ears as even their translation chips went offline. Virtually every system on the ship was dead, even the Chrono Drive it seemed, leaving the *Malshekt* adrift in the time stream at a ridiculous speed.

"Can you wake Daevol up?" Dillon asked as he rubbed away the pain in his chip.

Sherisza didn't answer, staring with wide eyes out the front viewport. The enemy ship came up in front of them, flying backwards with the same speed and vector as the *Malshekt* to stay before her. Dillon watched in what felt like slow motion horror as the enemy ship's gun ports began to power up and several missile tubes extended out of its wings. Sherisza opened the little panel on the side of her console and pulled the switch that would activate the Chrono Drive's defenses, but nothing happened. It, too, was offline.

The enemy ship fired several shots, and Sherisza cried out

as the *Malshekt* was rocked by the unmitigated blasts. Dillon threw caution to the wind. He released his harness and knelt next to her chair, wrapping her in his arms. If he was going to die, he was going to do it with her in his arms, wherever they went and whoever took them there. Sherisza clung to him, burying her face in the side of his neck as they waited for whatever end would come.

CHAPTER 4

INTERVENTION

THE SECONDS TICKED by in agonizing slowness, until at last, Sherisza looked up again. She gasped, and Dillon, too, raised his eyes to find there was no longer a ship in front of them.

"How do we get the systems back online?" Dillon asked, rising to his feet.

"We can manually restart the Chrono Drive. That will get us power back, at least," Sherisza answered. It was still amazing to Dillon how well-spoken she was in Terran English. When their translation chips weren't working, it was more than amazing, it was a godsend. "From there, we need hope that ion blast did not permanently cripple the ship or Daevol. We will need damage assessments, and we are heading in the wrong direction."

He nodded, and she unbuckled herself and started to half-walk, half-float to the back, the ship's artificial gravity offline. Sherisza was shaking, and Dillon's own legs felt like jelly as they went to engineering. He wasn't sure where that ship was or if it was coming back, but there was little to be done about it either way at that moment. He took Sherisza's hand in his, and she held onto him while they made their way to the back. It felt ominous to move farther into the darkness of the ship's rear, but even the emergency lighting wasn't on.

They forced open the door to engineering and went in, though Dillon couldn't see a thing. He followed Sherisza as she guided him by the hand she still held. Either by instinct or some extremely potent low-light vision like the feline she resembled, she led him right to the Daevol Drive. He could hear her clawed hands sliding across its surface as she looked for the release of the casing. He heard two clasps open, and then she began toggling some switch within.

"I'm... not feeling so good," Dillon said as the ship started to feel unnaturally warm. He had expected it to start getting cold immediately with life support offline.

"It is radiation. The ship's plating protects us from most, but there is some that the shields protect us from. Hang on, Dillon, I nearly have the drive awake again," Sherisza said. The blue indicator light came on, then, and Sherisza put the casing back on the Chrono Drive as if afraid it was going to melt the two of them. "Come on, come on."

The life support came back online, then the artificial gravity, followed by the interior lighting. Dillon saw the terminal in the corner switch back on, rebooting along with Daevol. Some of their exercise equipment was askew, but otherwise, the ship didn't appear to have taken much damage, if any. There was no telling what the cabins would look like, but there were no hull breach alarms as life support got back to nominal function. And then they heard the sound they both wanted to hear.

<Reboot sequence complete. I apologize for my absence, Captain.>

"Thank the Goddess," Sherisza said, falling into Dillon's embrace.

He nearly collapsed under her weight, weak as he felt

between the adrenaline and the minor radiation poisoning. "Damage report?" he had the wherewithal to ask.

<Assessing... The Kwaagi disruptors have been destroyed. Point-Defense Laser System is online. Missile ports intact. Shielding is now online, radiation returning to safe levels. Minimal damage to rear thruster ports. There is no substantial damage to any armor or systems but for the disruptors, Commander.>

"Think they were sending us a message?" he asked.

<Unknown. The incoming transmission was not decipherable and remains unclear even after running it through my translation algorithms.>

"You okay?" Dillon asked, still holding Sherisza.

"That was terrifying," she whispered. "When I was enacting my revenge against MacNault, I did not care if it cost me my life, but now... I was scared, Dillon. Scared for you, my people... and us."

"Me too," he said. "I'm lucky I don't need a change of pants."

She ignored his attempt at humor. "Daevol, get us back on our original course. Increase speed. If you see that black ship, use every evasive maneuver you have to lose it."

<Acknowledged.>

"How do we reboot our translation chips?" Dillon asked.

"It should happen automatically. Just be prepared for a bit of pain when it does. In the meantime, come, Dillon. The shower will decontaminate us of the radiation while the life support system does its work on our atmosphere," she said.

He didn't argue. They took a shower together, and Dillon held her for a while until the fear finally seemed to bleed out of them both. Their translation chips came back online with a burst of pain like an ice cream headache, but it passed quickly. Dillon kept waiting for a message from Daevol that the black ship had returned, but they were left in peace for the time being. He wasn't sure what thoughts were swirling through Sherisza's mind, but he could guess easily enough–probably the same ones in his own. Not only was that black ship able to enter the time stream, but it knew how to find them and, worse than that, disable them.

"We'd better not get into any more dogfights until we reach the Kwaagi station," Dillon said when they stepped out into the air dryers. Sherisza didn't answer, only nodded. The missiles they had were short range and intended for escape, while the point-defense lasers were almost purely defensive. Without the Kwaagi disruptors, they were essentially helpless in a battle.

Thankfully, Sherisza had arranged for them to proceed directly to Outer Dock Five. The Chrono Drive was set to deposit them not far from the station itself, with no planned stop at the border of Kwaagi space as would be typical. With any luck, the Kwaagi might know something new about their mystery craft. Would it have something to do with the species the Kwaagi were in the middle of skirmishes with? Dillon could only speculate at this point.

Once they were dried off and their clothes were in the wash, they returned to their cabin to get dressed again. Sherisza's movements were slightly mechanical, but Dillon knew she was just working through every possibility and angle in that brilliant mind. He rubbed her shoulders and she flashed him her little smile, and soon, they returned to the flight deck to watch for trouble.

———

Dillon looked around, even checking the smaller inset holodisplays. "Where is it?"

<Unknown. Scanning nearby space.>

"Did we come out of the time stream in the wrong place or time?" Sherisza asked.

<Scanning... Negative. We have arrived at precisely the time and location desired. Outer Dock Five is not here. There is a significant amount of wreckage to port and below, Captain. I believe it to be the remains of the station.>

"Holy crap," Dillon blurted.

Sherisza turned the ship in that direction, and before them was an expanse of twisted metal and bits of detritus. Based on its size and breadth, there was little doubt it was the remains of what had been Outer Dock Five or at least something comparable. Considering the station wasn't where it was supposed to be, it was the most plausible explanation. Dillon scratched at the back of his neck nervously, trying not to consider the loss of life involved, but there wasn't really anything else to keep his mind off it. Sherisza stared at the wreckage with a palpable mix of fear and regret as well.

"Daevol, scan for—"

<Captain, there is one life sign among the wreckage. Kwaagi, low vital signs, floating free in naught but a spacewalk suit.>

"Moving in," Sherisza said.

"What could have done this?" Dillon mused absently as they navigated the wreckage toward the lone life sign registering on the HUD.

"Significant concentrated firepower," she answered. "I shudder to think what species the Kwaagi have been tangling with if they are capable of this."

"There they are!" Dillon shouted, pointing at the suited Kwaagi hanging on desperately. They were tied to a length of hose attached to a section of the destroyed station.

Sherisza brought the *Malshekt* in close, matching the slight rotation of the wreckage until the ship was moving in perfect harmony with their intended target. Just as when they had escaped from President MacNault's office, Sherisza dropped the shields before extending the boarding tunnel out to encompass the Kwaagi survivor. The shields sealed the end of the boarding tunnel, forming an airlock, and the little green light beside the *Malshekt*'s hatch began blinking before there were three *bongs*.

Dillon went and opened the hatch, not even pausing to consider he could be sucked right out the door if something went wrong. By the slender build of the figure, he expected it was a Kwaagi woman, and he hesitated only briefly when he thought about their taboos over touching a woman. He hooked her under the arms and dragged her into the ship proper, then pressed the sequence beside the hatch to close it and the boarding tunnel.

Sherisza maneuvered them away from the wreckage again while Dillon went to a guest cabin to grab some blankets. When he returned, Sherisza was by the Kwaagi's side, working to get the helmet off the suit. It came off with a hiss, but she gestured Dillon to lift the woman up. They carried her to the lavatory, where Sherisza got the rest of the suit off and they placed her into the shower for decontamination. If nothing else, Dillon figured the warm water might wake the Kwaagi up if she had gone into hibernation.

Nothing happened for several minutes, but then the warmth seemed to finally get through to the Kwaagi woman. She spluttered and sneezed, but her motions remained slow and groggy. Sherisza went into the shower fully clothed so that someone was beside her, and the Kwaagi tried to fix her slit-pupiled eyes on the Kiandarian. Recognition dawned after half a minute, and the Kwaagi woman relaxed on the floor of the shower, either satisfied she was safe or resolved to be in captivity.

There was only the most minute scent of fear, and though it

still wasn't pleasant to Dillon's nose, it didn't rankle him all that much. He got a towel from the linen cabinet and hung it on the handle of the shower door. When the female's eyes turned toward him, Dillon bowed his head in greeting but then left the room to give her some privacy. She may have been a reptilian with no discernible sexual anatomy on sight, but that didn't mean she wouldn't consider his presence a breach of decorum. He already knew it was taboo to touch them without permission; there was no sense risking anything else when Sherisza could take care of her.

Dillon returned to the flight deck and strapped himself into his seat. He took control of the *Malshekt* and began flying simple circuits around the wreckage. "Daevol, transmit imagery to the Kwaagi. Let them know we've rescued one survivor and are looking for others."

<Confirmed. However, there are no others, Dillon.>

"Well, don't tell them that yet. Let's keep looking. Do you have an approximate number of Kwaagi who were on this station?"

<Including the wing pilots, who may or may not be dead and among this wreckage, there would have been roughly one hundred Kwaagi on the station. I have been monitoring the wreck for further signs of life but have found none.>

"Is it possible they're in hibernation like on the Crooked Talon, so you just don't detect them?" Dillon asked.

<Negative. There are none in space suits like the one we rescued.>

"Shit," Dillon spat before looking up the corridor. Sherisza wasn't there, so he didn't expect to be reprimanded for his language. "All right, let them know we're still checking the wreckage, but it doesn't look good. But tell them there's no sign of the enemy ships, either. Then let's scan to see if any of the wing fighters escaped."

<Affirmative.>

He kept flying around the wreckage, avoiding bouncing anything off the front of Sherisza's ship. The destruction was complete; there were no rooms left intact that might've let some of the station workers survive. There was no sign of any life pods, none of the fighter wing was nearby on patrol or otherwise, and there were no life signs whatsoever. Dillon set the scanners to begin trying to determine what exactly had destroyed the station, but in the meantime, he kept his eyes out for any enemy fighters. Just on a hunch, he kept a course laid in on the Chrono Drive, only needing to engage it to escape any sudden attacks.

<Subspace message coming in from Kwaaganarr.>

Dillon perked up at that. "Put it through," he said.

A holodisplay popped up to overlay the front of the flight deck, and an imperious-looking Kwaagi male in military dress started to speak. He halted when he saw Sherisza wasn't on the flight deck, and his slit pupils narrowed as he looked at Dillon.

"Captain Rousilarru is with the survivor, running her through a decontamination shower," Dillon explained after the pause started to get awkward. "I'm Dillon Mackey, her second in command, currently piloting the *Malshekt*."

"I see. Tell the captain that the force that attacked our outer dock has now assaulted our inner systems, headed toward our home planet of Kwaaganarr. Stay out of their path. There is no telling how many have come yet or how many more may come in their wake. Thank you for saving our citizen, but get well clear of the destruction, young human. I suggest heading to Outer Dock Six or Four; or, if you prefer to stay much safer, move to Three or Seven. But get out of the path of these invaders, whatever you do."

"All right. Is there any way we can help?"

The Kwaagi's feathers rose and then flattened back. "No,

human, but thank you. Best if you stay safe and do not in turn need rescuing. Our empire is mighty, and we will handle this surprise attack ourselves."

Dillon bowed his head. "Good luck. If you change your mind, just contact us."

The Kwaagi officer bowed his head but then simply cut off the transmission.

Dillon looked around his seat again when he heard movement in the corridor, and he saw Sherisza helping the Kwaagi female into one of the guest cabins. It was fortunate that Sherisza was as muscular as she was, able to handle the slender reptilian female with ease. Once their guest was safely tucked away, probably in bed under some warm blankets, Sherisza went to their own cabin and got changed out of her wet clothes.

She came and sat on the flight deck with Dillon when she returned, and immediately she started looking at the wreckage herself. "By the Goddess, what could have precipitated this?"

"Not sure," Dillon said. "No sign of survivors or any of the wing ships flying nearby, though. We did get a transmission from Kwaaganarr saying their inner systems were under attack and for us to get out of the path of the invaders as soon as possible. There's nothing for us to do here; we may as well move on to another docking station."

"Agreed. Daevol, take us to Outer Dock Six, it should be the next one to rotate to this position now that this one has been destroyed."

<Acknowledged.>

"Let us see if we can get their next wing outfitted to survive an encounter with the bastards who did this," Sherisza said.

Dillon nodded. "How's our guest?"

"Resting comfortably. We will explain things to her when she awakens. This does cause us a certain wrinkle, though, Dillon."

"What's that?"

"Keeping the existence of the Chrono Drive a secret," Sherisza said, chewing on her lower lip as she turned to him.

"I'm not going to say anything," he insisted. "We can just tell her it's a modified warp drive and to stay the hell away from it. Once she gets used to it and isn't passing out all the time, she'll just be curious like I was. If she gets too curious, we're dropping her off at Outer Dock Six anyway. It's not that long a trip, I don't think."

"True. We must be certain to say nothing, though."

"Well, let's just get to Outer Dock Six as quickly as we can; maybe she'll still be asleep by the time we arrive."

<Engaging drive now.>

Dillon smiled up at the ceiling, then centered himself as the effects of the Chrono Drive began to take hold. He hardly felt it this time, though the echoes and shivering of the stars were still there. This would be a much shorter trip, though, and he stayed buckled in for the ride.

———

The soft clack of claws on the corridor floor was the first hint that she was coming. Dillon and Sherisza both turned to see their guest approaching, wrapped in a blanket to hide her nakedness on the strangers' ship. Again, it impressed upon Dillon that though her people were reptilian, there was some taboo against nudity, at least among other races. Her head was dipped slightly, and her feathers were tightly plastered to the top of her head, which Dillon recognized as embarrassment from his time among her people.

She was colorful, a dark blue with bright orange stripes, her feathers in multiple hues like a peacock's tail, though without the trademark eye-like marking. Her eyes were golden and slit-pupiled like nearly all her people, but even with her relatively inexpressive face and the odd eyes, Dillon could easily see intelligence. He dipped his head in greeting to her, and she did the same in return. Sherisza repeated the gesture, but the Kwaagi woman approached to face the Kiandarian squarely.

"Thank you for saving my life," she said in her people's tongue, the translators interpreting.

"You are most welcome," Sherisza said with another dip of her head. "Despite the terrible circumstances, welcome aboard the *Malshekt*. I am Captain Sherisza Rousilarru, and this is my apprentice, Dillon Mackey. We are on our way to Outer Dock Six, where you may return to your people while we work on the fighter wing there."

"I am grateful. I know of you well, Captain Rousilarru, though your apprentice is new to me. I am Administrator Azilija. I am sorry to ask, but may I trouble you for something to eat and drink?"

"I'll get it," Dillon said, patting Sherisza's arm. "Keep an eye out for you-know-who."

The Kiandarian nodded, so Dillon led their Kwaagi guest toward the galley. She seemed quiet and submissive along the way, possibly because she was "just" an administrator, but then he guessed it probably had to do with being the lone survivor as well. She took a seat at the table and Dillon brought her a glass of water and some of the hard-skinned fruit that was staple of their diets on the mobile stations. Azilija dipped her head in thanks but proceeded to eat without saying anything else.

Dillon stayed with her, partially so she wouldn't be alone but also so she wouldn't wander into engineering or anywhere else she wasn't supposed to. There was no telling what she might do after having survived such a trauma. She might do something self-destructive, or she could just go wandering in a half-daze, finding and fiddling with things she shouldn't. It wasn't so much that Dillon didn't trust her, but he erred on the side of caution anyway. Her gaze flicked to him every now and then, and he wasn't sure what she was thinking. But then a possibility occurred to him.

"I'm sorry I touched you without permission when we brought you aboard," he said.

Azilija's feathers stood up straight, and Dillon feared he'd said too much. "Oh, it is of no trouble, human. I am not mated. You provided me a mercy, and for that, I thank you."

"Glad to help," he said with a smile, though he didn't make it too broad considering the rest of her coworkers were dead. "We got word from Kwaaganarr that the invaders are pushing toward your home world, but your people are fighting back."

"Our empire is strong. The invaders will not prevail over us," she said.

"Do you know anything about the invaders?" he asked.

"They are powerful. Our explorers were looking to terraform a small world we found across the reaches, and they took offense to this. It began as some minor ship-to-ship battles but has since become targeted skirmishes along our border. Most of these were repulsed. This last one was a concerted attack and destroyed my home base."

"I'm sorry about your friends," he said, and she dipped her head in appreciation. "Do you know anything about the people themselves?"

"No communication was ever established. Their ships are strong, but not much stronger than our own. With the modifications Captain Rousilarru could make to our wings, we would defeat them easily."

"Well, I think that's what we're headed to the next outer dock to do. All right, then. Do you need anything else to eat or drink?"

The Kwaagi woman made a dismissive gesture. "This was sufficient. Is there any way I may be of aid to you?"

"As an administrator? I don't think so," Dillon said. It wasn't as if he was going to ask her to scan in Daevol's notebooks or do paperwork for them. Though he could always ask her to take some of his tests in school if he wanted to be a smartass, he kept that tucked away. "Unless that position means something different to your people than mine."

"I am a skilled data analyst, diplomat, and linguist. I was assigned to Outer Dock Five in case of the very contact we made with our enemies, though I was not given sufficient data, time, or resources to decode their language, nor were they interested in speaking when they came for my base. Have you made any contact with them?"

Dillon put his hand to his chin. "I'm not sure. We did receive a strange message from a black ship that may or may not have been theirs. I guess we could see if the captain wants you to try translating it for us."

"I would be honored. Let us go ask her," Azilija said, gesturing back toward the corridor.

Dillon led her to the flight deck, where they repeated the Kwaagi woman's offer.

"I do not think your translation chip will have more languages than my own, but you are more than welcome to try listening to the messages," Sherisza said. "You say you are a linguist as well?"

"Yes, Captain. I am a first contact decoder of languages. Even if this message of yours is not translated by my chip, I may be able to deduce certain things from it," Azilija said.

"Well then, by all means. Daevol, play the recorded messages for our guest."

<Aye, Captain.>

CHAPTER 5

WARNINGS

NOT SURPRISINGLY, Azilija's translator didn't have any more luck with the message than Dillon's or Sherisza's had. It was fortunate that the recording of the message hadn't been lost after the blast from the enemy ship's ion cannon. After listening to it a few times, Azilija had requested it be sent to her cabin where she could listen to it and study it in quiet seclusion. Once she left, Dillon and Sherisza stared at each other across the scant distance between their chairs.

"Good thing you're sexy as hell, because you're dangerous to be involved with," he joked.

Her brows rose, but then she barked a laugh. "I was thinking the same thing of you. While I did endure my share of attacks before taking you as an apprentice, Dillon, they were never near this frequent or deadly. True, it is likely it was because President MacNault sensed I would try to use you to get close to him, but then again, I am starting to wonder if *you* are the one they truly want to eliminate."

"Or maybe it's just both of us together," he mused.

She reached over and laid a hand on his arm, and Dillon

leaned in to share a kiss with her. "Whatever the case and whatever may come, I love you, Dillon Mackey."

"I love you too, whatever may come," he returned.

"I am tempted to spread this news to the other governments. Anything that is strong enough to cause considerable damage to the Kwaagi Empire is a concern to all. However, I should not like to embarrass or annoy the Kwaagi, not with the good will we have formed with them. I will bring it up with the brigadier when we reach Outer Dock Six, though."

"Whoever the officer was from Kwaaganarr that contacted us, he was insistent we just stay clear and safe. They might tell the other governments to do the same, but it wouldn't hurt for there to be an offer of aid, at least. It'll help with future diplomacy if nothing else. Especially with how spectacularly my people botched the first contact."

"I told you your father was going to waste you on law," she said with a smile. "I think you have made more of an impression with the Kwaagi than all the Terran diplomats before you."

"Well, they didn't exactly set the bar high," he said with a snort. It was hard to forget the story of humanity's first contact with the Kwaagi. The reptilian people used scent to convey their emotions, and many of those scents were not pleasant to the human nose. To say the first encounter between the two races had gone poorly would've been an understatement. Frankly, it was a miracle the races hadn't ended up at war over the insult.

<Approaching Outer Dock Six, preparing to drop from warp.>

Dillon looked up, confused, but then he remembered why the AI was calling things by the wrong names.

"Is the station intact?" Sherisza asked.

<Affirmative, though it is on high alert. Sending credentials

and dropping from warp at a respectable distance for identification purposes.>

"Excellent. Request permission to dock directly in the hangar for disruptor repair."

<Acknowledged.>

The station came into sight on the holodisplay as the *Malshekt* dropped back into the normal space-time stream. A pair of Kwaagi fighters flew past them, but they didn't stop to speak or even escort the *Malshekt* closer. Warnings came up on the HUD that the station's weapons were armed and primed, but they weren't aimed at the *Malshekt*. It was a tense couple of minutes while they awaited a reply over the hailing frequency. Azilija approached and stood between and behind the pilots' seats, but she didn't say anything.

"Outer Dock Six to *Malshekt*, you are clear to land in the primary hangar," came the voice of the Kwaagi flight director.

"Confirmed. Coming in slowly now," Sherisza said.

"Flight Director, please let the brigadier know that Administrator Azilija Telusurrii is on board the *Malshekt* and would like to meet with him as soon as possible," the Kwaagi woman said.

"Understood. Proceed to hangar as directed."

It was intimidating to approach a space station on full alert, twenty-one ships flying about on patrols and various cannons aimed in every possible direction. There was even a twin-barreled disruptor turret above the hangar doors. Staring at the business end of it on approach was a harrowing experience no matter how friendly the Kwaagi were to them. Dillon was pretty sure he hadn't breathed the entire way in until they passed through the force shield and Sherisza spun the ship to land it facing outward.

"Thank you again for rescuing me and bringing me home," Azilija said before turning on her clawed feet to go retrieve her space suit and clothing. She left the traces of the Kwaagi gratitude scent behind, but it was mild and didn't faze Dillon.

"Dillon, go grab the tools. I want to begin our work immediately. Every Kwaagi fighter we can modify is one more defender between this station and the fate that befell its sister," Sherisza said with a grimace.

"I'm on it," he said, and he headed off the flight deck.

They only had to wait a few minutes to disembark, and after some stiffer-than-usual greetings, Azilija was escorted away by two armed guards to see the brigadier. Sherisza and Dillon were introduced to the dock hands and mechanics, and then they went to order all the parts they'd need to begin their modifications. As on their previous job, they noted that they would need the same parts twenty-one times over, and Sherisza requested two sets immediately.

"You thinking we should work separately this time?" Dillon asked.

"I am confident you do not need my oversight to complete this work. Are you comfortable working on your own?" she returned.

"Yeah, the faster we get this done, the better. You're going to double-check everything anyway, so I'm not too worried about it. We've done this, what? Forty-two times so far? Forty-three if you count having to redo the one."

Sherisza nodded, watching two Kwaagi fighter ships come into the hangar and land on either side of the *Malshekt*. Her own ship was already under repair by the Kwaagi mechanics, her damaged disruptors being removed for replacement. "Let us get this done as quickly as we can. We are both in need of some proper rest."

"And maybe some fun before that."

She chuckled. "Perhaps. I suppose you had better work

quickly–but not *too* quickly. I do not want to have to redo the work because you were eager for entertainment."

Dillon laughed and crossed his heart with his fingers. "I promise."

Sherisza didn't seem to know what the gesture meant, but the words satisfied her, at least. Once the inventory clerk brought them the two carts of equipment, she and Dillon split up to their own jobs and got to work.

————

Dillon lay in bed with Sherisza's head on his chest, enjoying the light rumble of her purr while she slept. She was warm and soft against him, yet her muscular body leaned just enough weight into his side to start easing him to sleep as well. They were both tired after a long day of travel and work, but they had still explored their intimacy further, trying new things and learning more and more about each other. It had been everything Dillon had ever imagined and more, and yet as wonderful as it had felt, he enjoyed their cuddling afterward just as much, and her purring next to his heart possibly more.

Sleep still evaded him, though. His mind was a whirl of thoughts and emotions in the wake of the second attack by the mysterious black craft, the destruction of the Kwaagi mobile outpost, and–not the least–his latest adventure in lovemaking with Sherisza. She was mentally spent; staring down that mystery ship while completely helpless had rattled her, but she was holding up well so far. Rest would do her a world of good. Dillon tried to loan her his strength while keeping enough for himself. After all, he was rather shaken up himself.

It had been a wild few months so far with Sherisza, fraught with danger not of her own making. He still resolved there was nowhere else he'd want to be, especially not home on Earth going to college. He was getting to see the stars just as he'd always wanted, it felt good to work with his hands *and* his brain, and he had a wonderful friendship and sexual relationship with his mentor and partner. Some may have argued that it wasn't a good relationship to have with one's employer, but in this case, Dillon disagreed.

Just as she'd requested, Dillon made sure to show her all the proper respect. She was the boss and the ship's captain, and just as he let her lead and guide him as his employer, so too did he let her lead in their relationship. She had been a "wife" and a mother before, whereas this was Dillon's first real relationship. She had made her intentions known, and though there was this little nagging voice that said it was just young love, he trusted his emotions. He loved her, and it didn't frighten him to say so or to think about having children with her.

What was even better than that, he recalled his father's advice about making sure he loved her as much outside the bedroom as within it. It was another indicator that what he felt for Sherisza was real, because as much as he enjoyed the sex–and he enjoyed it thoroughly–he had just as much fun with her in virtually every other facet of their life together. The dinners, the chess games, listening to her people's music, the theory crafting when working on the phase-cloaking device, all of it. Work was work, but he enjoyed that too, and he was thankful that she'd chosen him to be her apprentice. As dangerous and unpredictable as everything had been to this point, he loved almost every minute of it and, most of all, her.

There was a two-chirp alarm that Dillon was pretty sure was only in his head. "Daevol?" he whispered, trying not to wake Sherisza.

<Sorry to invade your mind, Dillon, but your parents have been trying to contact you. The Kwaagi are, understandably, blocking all transmissions from outside their space. However, I

was able to answer a call before it was intercepted. The Kwaagi may be listening in, so you will not want to divulge secrets, but I thought your parents might be worried.>

"Thanks, Daevol," Dillon said, and he soon found himself looking at a holodisplay that was apparently in his mind. "Hi Mom, hi Dad."

"Dillon?" his mother, Sasha, said. "Where are you? We can't see you."

"You've only got audio for this call," he answered. "The Kwaagi have a situation here, one I can't talk about, so they're blocking most communications. I just didn't want you to think anything terrible had happened."

Even though it'd be the truth, he added silently.

"That's what we wanted to talk to you about. The Kwaagi have been attacked," Malcolm, his father, said.

"I know. We're at one of their mobile outposts sprucing up another of their fighter wings," Dillon interrupted. "We were going to pick up some more Kiandarian refugees and we sort of got caught in the middle of all this, so we're helping our friends as we can."

"You two always seem to get mixed up in things," Sasha said.

"Yes, and I do apologize for that," Sherisza interjected.

"Sherisza? Oh, God... are you two in bed?"

Dillon laughed and Sherisza made a dismissive gesture despite there being no video feed. "Yes, I was asleep, and Dillon was reading. You did not interrupt anything. And even if you had, it is worth it to soothe your worries."

"She's so sweet," Sasha whispered.

Malcolm laughed. "The Joint Senates are meeting in an hour to talk about what's going on in Kwaagi space, but is there anything you can tell us?"

"We were asked to say nothing to anyone," Sherisza said.

"Yeah, we're trying to respect their wishes, you know how the Kwaagi can be. Hopefully, if they need your help, they don't wait too long to ask," Dillon added.

"Well, sorry to wake you two up," Sasha said.

"It's worth it to hear your voices," Dillon returned, and he saw tears roll from his mother's eyes. "I swear we're not getting in dogfights every day, Mom. Don't worry too much for us, the Kwaagi are our friends, and they're powerful friends. We're here to make sure they come out on top in whatever this incident turns into."

"Try to send us a message as soon as the Kwaagi will let you talk on a video call," Malcolm said. "We're proud of both of you. Sleep well."

"Goodnight, baby," Dillon's mother added.

Dillon and Sherisza wished them goodnight and then Daevol closed the connection.

<Disconnecting from your implant unless there is another emergency.>

"Thanks, Daevol."

<My pleasure, Commander.>

Sherisza was looking at Dillon, so he leaned in and kissed her. "Up for another round?" he asked when he finally broke off the kiss.

"Sweet Goddess, you are insatiable," she said. "Is this a teenage thing or are human males like this all the time?"

"Depends on the person, but I guess *Yes* is a simpler answer."

"Dillon, that was not a yes-or-no question," she said, but he simply smirked at her. She shook her head. "Do you remember what I said about being too casual?"

Dillon cupped her face in his hand. "Sherisza, this is anything but casual to me. I love being with you more than anything else in the world, or even the known galaxy, I guess.

You don't have to worry about me taking this for granted. I want this so I *don't* feel like I'm taking my time with you for granted."

Sherisza blinked, her eyes searching. "I never knew you were a poet."

"You mean that didn't sound completely corny?"

She slipped underneath him and then initiated a deep kiss of her own. When they split apart, her golden eyes were shining. "No, it did not."

———

They paid the price for their passions a few hours later when the door chime of their shared quarters rang insistently.

"*Maqua*," Dillon said.

Sherisza chuckled as she slid out of bed and yanked her clothes on as quickly as she could. She went and answered the door, and Dillon made sure to stand out of sight while he got his own clothes on. It was another Kwaagi female, one of the clerks with an electronic clipboard, and she tapped her large inner talons on the floor before she spoke.

"The brigadier requests your presence," she said, her feathers pressed back and down in a show of anxiousness.

"Of course; we will be happy to see him," Sherisza said.

Once Dillon was dressed, they followed the clerk. Dillon practically knew the way by heart from the previous visit. The Kwaagi stations were uniform, and Dillon was sure he could find his way to any of the amenities and facilities he'd visited on the other outposts. He teased Sherisza's wrist with his fingers and she smiled, but she kept her eyes forward. They were both tired, but after the night they'd had, he thought it was worth it. He was pretty sure she did, too.

And the scent of her is still all over me, he thought, grinning like a fool.

After taking a lift up to the brigadier's office atop the station, Dillon found it was one of the few things not uniform with the other outposts. The brigadier of Outer Dock Eighteen had plants all over his office to make it seem like he was in a jungle clearing. This station's brigadier, however, had a sterile and nearly undecorated office. He was standing behind his desk, and even from across the room, Dillon could smell the scent of his anger. He folded his clawed hands behind his back and managed to beckon Dillon and Sherisza forward and shoo the clerk away without making a single gesture.

"Sir," Dillon said, bowing his head politely when they reached the desk.

"Let me make something perfectly clear," he said with far more of a hiss to the language than was typical. "When we block incoming and outgoing transmissions, it is to safeguard our station, our space, and most of all, our emperor. Any breaches of this protocol are considered an act of espionage and even war. I do not care if you feel you need to speak with your parents, Dillon Mackey, but you will not do it when our lines of communications have been locked down, do you understand?"

"Yes, sir. My apologies."

The Kwaagi general nodded. "I understand you were caught up in this unawares and are here to help us, however, procedures must still be followed, even by outsiders visiting. I wish we could be more accommodating as you aid us, but the emperor's word is law, and the law is my only concern. There are to be no unapproved communications with outsiders whatsoever."

"I will make sure my ship's computer is aware of these rules," Sherisza said.

"Thank you. I also wanted to let you know the *Malshekt*'s disruptors have been replaced. However, the replacements are stronger than the previous ones. It seems our mechanics who outfitted you with disruptors used old, out-of-commission ones from their stockpile. You will find the ones you have now are far more powerful and destructive. Use them wisely."

"Thank you, sir," Sherisza replied.

"Is there any other way we can be of help, General?" Dillon asked.

The Kwaagi shook his head. "Simply keep outfitting my fighters. The more of them you upgrade, the better chance we have of repulsing these attacks from the reaches."

"Then we will get to work now, with the general's leave," Sherisza said.

"Dismissed," the Kwaagi said with a gesture toward the lift.

They both bowed and then returned to the lift, but the general called after them. "Oh, one last thing," he said, and they turned back toward him. "Administrator Azilija, our citizen you rescued from the wreckage of Outer Dock Five... she said you received an indecipherable message from an enemy ship. She requested she be allowed to accompany you while she works on decoding the message, on the off chance you receive any more."

Sherisza and Dillon exchanged a look, and he could see the question in her eyes. Despite what anyone else probably would've come up with as an excuse, Dillon simply gave her a barely perceptible nod. The last thing they'd want to do would be make some subtle insult to their friends. It might be a little strange to have a Kwaagi on board full time, but if it fostered stronger relations and helped them figure out who was attacking them, it was a small price to pay.

"We would be most appreciative of her help," Sherisza said. "Please let her know she is welcome to come with us when we depart for our next project."

The general nodded but said nothing else. Dillon and Sherisza took the lift back down, and he turned to her. "This means we can't rescue any more of your people until she's finished with her work. Not unless we want to explain the Chrono Drive to her."

"Which we do not," she agreed. "*Maqua.*"

Dillon chuckled but then held a finger up. "You know, though, this might at least help us figure out if the attacks have anything to do with rescuing more of your people."

Sherisza considered that. "True. Their motivations might go a long way to figuring out if there may be more of them looking to stop or kill us. Though, I must be honest, I am eager to test our new disruptors on their ship."

"You and me both," he grunted.

They returned to their quarters for their tools and work clothes, ready for a day of work despite their fatigue. When Sherisza leaned over to pick up her tools, though, Dillon admired her rump and then tugged playfully on her tail.

"Hey!" she barked, straightening out.

Dillon raised his brows at her tone. "Sorry, is that considered rude to Kiandarians?"

"No, it just has a very specific meaning, one we do not have time for," she growled—playfully, if he was reading it right. He pulled her in for a kiss, but though she gave him one, it was quick and then she backed off. "We have work to do, Dillon, and though I am not certain you noticed, the brigadier did not like the fact that we are being so overt about our relationship in front of his people."

"I didn't notice," he admitted.

Sherisza nodded. "I think he was mindful not to chastise us too many times when we are here to help, especially after how adamantly he forbade outside contact. But whether it is the fact that we are different species, or they are simply afraid we will concentrate more on our love than our work, he was not pleased." She put a finger over his mouth. "This is not to say I will be giving you the *cold shoulder*, but we must be a little more low-key about it, hmmm?"

"So, no goosing you in the hangar, got it," Dillon teased.

She shook her head, but she couldn't fight off the smirk. "Come, let us try to get another pair of fighters done today."

"Aye, Captain."

CHAPTER 6
MODIFICATIONS

DILLON AND SHERISZA continued to work on the Kwaagi wing, double shifting where they could to try to expedite things. It was exhausting and Dillon was afraid he'd fall behind in his studies, but it was worth it. For one thing, the work was getting done more than three times as fast with them working separately and overtime. For another, the Kwaagi no longer had to complain about them being intimate, because they had neither the time nor the energy. And lastly, the work allowed them both to calm down from the terrors of the prior weeks.

Sherisza was curious to how her people were doing on Kiandar, but communications were still locked down even after ten days. The Kwaagi were silent about their efforts to repulse the invaders, but the lockdown said enough. Things didn't seem to be going well for them yet, but Dillon held out hope that would change. At the least, they weren't detecting any more ships coming across the border, and Outer Dock Six was moving to take its sister station's place securing the line.

And now it's got almost an entire wing of upgraded ships, Dillon thought as he headed to the hangar for what would hopefully be the last day of work.

Sherisza had left him early in the morning, probably to get a jump start on the day's work. She was happy to sleep in with Dillon when she could, but she didn't sleep as much as he'd expected from a lioness. Of course, he was mindful not to make any such direct comparisons to what she looked like and possibly insult her entire species. Yes, she looked like a lioness and there were several other similarities beyond the cosmetic, but she was a person, and he had long since resolved to never even suggest he thought otherwise.

Sure enough, she was in the hangar running final checks on the ships they'd modified the day before. She smiled at his approach, and he took that to mean everything was in working order. That would leave only one ship to work on today, and with the two of them doing so together, it would go quickly. Dillon walked up to her and gave her a peck on the side of her muzzle, but then he went to the last ship to get started while she finished up her tests.

The more time he spent working on the ships and their systems, the more he understood what all the parts beneath the surface did. While his first job among the Kwaagi was an endless stream of couplings, relays, amplifiers, and various other electronics, now he saw the systems for what they were. He was imprinting the designs in his mind, leaning how the warp drive powered the other systems and how it all interacted. He still had little clue how the warp drive did what it did as far as propulsion, but it was now a part of the whole–a mysterious part, but one that fit into the schematic in his mind.

Dillon only had a few months under his belt, but it felt like a lot more. And that wasn't just to speak of his apprenticeship, but of his entire life. He had learned so much about the other governments of the known galaxy, space travel, politics, other cultures, his love life, and, of course, all these fascinating systems that Sherisza could reverse engineer. He wondered if it would be worth his time to one day attend a school like she had, learning the academic side of all she was teaching him hands-on. He supposed he'd have to see where he was at when she deemed his apprenticeship was complete.

"You seem pensive," she said as she came up the boarding ramp into the fighter ship.

He looked up and flashed her a smile. "Just thinking about the last few months and everything. It's been quite a ride so far, and I feel like I still have a lot to learn."

"You do," she agreed. "But you are learning at an astonishing pace. I hope... I hope that when you asked Daevol about our academic aptitudes, you were not put out. I never liked to be compared to my brother, and I do not wish you to compare yourself to me. You are far more than some number they put on your academic records, Dillon. Do not ever lose sight of that."

"Oh, I know," he said. "It doesn't bother me that you're smarter than I am, anyway."

Sherisza grumbled lightly as she got to work beside him. "I hate when people are compared or compare themselves to others that way. On paper, Daevol was smarter than I was, Dillon, but he could not do the things I do, just as I did not see the universe the way he saw it. We were not parts to be compared, but to be utilized together, two halves of a whole, neither complete without the other." She reached over and took his chin, turning him face to her. "Just as you and I are now two halves of one whole."

He nodded but refrained from kissing her just in case anyone was watching. "Are you comfortable with having a human relationship with me, though? Your people didn't ever live with their children's other parents, did they? Always with your twin sibling?"

"Virtually always, yes. This will be different for me, Dillon, but the only alternative is to be alone the rest of my life. I am excited to test these waters with you. And if... if your parents and family expect some sort of ceremony to bind us, I am comfortable with that as well."

"We'll talk about it when we have less of an audience," he said, nodding down the ramp at the few Kwaagi laborers in the area. They may have seemed focused on their work, but those tympanic membranes didn't miss much from the distance between them.

"Well, we will have Azilija with us for a time, but I expect she will mostly keep to herself. I hate to bring someone else into these troubles we have found, but if she can translate what that other ship said or says in the future, it should prove invaluable. Even with upgraded weaponry, I am not looking forward to engaging that ship in battle again."

"Me neither," he agreed.

They went quiet for a while as they worked. Sherisza let Dillon do the majority of the labor, watching and guiding, though she didn't have to say much. The Kwaagi ships and these specific modifications were second nature to him now. It still took time to put everything together with the care and precision Sherisza demanded, but they finished early. Dillon looked forward to a nice, relaxing dinner and perhaps a movie if the Kwaagi would allow a signal from the *Malshekt*.

As they descended out of the fighter ship to head for the mess hall, though, they saw Azilija coming toward them. It was hard to miss that distinctive blue *skin* or the orange stripes that highlighted it so magnificently. The Kwaagi woman stepped before Dillon and Sherisza and bowed her head, so they returned the gesture.

"I understand humans think my people smell bad," she said to Dillon.

His first instinct was to say *What* and play it off, but he knew that wouldn't work. Her words had gotten the attention of several other Kwaagi around the hangar, try as they might to pretend they weren't listening. He'd just been thrust into quite a spotlight, and Dillon was mindful not to say the wrong thing. He even pushed down the instinct to look at Sherisza, instead matching the Kwaagi woman's gaze evenly but not in challenge.

"Look, I can't speak to what happened at the first contact between our peoples," he said with a semi-helpless hand gesture. "But no, I don't think your people smell bad. In fact, it's not your people at all... it's the scents you release as a response to emotion. Some of them are just shocking to a human nose. But I think that says more about our noses than your people."

Her feathers stood up at that, her pupils dilating slightly. "So, you would be agreeable to me accompanying you on your ship to help?"

"Of course," Dillon said without delay. "But either way, it's not my ship or my decision. It's the captain's choice."

"Captain?" she prompted, turning to Sherisza.

"I would be glad of your help," the Kiandarian said. "I am not certain we will receive any other messages from our mystery ship, and I hope we do not encounter it again at all. However, if we do, it would be most helpful to have you aboard."

"I will inform the brigadier and gather some things to take with me," Azilija said. She turned to Dillon one last time. "Thank you for your honesty."

"Thanks for not taking it the wrong way," he said, bowing his head slightly.

She returned the gesture but then left without a farewell. She was stiff and to the point, but Dillon had a feeling she was very good at what she did. Having a Kwaagi onboard the *Malshekt* would take some getting used to, but he'd now spent nearly eight weeks among their people and hadn't so much as retched or gagged. He was sure he'd acclimate to it, especially when it was only one in the constantly refreshed confines of the *Malshekt.*

Dillon flashed his gaze around the hangar, but none of the other Kwaagi were still looking his way. There were the telltale signs, though, that his words had pleased them, their feathers standing up a bit more or even the traces of satisfaction on their mostly inexpressive faces. More importantly, though, when he turned back to Sherisza, there was pride in her eyes. That meant so much more to him, as important as the Kwaagi's feelings toward him were.

"Think we can convince the brigadier to let Daevol broadcast a movie to our quarters after dinner?" he asked.

"It cannot hurt to ask," she said, that little smile tugging at the corners of her muzzle. "You continue to impress me in so many ways, Dillon. Your work is exceptional, you learn quickly, you bridge gaps between races easily and honestly... the more I think about it, the less I think it was chance that you applied for this apprenticeship or that I selected you."

He wanted to kiss her, but he refrained from doing so in the hangar. "Like my father said: sometimes God brings the right person into our lives. I don't think it's any less true from where I'm standing than from your point of view."

Sherisza nodded. "Come, let us get something to eat, and we will inquire whether we can watch a movie afterwards."

For Dillon, it was almost painful to not be able to hold her hand as they walked.

––––––––

They were ready to leave the following day after Sherisza did her final tests on the last of the wing fighters. Azilija was standing near the *Malshekt* waiting for them, wearing light clothes that seemed as much for utility as modesty, a simple bag sitting by her clawed feet. Her feathers were half-erect, as if she was excited but trying to avoid showing it to all those in the hangar. Nevertheless, she couldn't help but emit the scent of happiness when Dillon and Sherisza approached their ship.

"Forgive me, I did not mean to assault your olfactory senses," she said, that stiffness returning to her posture and speech.

"No worries," Dillon said. "I'm glad to smell that you're happy."

She seemed surprised he knew how to differentiate what he was smelling, and thankfully, the awkwardness of what he'd said didn't seem to register as offense.

"Follow me, and welcome aboard the *Malshekt*," Sherisza said, leading her up the steps as Daevol opened the hatch for them.

"Thank you, Captain," Azilija said.

They boarded the *Malshekt* and Daevol scanned their new guest. <Adding biometrics for Azilija to the basic security protocols and the primary guest cabin.>

"Thank you, Daevol. This will be your cabin here," Sherisza said, leading the Kwaagi woman over to the door of Dillon's old room. She showed Azilija how to operate the locking mechanism, then had her stow her things inside. Once marginally settled in, Sherisza took their Kwaagi guest on a short tour of the ship.

Dillon took the time to sit on the flight deck and get things ready for departure. He was just going through the readouts on the new disruptors when the women returned. He stood up out of respect, and Sherisza turned so she could face both of them.

"As I am sure you have noticed, there is no seat here for a third crew member," Sherisza said. "If the ship is engaged in combat, I would ask that you remain in your quarters unless I specifically call for your presence near the flight deck. When we engage the Daevol Drive, you may experience disorientation or even briefly lose consciousness, so when we are about to use it, I will likewise ask that you remain in your quarters in a safe position. At any other time, you are welcome to stay near us or walk the ship. I only ask that you do not touch any of the things you see in the engineering section."

"Understood, Captain," Azilija said.

"I assume you are still under orders from your empire, however, when you are on this ship, my orders must supersede theirs," she added.

"Yes, Captain," Azilija said, straightening out.

"There is one other thing. Before we move on to Outer Dock Seven, we will be going on a short journey to a secret location to bring some of my people home to Kiandar. This location must, absolutely *must* remain a secret to all but Dillon and myself, so I will ask that you confine yourself to quarters when ordered with no argument."

"Yes, Captain."

"Have you any questions for us?"

Azilija glanced at Dillon. "Are you mating with this one?" she asked.

Dillon balked slightly at her directness, but Sherisza answered without delay. "Yes, Dillon is my mate as well as my apprentice. We will perhaps explain more of this at another time, but for now, we would ask that you respect our privacy."

"Of course. I simply found it curious. Kwaagi do not mate with non-Kwaagi, ever, not even the other members of our empire. Forgive me if my fascination was considered rude," Azilija said with a dip of her head.

"No worries," Dillon answered for them both. "You'll just have to forgive us if we're a bit more overt about it again now that we're away from your station and its brigadier."

Azilija let forth a little hissing laugh. "Thank you for welcoming me aboard. I will spend some time in my quarters to go over the recorded message you have. I believe I am starting to understand a bit of its tone and inflection, if not its words."

"Thank you, erm...," Sherisza hesitated. "Do you prefer to be called Administrator?"

"I have been relieved of that post," the Kwaagi woman said. "You may call me Azi."

"Very well. Thank you and welcome aboard, Azi."

Once the Kwaagi woman ducked into her cabin, Dillon turned back to Sherisza and tried not to burst out laughing. "She's blunt, eh?"

"Kwaagi do not believe in pretense or false faces," Sherisza explained. "It makes them much easier to deal with than most people, but yes, you must be prepared to have your feelings and privacy violated at times."

"Well, hopefully she stays in her cabin for a bit, because I've got something in mind."

"Unless it involves the shower, it will have to wait," she warned.

"Nope, and it won't wait," Dillon said. "Daevol? Cue the music I asked about."

Sherisza tilted her head curiously as a song began to play. She didn't seem to be familiar with much music from Earth, and even less so when it was something truly classic from centuries ago. But when Dillon took her in his arms and began to slowly dance with her–the way he had so chastely with Maddie Thomas back in the seventh grade–her eyes dilated in wonder. She rose up on her toes to give him a muzzle rub along his cheek, then laid her head on his shoulder and began to purr softly. He danced with her for the duration of the classic song, taking in the scent of her hair and her fur, diluted as it was by having spent so much time among the Kwaagi.

When the song was done, she straightened out to look him in the eyes. "Dillon, no one has danced with me since...," she began, blinking away the traces of tears. "Since the night my children were sired."

"Well, that's way too long to have waited. Sorry I didn't do it sooner," he said.

"Sweet Goddess, you are wonderful," she breathed, muzzle rubbing him again. "But I need to take a shower. You are, of course, welcome to join me..."

He glanced at the door of his old cabin. "Let's not shock our new crewmember too much too soon, as much as I'd love to join you," he said, and she nodded. "We'll have plenty of time and privacy tonight. I'll get us on course to our next pickup while you're in."

"Thank you, Dillon."

He watched her walk away, her steps tentative with the rubbery feeling in her legs, and he smiled. Dillon sat down at the console, then, and began laying in orders silently for Daevol to set their course. The next of the pickups would be another pair of Kiandarian families, some forty-five years in the past. Thinking on that, he silently ordered Daevol to gently but firmly keep their Kwaagi guest from leaving her cabin once they reached their destination.

"Dillon to Azi and the captain," he said officiously. "About to engage the Daevol Drive. Hang onto something or prepare for brief loss of consciousness. Engaging in ten seconds."

He gave them the indicated time to get ready, and then Dillon engaged the drive. Even he had to close his eyes against the flood of echoes, memories, and the shivering of the stars. And then the *Malshekt* was hurtling back through time and space to the Kiandar that was.

CHAPTER 7

MERCIES

THEY ARRIVED at Kiandar in the past, having given Azi time to shower, eat, and tend to her other needs before confining her to quarters. Though Sherisza was making significant progress on the phase-cloaking device, it still wasn't functional, so they had to be careful approaching the planet. Kiandar may not have been as well-defended as Usheva-4, but they had satellites, stations, and tracking probes of their own. Only Sherisza's knowledge of how all of it was set up and utilized gave them any hope of not being detected.

"We will be detected on our way off-world," Sherisza said, angling her approach to take advantage of gaps in the planetary monitors.

"Oh?" Dillon prompted.

"This was one of the times I knew to visit because there had been a sighting of this ship," she explained, and Dillon sat back, astonished. "Not much was ever made of it, the stories of people being abducted largely attributed to conspiracy theories and superstition and not much more. Still, we must be careful not to be too brazen in our approaches. I know much of our history, but I do not know all of it, and even Daevol's considerable research does not account for everything. We do not want to end up trapped or destroyed here in the past, especially when we do not know where that black ship is or where it comes from."

Dillon could only shake his head. It was incredible to think that Sherisza knew where to go to rescue people because history had already recorded it. It certainly suggested her brother's theory was correct. At the same time, it made Dillon wonder what would happen if they tried to do something differently. Would it change history, or would they in fact just end up doing what the records said they'd done, unintentionally or not?

"This is too far back for me to go with you, right?" he asked, done with musing about it and making his head hurt.

"Yes. There will be certain rescues you may accompany me onto the planet for, Dillon, but most will require I contact the people alone. Even in recent times, my people as a whole were never terribly familiar with humans, and if they are, it could cause problems, not make things easier." Dillon nodded, and Sherisza sighed, sitting back in her seat. "We are at a recent enough time that I could see my parents as youngsters, but I do not think I could bear the heartache. It is better that I continue to see them in my heart, and do not put our work here at any sort of increased risk."

Dillon reached across and laid his hand on her shoulder. "My parents are your parents now, too," he said. "They may not recognize it officially yet, but they will. And if we can risk a trip back to Earth in a few weeks, you'll get to meet my other relatives."

"Is there a date of importance drawing near?"

"Grandma Malinda's birthday, it's always a big bash," Dillon said with a smile. "And I'm sure she'll love you when she meets you."

The line of her mouth tightened. "I hope so."

"Remember," he said, but he waited for her to turn to him. "No matter what, I'm with you. Family is family, but a spouse, a mate... that's our first priority."

She released the harness and stood, then leaned over to give him a kiss on the forehead. She went into their cabin and retrieved her blasters, dressed to kill as he liked to think of it, though the irony of that thought in this situation wasn't lost on him. When Sherisza came back out, she took a deep breath and blew it out in a long sigh. She looked as though she was going to say something else, but then she just smiled, opened the hatch, and descended to her world that once was to rescue some of her people.

Dillon brought up the details on the HUD as the hatch closed. There were two families of four that would be joining them, just as on their first rescue mission. The records said these evacuees had been lost and were presumed dead after being caught camping when a massive storm hit. Daevol illustrated with a weather radar and overlay, confirming something powerful and nasty was coming. It was odd, since the place where they'd landed was far from the coasts, but Dillon wondered if it was like one of the famed *Derecho* storms of the American Midwest back home on Earth.

"You all right in there, Azi?" Dillon asked over the comms.

"I am well, thank you," she answered.

He didn't press for details. He felt bad that Daevol had blackened the viewports of her cabin and turned off all computer equipment, so she'd have no idea where—or when—they were. But whatever the Kwaagi woman thought of the circumstances, she raised no complaints and there was no noise from her abode. From here, it would just be a few days more of limited freedom, traveling with the refugees to set a false trail for snoopers, and then Azi would be free to roam the ship at will again.

Dillon looked out the front as the wind started to pick up wickedly. They were in what he'd have described as the middle of nowhere, so the ship was safe from being discovered where Sherisza had landed it. It truly underscored how isolated the families caught unawares were, and how lucky they were that Sherisza hadn't just created a time-travel device with her brother, but she'd also found these folks in the historical records. It nearly hurt Dillon's brain to try to put cause and effect in the right order where these events were concerned. All he could do was praise the brilliance of Sherisza's brother—and Sherisza, too—in making any of it possible.

"Daevol, can you let sound in from outside?" Dillon asked. "I've always loved the rumble of a good thunderstorm."

<Of course.>

"Just tell me Sherisza is all right," he added. There was a powerful, rolling boom, stretched out over long seconds, but it indicated the storm was still a good distance away, echoing off the mountainsides.

<The captain is fine. Her story has been corroborated by the boom you just heard.>

"Good, good," Dillon said, tapping his foot while he watched for her return.

The trees began swaying as the wind picked up. They were so like the trees back home on Earth, though not quite the same. That seemed to typify Kiandar as a whole: like Earth, but not exactly. Right down to its people, who were leonine yet pretty close to human otherwise. Being chosen as Sherisza's apprentice had been more than mere coincidence, she was right about that. Dillon didn't know how God—or her goddess, he still allowed in the back of his mind—had brought it all about, but it couldn't have just been happenstance.

No more than these people disappearing forty-five years ago only to come with us now to save their race, he thought. *What-*

ever the truth behind Your mysteries, God, you just keep on using me however You see fit.

There was no affirming voice or even tingle in his gut, but Dillon didn't need either. He got to his feet as the *Malshekt*'s hatch opened and extended down to form steps. Four Kiandarian adults and four children came aboard, stopping in shock when they beheld Dillon. Sherisza came in behind them and shut the hatch, then came to stand near Dillon.

She gestured to him. "This is my apprentice, as I told you. He is a human from the world of Terra Prime," she said to them in Kiandese, and Dillon bowed his head to the new guests. "He is my co-pilot and, for the duration of this trip, will also be staying in my cabin to make room for you and our other guest. Please, proceed up the hallway to the next two doors, and I will help you get settled in while Dillon takes us off-world."

Dillon waved a casual greeting but stayed quiet while Sherisza led them away and continued giving them instructions and details. Once she showed them to their cabins, Dillon strapped back in and got the *Malshekt* ready for takeoff. He waited on a persistent gust of wind, but once it had blown out its fury, he got the ship off the ground. He was about to pitch up for the quickest escape from the planet's gravity as he could get when he saw something.

"Wait, there's another person down there," he said.

<Affirmative.>

"We should grab them, too. Otherwise, they'll get caught in this storm."

<Negative. We have brought aboard the indicated guests. The Kiandarian below has just taken a photo of the *Malshekt*. Per Daevol Rousilarru's theories, we cannot take them aboard. Their photo is what led us to this point in the time stream.>

Dillon shook his head, astounded at how history and their

present actions intermingled. "I'll take your word for it. I just hope that guy's all right."

He didn't wait for an answer from the AI, instead punching the throttle to get them out of the atmosphere before someone did more than take a photo. He was reprimanded by Sherisza for not giving her or their guests sufficient warning, but soon, he had the *Malshekt* in space and took her far out of range of the tracking probes and satellites. He headed toward some open space and laid in their course with the Chrono Drive.

As usual, they would arrive somewhere near Kwaagi space in the reaches, but with the help of Daevol, Dillon found a spot safely away from the wreckage of Outer Dock Five. Now that they had many guests aboard, the last thing they needed was trouble. With any luck, it'd be a quiet trip to the reaches and the "current" time stream, and then they'd fly their guests to Kiandar and drop them off. Hopefully, the previous Kiandarians they had rescued were adjusting well to the new time in an old place.

With their course laid in, Dillon gave Sherisza a couple of minutes. When she didn't return to the flight deck, though, he figured she trusted him to get them underway. "Dillon to Captain Rousilarru and guests, we are about to engage the drive. Please hold on to something or prepare for brief unconsciousness."

He gave them twenty seconds, and then Dillon pulled on the throttle of the Chrono Drive. The stars shivered, he heard echoes of his previous words, and he swore he could smell Sherisza on the light breeze from the life support system. And then they were in the time stream, but they were not alone.

Off the starboard bow, matching their course and speed, was that mystery black ship.

———

Dillon stared out the starboard viewport but didn't make any adjustments to their course or speed, nor did he try evasive maneuvers. For the moment, their mystery attacker was only flying by their side, no sense of hostility yet. It was remarkable just how like the *Malshekt* it was now that he had the time and luxury to study it, from its weaponry to its design to its ion cannon. It was smaller and sleeker, but it was hard to believe its design was a coincidence. Only the lack of Kwaagi disruptors really made it stand apart now that he got a good, long look at it.

"Captain, Azi, I need you both on the flight deck," Dillon said.

Daevol released the lock on Azi's cabin, and she came out a moment later to stand behind Dillon. She had to lean between his chair and Sherisza's to see the other ship, but then she stood up straight so the captain could get to her seat.

"Attempt to get them talking," Azi said.

"Hold on tight, Azi, this could get dangerous," Sherisza said, strapping herself in. She then opened the hailing frequencies. "Unidentified craft, this is the *Malshekt*, a scientific vessel from the world of Kiandar. Why do you insist on attacking us?"

Another garbled message came across the frequency, and Azi's feathers laid down flat as she listened to it. "I cannot decipher what they are saying, but they are angry. I would suggest we get away from them, but if you can keep them talking, that would benefit my research."

"This is Dillon Mackey, a human from Earth... Terra Prime," he said across the comms. "We don't want to fight you. Please just leave us alone or at least stop attacking long enough for us to figure out what you're saying."

Another message came across the frequency, longer but still garbled. "Good, keep them talking as long as you can," Azi said, rushing back into her cabin. "This will not be easy with no commonalities in our tongues, but the more they say, the more I can try to infer what it means."

"Don't think figuring that out's gonna be an issue," Dillon said, sliding the *Malshekt* hard to port as the other ship launched a salvo of missiles. The point-defense lasers destroyed them all, but Dillon didn't think that would be the end of the pleasantries. "Boy, did they get pissy when they heard Azi."

"Perhaps it is the enemy from the reaches, recognizing Kwaagi speech," Sherisza said. She activated the hailing frequency. "This is the last time I will warn you. We cannot understand your language, but if you attack us again, I will put this ship's new weaponry to the test."

The other ship turned toward them and started to charge its weapons, and Sherisza moved to beat them to the punch. The targeting HUD came up and locked on the other ship, and Dillon saw in the bottom right of the display that Daevol was diverting all possible power to the forward shields. The other ship got off a few ineffective blaster shots, charging the *Malshekt*'s ion cannon, but then Sherisza unloaded on it with the Kwaagi disruptors.

Dillon saw flashes of blue and purple lightning arcing across the enemy ship, almost like the ion cannon's discharge had hit it. The disruptors had overloaded its shields, and then Sherisza let loose with the ion cannon, the *Malshekt*'s interior going dark for a moment. Soon, both ships were "drifting" at phenomenal speed while facing each other. But the black ship was dead in space, and Sherisza held her finger over the trigger of the disruptors while the targeting reticle spun its green circle.

"I could send you to the six hells right now," she said over the hailing frequency, though the other ship would be deaf to it after taking a hit from the ion cannon. "Goddess, guide my hand."

"Wait," Azi said, re-emerging from her cabin. "The inflection... it was not a message of anger, but desperation. I believe they are trying to warn you of something."

Sherisza slowly moved her finger away from the trigger, staring with equal parts anger and curiosity at their enemy. She didn't have long for it, though, before the other ship powered back up, likely the same way the *Malshekt* had after their previous encounter. And then it disappeared from the time stream to some place and date that was impossible to deduce. Sherisza looked at their Kwaagi companion over her shoulder and nodded her thanks.

"I will continue trying to decode the message," Azi said. "Should we encounter that ship again, I would suggest we stop our ship and wait upon them. I believe–and again, I cannot say this for certain–they think we are ignoring or fleeing from them, and defending yourselves has led them to believe they may have no choice but to destroy you. This is my hypothesis."

"Two things I noticed, though," Dillon said. "One, they got really mad when they heard Azi speak. And the other? Every time we've encountered that ship, we've been heading toward the reaches beyond Kwaagi space."

Sherisza clearly understood what Dillon was subtly leaving unsaid. "Did you collect any more data on that ship, Daevol?"

<Affirmative, Captain. Its design is virtually identical to the *Malshekt* but for its smaller size and sleeker build. It appears to also have a Daevol Drive.>

Sherisza turned to Azi. "Let me know the moment you figure anything out."

"Aye, Captain," the Kwaagi woman said, returning to her cabin and closing the door.

"There must be some connection between these attacks and the one upon the Kwaagi," Sherisza said when they were alone again. "Keep us on course and I will start preparing supper for you and our guests."

It seemed a little strange, but Dillon figured she wanted to do something with her hands to work out the tension. "Sounds good," he agreed, turning the *Malshekt* to face forward again.

Once he was alone on the flight deck, Dillon's thoughts started to wander. He considered the enemy ship and how things had played out this time. Each ship had now *counted coup* against the other–earning honor in battle without actually taking lives. It did seem to point to the enemy ship trying to tell them something or warn them off some course of action, but all the other circumstances left it a mystery. Until Azi figured out how to translate the messages they'd recorded, there was little to go on but circumstance.

Most concerning to Dillon, though, was the design of the other ship. If it looked like the *Malshekt*, was armed like the *Malshekt*, and had the same drive as the *Malshekt*, how much of a stretch was it to think it *was* the *Malshekt*, perhaps of the future? Could this even be him and Sherisza, or one or the other, coming back to try to stop them from doing something? If so, why could they not understand the other pilot? And why had the other pilot resorted to violence immediately?

There were so many questions, but for the moment, Dillon didn't have any answers. He sat on the flight deck and contemplated the stars and all the mysteries while he waited for their new Kiandarian guests to eat. Soon enough, they had finished and returned to their cabins, and Sherisza called Dillon and Azi to come to the galley for a meal.

Got to keep Azi away from anyone who might mention they're from a different time, he thought as he padded up the corridor, the Kwaagi female by his side.

CHAPTER 8
ADDITIONS

IT WAS a tricky few days as they proceeded back to Kiandar in the current timeline. They kept Azi from interacting with the Kiandarian refugees to try to prevent her learning that the *Malshekt* could travel through time. Sherisza apologized repeatedly for the inhospitable treatment, limiting their eating and lavatory times, and keeping them all mostly confined to quarters. For their part, Azi and the guests were understanding, even if they had no idea what the true purpose was.

They reached Outer Dock Seventeen orbiting Kiandar and were welcomed to land in its main hangar. Sherisza let Dillon pilot the *Malshekt* into the landing bay while she went to gather their guests for departure. Azi came out to stand behind Dillon's chair, and she smiled as she saw the familiar sights of one of the Kwaagi space docks. Dillon could only imagine the roil of emotions that must've seeped beneath the surface as the woman thought of her destroyed home.

I guess that's something she and Sherisza have in common, he thought.

He set the *Malshekt* down easily, and Daevol opened the hatch when Sherisza brought the Kiandarians up the corridor.

There was a brief farewell, and then Sherisza disembarked with their guests to get them situated with their hosts. These Kiandarians didn't have translator chips the way Dillon and Sherisza did, so communication was a minor issue. But the Kwaagi had been able to work with the prior group of refugees, so Dillon was sure these ones would be well taken care of, too.

Once they were alone, Azi walked over and closed the hatch. Dillon turned to see what she was up to, and she leaned on the back of Sherisza's seat. "How far back in time is this ship able to travel?" she asked. Dillon's mouth dropped open a bit, and he couldn't find his voice. She met his gaze evenly, a challenge in those eyes. "You think my people are stupid?"

"Far from it," he finally managed. "How did—"

"I felt as though I was living moments in reverse, heard echoes, and then we went to an empty section of space numerous times to lay a false trail. Even with the faster speed of this ship, we did not go anywhere far enough or isolated enough to suggest we would find an unknown colony of Kiandarian survivors. It was not difficult to figure out. There has long been speculation about the capabilities of this ship and its drive. Now I understand why."

The hatch opened again, and Sherisza came on board. "Why did you close the door?"

Dillon glanced at Azi. "She knows," he said. "She figured it out faster than I did."

Sherisza looked at their guest but only nodded. "Can I ask you to keep this a secret?"

"Yes, Captain. Though I am immensely curious about this ship and its capabilities. Are there limitations to its use?" Azi asked.

"That will take quite a bit of explaining. Can you wait until we are safely away? I am worried that mystery ship may be waiting for us again as we engage the Chrono Drive back to the reaches. Once we are safe, Dillon and I will explain things to you, contingent on your promise not to speak a word of it to anyone. We are hunted enough as it is."

"The Chrono Drive... Of course," the Kwaagi woman agreed. "If my oath is insufficient, I... I will join your crew on a permanent basis if you wish. That is, if the human can tolerate me indefinitely..."

She tried to approximate a smile, and Dillon laughed. "Don't be silly. Might be nice to have another face on board full time."

Sherisza nodded. "We will discuss this as well. For now, let us depart and hope we do not encounter our mystery ship again."

"Aye, Captain," Dillon said.

<We have been cleared for departure, Captain. Just as last time, however, there are Dominion warships in the area. We must be cautious in leaving.>

Sherisza took her seat at the controls. "Let me handle this. Best we are fully prepared in case our enemy comes calling immediately." They left the station, but Sherisza coasted away at first. "Daevol, can you show me an image of the first group of settlers?"

<Of course, Captain. Allow me to interface with the satellites. Negotiating...>

Soon, a holodisplay came up, zooming in to show two houses side by side in Sherisza's old neighborhood. There were gardens being tilled, repairs being effected to the homes, and they could even see some of the children playing ball in the yard. Sherisza took in a deep breath through her nose, and Dillon reached across to lay his hand on her shoulder. It was but the first step of many, but it clearly already had an impact on his love.

He gave Sherisza's shoulder a squeeze. "Legacy," he said.

"This is truly happening," Sherisza said with a shuddering breath.

"It is hard to believe what I am seeing is real," Azi commented. "That you designed and built a time travel device to save your own people in this manner... this is the most amazing use of technology I have ever witnessed. I am honored to travel with you, Captain Rousilarru."

"Thank you," Sherisza said, barely above a whisper. "Thank you both for helping me."

"Daevol, set course and engage on the captain's word," Dillon said.

<Acknowledged.>

Sherisza engaged the drive herself, and Azi held onto the backs of both seats as she fought off the press of unconsciousness. Soon, they were in the time stream, and Dillon and Sherisza both glanced at their guest, who was now staring with dilated pupils out the front viewport. They both turned back, expecting the black ship to be there again, but there was nothing. Whatever Azi was thinking, it was related to their traveling through time and not the danger they might soon be in.

"Anything on sensors, Daevol?" Dillon asked.

<Negative. There is no sign of the enemy ship.>

"Thank God for small favors," he muttered.

"Perhaps they learned their lesson the last time," Sherisza said. "Though I will not pin too much hope to that. Daevol, continue scanning for trouble."

<Acknowledged.>

"You two, come along to the galley so we can talk," the captain said, unstrapping herself and leading Dillon and Azi up the corridor.

———

"Do you think we can trust her?" Dillon asked.

Sherisza lay in his arms, basking in the afterglow of their love, purring softly as she started to drift off to sleep. He almost hated to wake her and make her think about complicated matters, but his mind was a whirl after their discussion in the galley. Azi had deduced a lot, including the fact that the AI was more sophisticated than Sherisza let on, so there was little holding back when they spoke of the ship and its capabilities. Sherisza still hadn't revealed how the Chrono Drive did what it did, but she didn't keep much else about it a secret.

Azi had accepted everything she was told at face value thus far. It was important to impress Daevol Rousilarru's theories on her, to make sure she knew that history couldn't be altered. Even if it could, Sherisza had no intentions of doing so, not even to try to save her family. That was something that clearly confused the Kwaagi female, but she offered no nosey inquiries or arguments. In the end, she trusted Sherisza to use the drive to save her people, and until that was accomplished, it was enough. Whatever Azi thought about trying to save Outer Dock Five, she hadn't put it into words.

"Kwaagi are not known for subtlety," Sherisza whispered. "When she says she wishes to join our crew full time and promises to keep our secrets, I believe her. It does not mean we should tell her everything, but we will take it a little at a time. My primary concern with her is not even that she will steal our technology or divulge its function to others."

"What are you worried about, then?" he asked when she went quiet.

Her gorgeous golden eyes opened, stars shining in their depths though it wasn't a reflection from the viewports. "When we have children, Dillon, this ship will be our home. I am not certain I want anyone else to share it with us."

"Maybe she'll be a babysitter," he offered.

Sherisza snorted. "For when we go out on the town...? You are silly. I trust that she will respect our privacy, but I want you, our home, and our children to myself."

"Well, no one says she has to stay on board forever," he said. "Or that she'll want to. Maybe she'll get sick of us after a while. How long... do your pregnancies last?"

"Hmmm, about eight Terran months, give or take. Do you still want to finish your studies before we take that step?"

"I'd like to, but we'll make that decision when the time comes," Dillon said. "And you have just as much say in it as my studies do. If you're really eager to start a family, we can do that. Just consider our relationship is still young and *you* may still get sick of me, too."

"I do not see that happening. Tell me I am not becoming boring to you," she said with a glistening in her eyes.

"Never," he said, rubbing a thumb along the side of her muzzle. "God only knows how much I love you."

"Good. Now stop talking. Just hold me and get some sleep."

Dillon pulled her closer and she laid her face against his chest. He could feel the vibration of her purring in his heart, and he couldn't help but smile. His mind was still a whirl, now with the added thoughts of children and raising them when he would only be twenty, but the sound and feel of her purr calmed him. The smell of her only aided in soothing him, and he laid his hand along her jaw and drifted off to sleep.

———

The mystery black ship made no appearance at all on the way to the reaches. The *Malshekt* came out of the time stream in the middle of a vast emptiness as usual. No other ships were nearby, nothing to suggest trouble or danger. Dillon and Sherisza blew out the breaths they were holding, and even Azi let loose a small dose of some scent. She seemed embarrassed after she did, but Dillon made a conscious effort to pretend he didn't notice.

"Let us stay here a few hours before we make the next trip," Sherisza said, turning in her seat. "Dillon, you should message your parents, and Azi, we will monitor the news feeds to see if there is any word of the state of your empire."

"Thank you, Captain," the Kwaagi woman said. "I will return to working on deciphering the messages from that black ship to give you some privacy."

"You don't have to hide in your cabin all the time, you know," Dillon said.

"It is no trouble. I do not wish to intrude upon your relationship. Any time you two wish to have the ship to yourselves, simply say so. I will sequester myself," Azi said.

She went into her cabin and closed the door then, and Dillon shared a look with Sherisza. "Like I said, she's blunt."

Sherisza chuckled. "Daevol, open a subspace channel to Terra Prime, addressed to Malcolm and Sasha Mackey."

<Initiating... channel open. Video feed established.>

An image of Dillon's parents in their kitchen came up on a holodisplay in the front of the flight deck. They were dressed for work, but they looked to have just gotten home. It was good to see them again, and Dillon looked at his tall, muscular father who somehow managed to look like a linebacker and a galactic lawyer at the same time. His mother, too, looked good, still in the robe she wore as the arbiter of the Terran Senate. Her smile was warm and wide as she saw Dillon and Sherisza seated on the *Malshekt*'s flight deck.

"There you are, baby. How are you? Nice to see you again, Sherisza," Sasha said.

"Mom, Dad, good to see you," Dillon said.

"Hello Sasha, Malcolm," Sherisza greeted them.

"We haven't heard much about what's going on in Kwaagi

space if that's what you were wondering," Malcolm said. "You know the Kwaagi, they're quiet and proud, so they're keeping it mostly to themselves for now. We're preparing aid in case they ask for it, though."

"That's good," Dillon said. "Actually, I was just calling to see if you were planning the usual big bash for Grandma's birthday."

"Oh, of course, the backyard barbecue at the estate house. Almost everyone is coming," his mother said. She glanced at Malcolm. "Were you two planning to come?"

"If she would not mind," Sherisza offered.

Dillon waved at her dismissively. "As long as it's not going to create some kind of incident with the Dominion."

"She won't mind, Sherisza," Malcolm said. "It could cause some trouble with the Quarran Dominion, but nothing violent. They're still screaming for the two of you to be arrested. Laws were broken and all that. They don't much care that we showed them what precipitated the entire ordeal or what MacNault said when he thought he was in control. But we'd love it if you could both make it, too."

"We're planning on it, then."

"How are your rescue efforts going?" Sasha asked.

"We have brought four families back to Kiandar so far," Sherisza answered. "I am trying to prioritize certain professions so they can remain somewhat autonomous. Farmers, hunters, engineers, an architect; they will need to learn additional skillsets to survive, and we will need to bring in some teachers from the outside for the children. I have hope, though. It is proceeding well so far, but there is much work to be done."

"I can pass along a request for teachers, if you think they'll be receptive to having humans around," Malcolm said.

"None of them have translation implants, so the teachers

will need to be fluent in Kiandese to be of use," Sherisza said. "If you can find suitable candidates, that would be very helpful."

"I'll check into it for you."

"There's one other thing if we come to visit for Grandma's birthday," Dillon said. "We'll have another guest along for the trip."

Sasha put her hand over her mouth. "Oh my God, congratulations you two!"

Sherisza barked a laugh and Dillon rolled his eyes. "Not that kind of guest, Mom. No, we've got... hang on. Azi, can you come out to the flight deck for a second?"

The Kwaagi woman came out of her cabin and stood between the two seats. She studied the humans in the holodisplay as closely as she was being studied in turn, her feathers bobbing a few times before she bowed her head slightly.

"Mom, Dad, this is Azilija. She's helping us with a bit of a linguistics mystery and staying on board the *Malshekt* for a while. She'd probably just insist on staying on the ship when we come to visit, but I'd like to bring her to the party as well if that's all right."

"Greetings," Azi said. "What party do you speak of, Dillon?"

"There's always room for one more," Malcolm said. "Hello there, Azilija. I'm Malcolm Mackey, Dillon's father, and this is my wife, Sasha. Nice to meet you."

The Kwaagi woman bowed her head again. "Thank you. Your son has been demonstrating that humans are not all as offensive as my people have long believed."

Dillon laughed. "Are you having the party on her birthday or on the weekend?"

"Sunday afternoon," Sasha said.

"We'll see you guys then. Right now, we've got the next group of Kiandarians to rescue, and then we're headed to another Kwaagi dock to upgrade their fighter wing. But we wouldn't miss Grandma's birthday for the world. Give our love to everyone."

"Take care, you three," Sasha said.

"Farewell," Sherisza said as Azi bowed her head again, and the connection closed.

"Thank you for your invitation, Dillon. I will try not to offend your family's noses while I am there," Azi said matter-of-factly before she went back in her cabin.

Dillon looked at Sherisza and they both snickered quietly. The Kiandarian sighed wistfully and smiled at him. "Your parents are always so kind to me. I am glad to see that kindness also extends to our Kwaagi companion."

"My folks are good people despite all the jokes we have about lawyers," Dillon returned. "Let's get another handful of your people to Kiandar."

"Daevol, set course and engage the Chrono Drive when ready. Azi, prepare to enter the time stream," Sherisza said.

<Engaging Chrono Drive now.>

They slipped into the time stream, but no matter how much Dillon wanted to hold Sherisza's hand at that moment, both of them sat ready for attack.

CHAPTER 9

PROGRESS

BRINGING Kiandarians forward through time was a bit easier when Dillon and Sherisza didn't have to try to hide it from Azi. She was excited, and it was easy to tell even though she was suppressing her scent usage. Sherisza and Dillon had both been concerned that the Kwaagi woman was going to want to tell her people about the Chrono Drive, but she was more interested in its use than its function. Despite her allegiance to the empire and the dangers she was subject to flying on the *Malshekt*, she acted as part of the crew and was thrilled with their mission.

Dillon stood as Sherisza came up the steps with the latest Kiandarian refugees, another pair of families whose lives had been in danger. Like the others before them, they were shocked to find a human and a Kwaagi on board the ship. Sherisza made introductions, and that appeared to ease their worries, but then everyone got a massive surprise.

"Welcome aboard the *Malshekt*," Azi said, and it took Dillon a second to realize she had spoken in Kiandese. "I am Administrator Azilija, and I will be taking care of your comfort and needs while we are underway. Should you need anything from the captain, please ask me first, and I will be happy to speak to her on your behalf."

"Thank you, Azi," Sherisza said, also speaking her native tongue. "Would you show our guests to their cabins and then give them a tour of the galley and lavatory?"

"Aye, Captain," the Kwaagi woman said with a slight bow of her head. She gestured for the guests to follow her and proceeded up the corridor.

Dillon and Sherisza exchanged a glance, and the lioness of Kiandar chuckled lightly through her nose. "Come, let us get underway. We do not want to remain exposed to discovery too long. We will proceed at impulse speed until our guests are safely in their cabins before we engage the Chrono Drive."

"Yes, ma'am," Dillon said, taking his seat. "All clear, Daevol?"

<Affirmative. Several tourists took photos of the *Malshekt* on our approach, but this is in line with the historical records. Proceed west before taking us out of the atmosphere to avoid a growing crowd of spectators.>

"Thanks, buddy," Dillon said.

<Of course, Commander.>

Dillon found he missed the AI's incessant teasing, but only a little. He got the *Malshekt* off the ground with a deft touch. He spun the ship in the indicated direction and kept it low, avoiding too much visibility from the ground. Once they reached a safe distance, he took them up but at a leisurely angle, trying not to jostle their new guests too much. Reaching escape velocity, he brought the *Malshekt* into space and then set her on the usual course to the reaches.

"I have a feeling we're going to see that black ship again," Dillon said.

"As do I," Sherisza replied, running a finger along the

combat controls. "If we do, let us see if we can get them talking again before we exchange our usual pleasantries."

"Azi, our course is laid in, if you could show our guests to their cabins and explain the side effects of engaging the Chrono Drive," Dillon said over the comms.

"Understood, Commander. Give us five minutes," she responded.

"She's working hard to fit in," he commented when the comms were off.

"I am quite pleased at her presence, though my secret is threatened by it," Sherisza said.

"I think she's more excited about helping us than trying to earn any favors by telling her people our secrets."

"For now," she said. "I suppose that is as much as we can ask for."

Azi came walking up the corridor a few minutes later. "Our guests are safely in their cabins, prepared for the jump to warp speed," she said, a little gleam in her eye like she wanted to wink but didn't know how.

"Thank you, Azi," Sherisza said. "Daevol, take us into the stream."

<Acknowledged.>

Dillon hardly felt the jump this time, though the other side effects were still there, the echoes and memories and shivering of the universe about them. He gripped the combat controls as well, but there was no immediate sign of the black ship. He had Daevol scan far and near, but the AI detected nothing through the sensors. Unless the other ship's captain had installed a cloaking device, they had avoided it yet again.

"Seems safe, but keep on guard, Daevol," Dillon said.

<Aye, Commander.>

He turned to Azi. "I'm surprised you can speak Kiandese."

Her feathers rose for a moment, then flattened out. "What

do you think I have been doing all this time in my cabin? I have studied the messages from the black ship extensively, but I have also been learning Kiandese, that I may be of more help to the captain in this mission."

Dillon looked at Sherisza, who smiled. "I am grateful for your efforts, Azi. Wait a few minutes until we are certain our enemy does not appear, and then you may use the replicator to provide some food for our guests. Partake of some yourself if you wish, of course."

"Thank you, Captain," the Kwaagi female said, heading back up the corridor.

"I think she's going to put me out of a job at this rate," Dillon grumbled.

Sherisza laughed. "Nonsense. She can serve several important functions, but she does not have the mechanical aptitude you do. She would not make a suitable apprentice, nor would I be interested in taking her to my bed."

"Sherisza!" Dillon barked, and she laughed harder. "God, don't tell me my bad sense of humor is starting to rub off on you."

"I figured I had best get used to barbing as often as I am barbed if we are going to see your family," she teased.

"That's true. Good thinking."

She looked out the front viewport pensively. "Hmmm, I hope we have seen the last of that black ship, but at the same time, I would really like to know what they were saying and why they attacked us."

"If they had something important to say, I'm sure we'll see them again," he said.

"I suppose so. While our guests are busy, I am going to work on my schematics some more. Feel free to go join them if you would like to get away from the helm."

"I think I'll head to the back and get some exercise in while we have some time," Dillon said. After a quick peck on her leonine nose, he made his way toward engineering.

———

After letting Outer Dock Seventeen know, Sherisza piloted the *Malshekt* down to the surface of Kiandar to drop the newest settlers off directly. Dillon knew it was something she'd wanted to do from the beginning, but he also suspected it was to keep Azi from reporting to the station's brigadier. The Kwaagi woman was working to fit in as part of the crew, but there was still a bit of suspicion there. It was no mystery to Dillon; he felt the same way.

Sherisza set the *Malshekt* down in the road near the occupied homes. Now there were four families living near each other, soon to be six. Sherisza was prioritizing professions that would help the settlers get by day to day, and it looked like they were getting a lot of work done already. Carpenters, architects, and farmers were working together to turn the old neighborhood into a working little town. They hadn't even been here that long, but Dillon could already see the evidence of their hard work.

There was another ship on the road a little distance away, Kystar by its design and markings. The Kystar, whose alliance included a race the Kiandarians had once warred against, had sent teams of archaeologists and anthropologists to study and preserve Kiandarian culture. There was no telling how much their society would change as it tried to rebuild, but the Kiandarians were getting outside help to keep their customs. And all that was to say nothing of the generous donations of food and supplies the settlers received to help them along.

Dillon was glad Earth was involved with the relief efforts. Humanity had once fought with the Kiandarians, too, though indirectly during another war. Though relations had been mostly normalized after the conflict ended, the Kiandarians had still viewed humans with suspicion. Now, humanity was doing its part to help, and Dillon hoped it would lead to friendlier relations in the future. Lord knew his relationship with Sherisza wouldn't be enough to bridge the gap between the two species, as special as it was to him.

He bid their passengers farewell as the Kiandarians disembarked with Sherisza and Azi, and then he sat down in his co-pilot's seat. He watched from the viewport as the other settlers came to welcome the newcomers. It was a heartwarming thing to see. They were retrieving people from the same geographical location but different points in time, and it was interesting to see how the people all reacted to each other. Eventually, Dillon knew, they'd be bringing settlers from different parts of Kiandar, which meant different customs and even dialects. For now, though, the people all had a lot in common, strangers across time though they were.

"Hey Daevol?" Dillon said.

<Yes, Commander?>

"You haven't busted my chops in a while. I kind of miss it."

<I have found no reason to. Your relationship with the captain now fits my parameters nearly perfectly. Besides, we now have a Kwaagi guest I can tease.>

Dillon sat up straight. "Oh God, you're not bothering her, are you?"

<Worry not, she gives as good as she gets. Despite what you may think based on her muted personality, she has quite a sense of humor and her wit is quick and sharp.>

He laughed. "For some reason, I'm not surprised. She's an interesting woman, for sure. Do you trust her with the captain's secrets?"

<As Captain Rousilarru has explained to you before, the Kwaagi are not a subtle or devious people. If she has sworn to

keep the secret, I trust she will. This does not mean, however, that we should be careless in what we tell her. Thus far, she has spent most of her time studying the messages from our enemies and the Kiandese language. I believe she is also studying Terran English as well, for your impending visit to Earth.>

"I wonder how much she'll learn by then."

<Azilija has an astonishing aptitude for learning languages. She may not be fluent by the time we go to Terra Prime, but she will be able to hold conversations.>

"Good God," Dillon muttered. He looked out the viewport again. "Things seem to be going well here."

<The Kiandarians are a hard-working and industrious people. They will start small but move on to larger things in a short while. By my calculations, if we can deliver one hundred of them to this time and place, the species has a nearly ninety-eight percent chance to not just survive but thrive. And we have at least that many selected from the historical records already.>

"Outstanding," he approved. "Why don't you send a subspace message to Outer Dock Seven and let them know we'll be there in a couple of days to work on their wing?"

<Acknowledged.>

Dillon couldn't help but smile when he saw Sherisza exchanging hugs with the settlers. Her expression was one of utter joy, and even the antics of the children only made her smile wider. In her heart, she was missing her own, Dillon knew. But she was basking in the joy of the hope that her people would survive, that her efforts weren't for nothing. More than that, she seemed proud of her brother and their invention, which made it all possible. Though he tried not to think about it too often, Dillon resolved that even if his relationship with Sherisza didn't work out, he was proud to have been a part of this.

Soon enough, though, she and Azi boarded the *Malshekt*,

and she came right over to give Dillon a muzzle rub along his cheek. He stood up to hug her, and she began purring against him, her joy expressed for everyone to hear, but only for Dillon to feel. He looked at Azi from over Sherisza's shoulder, and the Kwaagi woman approximated a human smile again, the slightest trace of her joyful scent touching the air.

"Do you two wish for some privacy?" she asked.

"Nah, it's fine," Dillon said. "We're going to get underway to Outer Dock Seven to work on the next wing of your people's fighters. Once we're on the way, maybe you can trounce me at chess again while Sherisza works on her schematics."

"Oh, with pleasure," Azi said.

"Perhaps at the station, we can have another seat installed here for you," Sherisza offered.

"With this ship's impressive holodisplays, a seat would be all I need. So long as it does not inconvenience you, that would prove beneficial to all of us, I think."

"We will see what they have available to install," the Kiandarian said. "For now, hold on to something, we are heading back to your people's empire."

"Aye, Captain," the Kwaagi woman said, gripping the backs of their seats.

Sherisza piloted them off the ground, waving out the viewport until the *Malshekt* was well into the air. They left the planet's atmosphere and Sherisza guided them to a safe distance from which to engage the Chrono Drive. She laid in their course with help from Daevol, and then she pulled back on the throttle. Soon enough, all three of them had shaken off the momentary effects of entering the time stream.

And so all three of them clearly saw the black ship coming directly at them.

———

"This little bastard is persistent," Dillon managed through his teeth as Sherisza executed another evasive maneuver.

There had been only one garbled message this time before the enemy ship opened fire. Its cannons didn't seem much stronger, but it was hounding the *Malshekt* and peppering her with shots, however ineffective. It was annoying, if nothing else, and Dillon suspected Sherisza just wanted to blow the damned thing up this time and be done with it.

Azi had stopped her, though. After the latest message came across, the Kwaagi woman had hurried to her cabin to compare it to the others. Her language skills were impressive, but Dillon wasn't sure she was going to figure anything out before Sherisza lost her patience for good. It certainly wasn't helping that she was getting jolted about as the *Malshekt* evaded fire. The artificial gravity could only do so much, after all.

Several more shots caught the *Malshekt* despite Sherisza's efforts. The ion cannon was now fully charged, but that meant the shields had to start absorbing rather than redirecting energy. It was a brilliant piece of technology, but it had its limitations. By the same token, Sherisza didn't like to discharge the ion cannon without a specific target, as the shot didn't simply fizzle out if it missed. It kept going and could strike another planet or ship an untold distance away, perhaps even years later.

The point-defense lasers went off as the enemy ship fired a salvo of missiles at close range. Dillon was thankful their enemy hadn't upgraded to Kwaagi disruptors the way the *Malshekt* had, at least. Warning lights and messages came on as the shields began to wear down, though, and he knew Sherisza was going to have to turn and fight soon. Nevertheless, she executed every brilliant maneuver she could, trying to buy Azilija more time.

A final warning flashed, and Sherisza spun the ship to face their enemy, her finger about to depress the trigger for the ion cannon. The enemy ship ducked out of the way, though, and the Kiandarian snarled as she began to give chase. She fired herding shots to keep the enemy from trying to circle around, content to be the chaser and not the prey for the time being. She was muttering something under her breath, though, and Dillon suspected it was a prayer. Whether for guidance or patience, he wasn't sure.

Azi came out of her cabin a minute later. "Open the hailing frequency!" she hissed. Once Dillon had, she shouted, "*Om-cubwe! Om-cubwe!*"

<Enemy ship has powered down its weapons, Captain.>

"What did you say?" Sherisza asked. She didn't look at the Kwaagi woman, though. She brought the *Malshekt* up slowly to fly beside the other black ship. There was a sour look on her face as she stared out the port side of the viewport, but she otherwise remained quiet.

"I will explain in a moment," Azi said, motioning for quiet as another garbled message came over the hailing channel. She listened intently, but then straightened up. "Daevol, transfer the work from my cabin to a holodisplay here, please."

<Affirmative.>

A holodisplay appeared before the Kwaagi woman, and she began moving things around on it with a clawed finger. Dillon couldn't make heads or tails of what she had written there, as even the translated part was in the Kwaagi language. She worked quickly, though, her feathers laid back flat along her skull in concentration.

At last, she looked up. "*Dajon-nuut. Kada-sin-we.*"

A final, quick message came across the comms, and then the black ship disappeared from the time stream. All three of them breathed out sighs of relief, Azi's accompanied by a brief bit of a scent that was reminiscent of burnt toast.

"What happened?" Sherisza asked, getting the *Malshekt* back on course.

"I do not understand the totality of it, but the desperation helped me decipher things. The other captain, who remains unnamed, has demanded we stop using something and destroy it or we will be destroyed. All I could do was tell him we acknowledged his message."

"You do not know what he wants us to destroy?" the Kiandarian asked.

"Not by name, though I can only speculate it must be the Chrono Drive, since all of our encounters with this ship have been while using it," Azi said. "I will continue trying to decipher the messages, Captain, but I barely had enough to use to formulate a positive response."

"Well, I will not be destroying my Chrono Drive, I can say that much," Sherisza huffed.

"What if they're trying to warn us off repopulating Kiandar or something?" Dillon asked, and Sherisza looked at him. "I mean, it doesn't really make sense since we always meet them when we're headed to the reaches, but they've got to be trying to warn us off for a reason. Maybe they're afraid of us fiddling with the time stream too much."

"Azi, I implore you to redouble your efforts," Sherisza said.

The Kwaagi woman bowed her head. "Of course, Captain. Daevol, please transfer the holodisplay to the galley. I am famished."

<You are always famished. You are going to run our replicator out of power.>

"Daevol!" Sherisza barked.

Azi only let forth a hissing chuckle. "So long as that power is diverted from *your* supply, we may all be much happier."

<Ejecting contents of resident Azilija's cabin into the cold reaches of space.>

"Daevol, leave our guest alone!" the Kiandarian said.

<Would approximately five hundred meters off the port side be alone enough, Captain?>

Sherisza put her hand over her mouth, but Dillon burst out laughing. Azi headed off to the galley, chuckling all the way. Sherisza began programming something into her console, her face set in a scowl.

<Must I really perform all of these self-diagnostics, Captain?>

"Yes. It is the only way I know you will leave our guest alone for a few hours," she said. "I really do not know where you get this from. My brother was not like this."

<Perhaps not to you. Very well, then, Captain. For what it is worth, though, she started it.>

Sherisza put her face in her hand again. Dillon laughed but leaned over to kiss her before he made his way to the galley as well. He was pretty hungry himself, and he was due to get beaten at chess yet again by their Kwaagi companion. He left Sherisza to relax in the aftermath of this most recent incident.

CHAPTER 10

DEVELOPMENTS

THEY ARRIVED at Outer Dock Seven without any other incidents. Sherisza was distracted the rest of the way, though, not even poking around at her schematics for the phase-cloaking device. She wasn't distant from Dillon, or even Azi, spending time with them in the galley or working out in the exercise area. She slept with Dillon and made love to him—and that was getting more enjoyable every time—but the encounters with the black ship were weighing on her mind. To be asked to give up the Chrono Drive and what it meant to her people's future was too much.

It weighed on Dillon's mind quite a bit as well. There was something confusing about it all. If Daevol Rousilarru's theories were correct and history couldn't be altered, why warn them off from using it? Everything they had done and planned to do would already be accounted for. He was sure Sherisza and Azi realized it as well, but if the theories were true, that had to mean the black ship was trying to warn the *Malshekt* away from some course of action to keep its own timeline. What that course of action could be, though, remained just out of Dillon's grasp.

Azilija's progress with the garbled messages was unbelievable. She only had around one hundred words to work with, but she had learned to discern tone and inflection easily. Now she was figuring out some of the words, though Dillon didn't even want to think about how. He was lucky to be able to speak a few languages from Earth, much less try to learn an entirely new and unknown one without so much as a teacher.

His musings cleared up as Sherisza brought them into the station's hangar, not bothering to intrude on Dillon's thoughts. She landed the ship expertly, as always, and Azi came out to stand near the hatch.

"I must go and report to the brigadier," she said. "I will try to get news of how our battle is progressing that I may share with you. Of course, they will insist this information does not get passed on to Terra Prime or the other governments."

"And we will respect those wishes, of course," Sherisza said. "Enjoy your stay among your people, Azilija. We should not be here more than ten or eleven days."

"Thank you, Captain. I will see you both soon."

Azi disembarked, and Sherisza's mouth tightened. Dillon reached over and laid a hand on her arm. "You afraid she's going to tell the brigadier what she's seen and learned?" he asked.

"My entire life's work is in danger, Dillon. It is possible we may not be allowed to leave this station if the Kwaagi are told what we have and decide they need it to defeat their enemies. If that black ship insists we no longer use the Chrono Drive, it may not matter what the Kwaagi do. And if we destroy that black ship, there is no telling what effect it might have on the future. My brother's theories say we cannot change the past, but is that ship not trying to do exactly that?"

"I was just considering that," he answered. "Hard to know, but maybe if we're lucky, Azi can figure out more of what those messages said while we're busy working."

"And what do we do if they try to keep us from leaving?" she asked.

Dillon shrugged. "Tell Daevol to engage the Chrono Drive. The threat of what that would do to the station might get us out alive, at least."

"I should hate to sour our relations with the Kwaagi."

"They'd be starting it," he argued. "Don't let them try to coerce you and make you feel bad about it. But you know what? We're getting ahead of ourselves. Azi said she'd keep her mouth shut about the Chrono Drive. You trusted her on that. So, let's assume she was being honest and try not to get too worked up."

Sherisza nodded. "Yes, you are right, I suppose."

"Hey, don't worry too much about it. Soon enough, we'll be done here and on our way to Earth to go to my grandma's birthday party. We're going to have a lot of fun, so just keep that in mind while we're working."

"You are so sweet," she said, leaning over for a quick kiss before she got up. "Come, let us get to work. This should be familiar enough to both of us now, and we will work separately again to speed things up."

They rose and grabbed their travel bags and toolkits, and when they made their way down the steps to the hangar floor, the dock clerk was there with her electronic clipboard. They were welcomed to the station and led to quarters first, and this time, there were no arguments or objections raised when they opted for a single room and bed. Soon enough, they were back on the hangar floor, attired and ready for work.

Dillon noticed all the dockworkers seemed nervous and on edge, but he wasn't sure if it was because of the war or if something was planned. Whatever the case, he figured they'd know soon enough, and worrying about it wouldn't help. If anything, it would make his work worse, and that would make everyone even more anxious.

Instead, he pushed the thoughts aside and concentrated on making Sherisza happy. And the easiest way he could do that was to put her teachings to use and do the best job he could.

———

After dinner, Dillon and Sherisza remained in their cabin, looking for a film to watch to pass the time once Dillon was finished with his studies. Working separately, they had completed two ships already, which meant they'd easily be on schedule. Sherisza was planning to work extra hours the following two days to put them ahead of schedule so there would be no issues getting to Earth for the birthday party. That meant early bedtime and less romancing, but it would be worth it, Dillon knew. If their stay on Earth went anything like their first visit, it would be well worth his patience.

Azilija came to their quarters before they got the movie started. She looked as nervous as all the dockhands had when Dillon was in the hangar, but she didn't say anything immediately. After an awkward silence, Sherisza invited her inside. The Kwaagi woman came in and stepped to the side, leaning against the wall, her feathers plastered to the top of her head.

"Everything all right?" Dillon asked.

"No. Far from it," Azi answered. "The war is not going well for our empire. What started as a single attack force pushing into our space has become a concerted effort. While our docks are now holding the line along the reaches, significant enemy forces penetrated our territory and appear to be headed for Kwaaganarr. If they reach our home world, there is no telling how much damage they could do."

"Is there any way we can help?" Sherisza asked.

"The *Malshekt* is not a warship; we know this. However, without compromising my oath to you, I did suggest there may be ways we could aid the war effort should you be agreeable to it. They would be endeavors of reconnaissance, not direct conflict, utilizing the ship's incredible speed to beat our enemies to their targets and give warning."

"We will see what we can do," Sherisza said. "However, if the mystery ship continues to attack us every time we use the... Daevol Drive, then we may be in greater danger."

"I understand. I assure you, Captain, I continue to work on deciphering the messages we received. I feel I am close to a breakthrough, but it will require additional research, since I have access to limited samples. However, there is also a way that Dillon may be of help with this."

"How's that?" he asked.

The Kwaagi woman met his gaze evenly. "The emperor... is agreeable to asking for aid from Earth if the request goes through you specifically. I do not know all the details, but there was mention of a princess you rescued, and also of the respect you have shown our people time and time again, particularly in front of the Joint Senates. The emperor knows your name, Dillon Mackey. This is no small thing, especially for an outsider, and even more so for a human."

"My parents will help any way they can, and they have significant sway with the senates," Dillon said. "If the brigadier allows a signal out to Earth, I can send a message tonight. I'm sure my parents would take it to the Terran Senate immediately, and then the Joint Senates from there. I doubt the Quarran Dominion will want to help if my name comes up, but everyone else probably will."

Azi dipped her head slightly. "That would be most benefi-cial. You know my people are a proud people, Dillon. We do not like to ask outsiders for help, but we need it. And the rest of our neighbors need to help us make a stand. We are the strongest of the empires. If we fall to these invaders, the other governments will fall soon after."

"I don't doubt it," he agreed.

"And I will help in any way I can with the aid of my ship," Sherisza said.

"Thank you. I am sorry to bring such dire news, but we are running out of time. I could not wait until after your grandmother's birthday, Dillon," Azi said. "I would not ask you to refrain from going, but I will stay here until you return. Things may be tense enough on Terra Prime without a Kwaagi there being seen as an undue influence on you or your parents."

Dillon tried to wave her off. "You don't need to–"

"This was by request of the brigadier, and thus, the emperor," she interrupted. "I thank you for your honesty and kindness, but in this case, I must follow my emperor's orders."

"We understand," Sherisza said. "We will miss you."

"I will not miss your obnoxious AI," the Kwaagi woman said, chuckling. "I appreciate the trust you have shown me and the wonders I have witnessed. I will continue my work and hope to have an answer for you by the time you return. In the meantime, if you send a message to Earth via the *Malshekt*, the brigadier will know to approve its broadcast."

With that, she bowed and left their quarters.

"Damn, and I was just getting used to her," Dillon said, turning to Sherisza. "I was looking forward to seeing how the family reacted to her."

"I think they will have enough of a shock when they meet me," she returned, sitting on the edge of their bed.

"Ah, don't say that. They're going to love you," he said, kneeling down in front of her. "Not as much as I do, but they will."

Sherisza leaned forward into his embrace. "I am sorry I have made your life so complicated. I know this is not what you expected when you applied for the apprenticeship."

"I'm enjoying every moment, even the ones that almost make me crap my pants," he joked, and she chuckled. "God's got something in mind for us, Sherisza. He'll see us through."

"I pray that it is so."

"Daevol, can you hear me?" Dillon asked.

The *Malshekt*'s AI spoke through Sherisza's chip. <I can hear you, Commander.>

"Send a message to Earth, to my parents, high priority. Tell them the Kwaagi are in need of aid and ask them to get the issue in front of the senate and Joint Senates as soon as possible."

<Acknowledged.>

"Thank you, Daevol. When the transmission is complete, you may begin the transmission of Dillon's silly... *karate* film," Sherisza said.

"It's not silly, it's a classic."

"It is a good excuse to cuddle up with you, and so I will not complain too much," she teased.

And then they both got undressed, turned down the temperature control, and snuggled up under the covers for the movie.

———

The rest of the modifications went swiftly. It was a good thing, too, as the station began to move farther into Kwaagi space to tighten the noose around the invaders. The outer docks didn't move that quickly, but with little trouble expected from their neighbors, the Kwaagi began bringing across ones from the other sides of their space. The enhanced fighter wings were to be left in the path of any enemy reinforcements while the other stations went to support the battle that was fast approaching Kwaaganarr.

Dillon never received a reply from his parents, but he assumed it was being blocked like most other transmissions into Kwaagi space. It was a silly policy on some levels, as the Kwaagi were preventing aid in this case, and could potentially cause other problems they didn't foresee. Still, it wasn't something Dillon planned to bring up to the brigadier and even hint that he thought the Kwaagi were being stupid. Azi had already challenged him once when she thought he was suggesting their people weren't as intelligent as humans.

In some cases, the best policy is to keep your mouth shut, he thought.

Sherisza was testing the last of the modified fighter ships while Dillon loaded their things back on the *Malshekt*. No third seat had been added; apparently, the dock crew knew Azilija wouldn't be going with them again, so they hadn't bothered. They hadn't ignored the *Malshekt*, though, as evidenced by the gifts left on the pilot's and copilot's seats. Dillon picked up the bottles of Kwaagi spirits and fruit baskets with a smile before taking them to the galley.

Sherisza was just boarding the *Malshekt* when Dillon left the galley. She came up the corridor and took him by the hand, leading him into the lavatory. She didn't need to speak a word; Dillon knew what to do. He shed his clothes and put them in the wash, and Sherisza did the same. Then he followed her into the shower and let out a long sigh when the hot water began to spray them both down. The only thing nicer in that moment than shedding the scent of the Kwaagi space station was doing so with Sherisza standing naked before him.

Dillon took her in his arms, and she laid her head on his shoulder. They were expected to leave the station soon, so they didn't progress beyond kissing and caressing, but they did plenty of both while washing each other. Dillon would've liked to take her to their cabin and make proper love to her, but while they didn't have time now, they would during the trip to Earth. He helped her wash her back and her mane, but otherwise resolved to wait until the proper time to make his intentions known.

Once dried off and dressed, they sat in their seats on the flight deck. "Time for the moment of truth," Dillon said, drawing a curious gaze from Sherisza before it dawned on her. "*Malshekt* to Kwaagi flight control, requesting permission to leave the hangar."

"Confirmed, *Malshekt*, you are clear to leave. Thank you again. We hope to see you soon," the flight director said.

Sherisza took them out slowly, as if wary the doors of the hangar were going to snap shut when they tried to leave. Nothing of the sort happened, though, and soon they were out in space, ready to begin the journey to Earth. Sherisza checked the galactic time and date compared to the local time at Dillon's parents' house on Earth, then set the Chrono Drive course and speed.

"Two days seems like a good amount of *us* time," Sherisza declared.

"Sounds good to me. Now we just have to hope our mystery ship accepted what Azi told them at face value," Dillon said.

Sherisza brought them a safe distance from the station and engaged the Chrono Drive, entering the time stream with minimal discomfort for either of them. The HUD came up immediately, but there was no sign of any trouble nearby. Nevertheless, Dillon and Sherisza scanned the darkness out the viewport and on their various holodisplays, looking for any trace of the ship. There was nothing, though, and Daevol didn't raise any alarms.

When there were no attacks and no sign of the black ship, Sherisza brought up the schematic for the phase-cloaking device and began fiddling with it. At least until Dillon dismissed the holodisplay and ran a finger down her arm. She smiled at him, but then she gestured for patience and brought the schematic back up. She made a couple of minute changes that Dillon couldn't understand for the life of him.

"Daevol, run the theoretical test, see if this will work. You may tell me the results and give suggestions when I come back," she said.

<Affirmative, Captain.>

"She might be a while," Dillon joked.

<I assume she will be. Enjoy yourselves.>

They entered their cabin and picked up where they'd left off in the shower. She smelled so good, and Dillon marveled at how each time they made love it got better and better. The more he grew accustomed to her, the better he became at controlling his rising blood pressure and desire. He started to take the lead where he'd initially let her have control. She responded well to his minor dominance, and when he treated her like the person he loved most in the galaxy, she returned the sentiments.

They made love for a while, trying new things, exploring different ways to please each other. She found it funny when he started chasing the furry tuft at the end of her tail, at least until she biffed him in the nose with it. Then it was on. Dillon never thought sex could involve so much laughter, but everything about it felt right. It was more than just an intimate dance seeking physical release; it was a melding. When they were done, Sherisza curled up against Dillon's side and laid her head on his chest. Her purring helped soothe him off to sleep as usual, and they snoozed contentedly in each other's arms for several hours.

Sherisza got up after a little while, though, no doubt leery of ending up too far off their usual sleep schedule. She dressed and headed out to the flight deck, and Dillon followed her. When he came out of their cabin, she was in her seat, the schematic up before her. She had that look of intense concentration on her face, studying every facet of the schematic with a furrowed brow.

"Did the test fail?" he asked.

"Yes, though I am not sure why. Everything looks correct, but the numbers are not adding up correctly. I think your suspicion about *going over the wave* was correct, but the warp inverter I built is not handling the load properly in the testing. I may need to build a stronger one if I can get the supplies while we are on Terra Prime. Once we get this machine working, perhaps we will never have to worry about our strange attacker again."

"One can hope," Dillon said. "I do have one suggestion, though."

"Oh?"

"Put that away and come have a drink with me. The Kwaagi gave us some spirits and fruit baskets in thanks for our work. I stowed them all in the galley."

Sherisza glanced at her schematic one more time and then dismissed it. "Lead the way, my love," she said, rising.

Dillon took her in his arms. "Want to share a little dance first?"

She sighed wistfully, eyes closed. "I would love to."

"Daevol, music please," he said.

<As you wish, Commander.>

The classical music began to play, and Dillon led Sherisza through the dance. It wasn't quite the same as dancing with human girls back in school, but Sherisza learned quickly, and she moved in time with him. It awakened another fire in him, but this wasn't the desire for physical intimacy. No, this was a different fire, one he instinctively understood despite never having felt its like before.

It was the knowledge that she was the one.

Dillon leaned down and kissed her.

CHAPTER 11

EARTH BOUND

THE JOURNEY back to Earth's solar system was quite enjoyable. Dillon had adapted well to having Azilija and the Kiandarian guests on board, so he hadn't really noticed just how much he missed having the ship and Sherisza to himself. He took full advantage of it, though, enjoying his time with her dancing, playing games, and making love, of course. She wasn't accustomed to being intimate all the time, and he understood based on the fact that Kiandarians were typically paired with their twin sibling. Nevertheless, she acclimated to his more amorous nature quickly, and she never gave him the impression she was bored with or put out by it.

Dillon did whatever it took to keep Sherisza's mind off work for a short while. There would be plenty of time to work on the schematics after his grandmother's birthday party. *And Lord knows she'll need something to keep her busy when we have Azi and others on the ship again,* he thought.

There had been no sign of the black ship the entire way to the Terran system, and Dillon couldn't help but think it wasn't the Chrono Drive they were opposed to. There had to be some other facet of their trips to and through Kwaagi space that was drawing the black ship to attack them. Could it be as simple as not wanting them to interfere with the war between the Kwaagi and their unknown attackers? There was no telling; the black ship may have been remarkably similar to the *Malshekt*, but it could have belonged to their enemies.

There was always the possibility that Azi's translations weren't quite right, though her ability to call off the attacker seemed to mitigate that. She was certainly on the right track, and though he was glad to have the ship and Sherisza back to himself, Dillon wanted Azi to return and finish her work. Maybe she wouldn't stay on indefinitely, but he wanted answers about the black ship, and she was best suited to finding them.

He glanced over at Sherisza. She was content. She had a little smile on her leonine face, and he knew part of it was going to see Dillon's parents again. They got on well, and she was grateful not just for their aid to Kiandar, but their acceptance of her as a mate for their son. She was probably a little nervous about meeting the rest of Dillon's family, but she looked hopeful, and he was glad she wasn't a bundle of nerves. He reached over and traced a finger down her arm, and she turned a fuller smile on him.

"I think Grandma is going to love you," he said.

"She sounds like a very special woman. She is your mother's mother?" Sherisza asked.

"Yep, Grandpa Charlie's widow. She lives in this big old southern-style estate house a little bit outside the city. Huge property that my mother and her siblings grew up on. Every year we have a big backyard barbecue for her birthday, and the entire family tries to attend, including all of my father's side. There's probably going to be twenty-five or thirty people there at least but try not to get too overwhelmed. Everyone's going to want to meet you, but we'll save personal introductions for after the initial greetings happen, all right?"

"All right," she agreed.

"And if you do get overwhelmed, you just come find me if I'm not already by your side."

She leaned toward him, and Dillon met her halfway for a kiss.

The moment was spoiled by a two-chirp alarm. <Sorry to interrupt you, Captain, but there is a Dominion warship ahead.>

"Dominion? In the Terran system?" Sherisza gasped.

<Incoming transmission.>

"This is Captain Lacroix of the Dominion warship *Godspeed* to Captain Rousilarru," came the imperious greeting over the hailing frequency.

"Yes, Captain?" Sherisza responded.

"You will stop your ship where you are and surrender yourself to my authority. You are wanted by the Quarran Dominion for violations of numerous sections of the Interstellar Code, including armed assault, trespassing while armed, conspiracy to commit murder, acts of espionage and war against the Quarran Dominion, murder, aggravated–"

"Why don't you throw jaywalking on the list while you're at it?" Dillon interrupted.

"Who is that?" the captain demanded.

"Dillon Mackey, the one you're really after," he answered.

"You will surrender yourself to–"

"Shut your damned mouth for a second," Dillon snapped. "Listen up. You're in Terran space making threats in violation of every interstellar code there is. I suggest you get your ship out of our space before the Joint Senates put out a warrant for you and your entire crew. And God forbid you so much as get the idea of locking a weapon on this ship, because we'll send your ass to the six hells before you can set down your tea."

There was silence over the comms, and Sherisza turned a

wide-eyed stare at Dillon. She muted the hailing frequency and whispered, "How do you know he is drinking tea?"

Dillon shrugged. "Sounds like the kind of arrogant asshole who parades around the bridge with a cup of tea like he owns the galaxy." She put a hand over her mouth, and Dillon reached over to lay his on her arm. "Nobody threatens my girl, certainly not in my home space."

Sherisza smiled but turned back forward and reopened the comms. "Captain, I have little doubt you have seen and heard what transpired in your president's office. I harbor no hatred for the Quarran Dominion or its many peoples. I took revenge solely against the man who tried to commit genocide against my people. If the Quarran Dominion continues to take umbrage with this, take your case before the Joint Senates, and I will subject myself to their judgment."

There was a long pause. "Understood, Captain Rousilarru. I am only following orders."

"We understand," Dillon said. "Just tell whoever's in charge in the Quarran Senate now to take the case before the Joint Senates. You all know who my father is."

Another pause. "Very well. You are clear to pass, *Malshekt*."

"Thank you, Captain Lacroix," Sherisza said, inching the impulse throttle forward.

They watched as the Dominion ship turned and began to head the other way. The HUD came up, showing a number of other good-sized cruisers approaching from Earth. Dillon didn't know if Earth Defense and Mars Military had overheard the conversation, but they wasted little time in sending out a deterrent force. It was a stupid risk for the Quarran Dominion to have taken, and it led Dillon to wonder how they'd found out the *Malshekt* was headed to Earth.

"Someone's still watching us from the Dominion," he mused.

"Yes, they do seem to know our schedule quite well. It is possible some of the others that were involved in MacNault's plot are still in positions of power. I do not want to end up in a state of war with them, not when Kiandar is so vulnerable. The Kwaagi may have to draw some of their defenses away. My people would be helpless."

"I'll mention that to my folks when we get there," Dillon promised.

"Earth Defense Carrier *MacArthur* to the *Malshekt*, is everything all right you two?" came another call across the hailing frequency.

"We are fine, *MacArthur*, thank you for asking," Sherisza responded. "We were able to talk down the Dominion warship from trying to take us into custody in your space."

"Roger that. Fly by our side, *Malshekt*, and we will escort you to home."

Sherisza's ears stood up a bit at that. "My thanks, *MacArthur*."

She brought the *Malshekt* alongside the carrier as it turned about, and she matched its course and speed. Dillon flashed the lights in greeting and the MacArthur repeated the gesture with its port-side docking flashers. He figured not even their mysterious black ship would have the nerve to come take shots at them with an Earth Defense carrier flying escort. When he turned back to Sherisza, she had a little smirk on her face.

"I have never heard you tell someone off in such a manner before," she said.

"Got it from my father, though he's much more diplomatic about it," Dillon chuckled. "They used to call it *Irish diplomacy* back in the day. The ability to tell a man to go to hell in such a way that he looks forward to the trip." Sherisza barked a laugh. "So why are there six hells in your theology? Did the first five fill up too quickly?"

She leaned away with her ears back at that, but then she scoffed. "Your sense of humor can truly be terrible once you get going," she said. "No, it was a reference to the six major lords of the underworld, each with their own pit. Someone sent to the six hells would be tortured slowly in turn by each of them. It was a fate everyone wanted to avoid."

"I can't imagine why," he muttered.

"It is a dark reflection of the light from above," she continued. "The light from above was broken into Love, Honesty, Perseverance, Patience, Purity, and Justice. Righteousness was the seventh light, and this belonged solely to the All-Father, shone upon the All-Mother as she shielded us from his fire. There is not even a dark reflection of the All-Father's righteousness, so there are six hells, one each to mock the other six virtues."

"That sounds vaguely familiar, like something they taught us in Bible school," Dillon said. "I'm glad you feel comfortable enough with me to share that. You've never spoken much about your goddess or her mate."

"I am still feeling through reestablishing my ties to them," Sherisza admitted. "And I did not wish to possibly insult your own beliefs. I understand yours is a monotheistic faith."

He shrugged. "I don't think my faith is wrong, but I keep an open mind about others."

She smiled but didn't say anything else about it. Instead, they cruised toward Earth in a calm, sweet silence beside the *MacArthur*.

They reached Earth and Sherisza let Dillon fly the *Malshekt* down to the capital spaceport. The sun was approaching the horizon, a long summer day coming to an end. Dillon's parents were expecting them for dinner, and he and Sherisza were looking forward to it. He was pretty sure she was hoping for pizza, but he didn't pass that along to his parents. Worse came to worst, he'd take her out for pizza the day after the birthday party, if they didn't have any by then.

They were cleared to land at the spaceport without delay, and Dillon brought them around over their slip and then gently descended with the hovering ports. Once they touched down, they got their travel bags together and disembarked. They held hands as they walked up the boarding tunnel, and when Dillon's parents saw them, their faces erupted in smiles. They waved their son and Sherisza over, and soon, hugs were being exchanged, no handshakes this time.

"Oh, it's so good to see you two again," Sasha said, hugging her son and the Kiandarian at the same time. "We heard there was a little incident when you reached the system?"

"Nothing we couldn't talk our way out of," Dillon said, nearly getting crushed in his father's massive arms. "This is going to come up before the Joint Senates, though."

"It already has," his mother said. "And they were told where they could stick their charges. The video was authenticated, and it not only absolves you of guilt as far as the Joint Senates are concerned, but it leaves the Dominion open to civil and criminal actions if Sherisza would like to press any sort of charges."

"I would not. I only want my people left alone or, better yet, aided in thriving once again," the Kiandarian said.

"You may have to just to press the point with them," Malcolm said. "But that's all stuff to worry about another time. You came back here for a party and to relax, and that's what we want you to do. Dinner should be ready by the time we get back to the house."

"I look forward to sharing a meal with you again," Sherisza said.

Sasha looked at their bags. "And you'll be staying at the house again? You can share the extra bedroom; we won't bother you."

"Thank you."

Dillon's father shook him lightly by the neck behind Sherisza's back, but he had a smile on his face. Did they know Kiandarians went about relationships differently? He wasn't sure, but whatever the case, his parents weren't raising too much of a fuss about them being intimate. If they were giving their permission for it to go on in their home, they had to be looking at Dillon and Sherisza as a married couple, even if it wasn't true just yet.

"Were you planning to come to church in the morning before the party?" Sasha asked. "You don't have to if you don't want to."

"I would not know what to say or do," Sherisza said shyly.

"Ah, just clap and dance to the music, listen to the message, and smile a lot. No one's going to expect you to convert, but some of the family will be there for the service before the birthday festivities. It's completely up to you; don't feel pressured."

Sherisza looked to Dillon, and he smiled. "Sure, we'll go," he said. "I'm sure the reverend will do a better job explaining things than I usually do."

She took his hand again, and they walked with his parents toward their personal shuttle. Only when they reached the spaceport's exit did Sasha turn around, confused. "Wait, where is that Kwaagi woman who was with you? Did she stay on the ship?"

"Oh, she had some other things to take care of, and was ordered to stay back on their mobile outpost," Dillon said. "I don't want to say too much in public, but you know what's going on."

"Yes, we do," Malcolm agreed. "Come on, let's go get dinner. That sort of talk can wait until after when we all have a drink."

Sasha turned a hard stare on Dillon, and he blushed, but then she laughed. "I'm just teasing you, baby."

"You guys are the best," he said.

————

Dillon's parents had provided another prime rib roast dinner, bestowing that rare honor on Sherisza once again. She may have wanted pizza in her heart, but she raised no fuss. She and Dillon enjoyed the rare treat and, as she had before, Sherisza helped clean up after. Dillon was going to put in some help with the cleanup as well but was warned off by his mother's stare. He sensed she wanted some woman-to-woman time, so he went to the sitting room with his father.

Malcolm was on the couch with a little glass of bourbon beside him. Dillon smiled and went over to the liquor cabinet, but he opted for a bit of brandy. He took a seat across from his father and had a small sip before setting the glass down. He didn't want to give his parents the impression he'd become a drinker, because it wasn't the case. He shared a celebratory drink with Sherisza now and then, but she wasn't much of a drinker, so neither was he.

Frankly, he got drunk off their relationship and enjoyed that far more...

"No drinking at the party tomorrow, all right?" his father said. "I don't mind you drinking, but I don't want you to set a bad example for your cousins."

"Oh, sure," Dillon answered absently.

"I've never seen you like this," Malcolm said. "Not even the first time you two came to visit and you spent that first night with her."

"What do you mean?" Dillon asked.

"You're in love with that woman. It's obvious, and it's not young love or lust. I can tell."

"She means the world to me."

Malcolm nodded. "I know. Your mother and I have talked a lot about this. I don't know what Kiandarian customs are like, but she seems to have claimed you as hers. And we're fine with it, Dillon. We want you to know that. Whether you two get married or not, we're happy to see you together. And your mother... she's been talking about grandchildren ever since you told her it was a possibility."

Dillon's breath caught. "Oh God, we're not going to get stuck talking about that all day at the party, are we?"

His father laughed. "No. We haven't told anyone else, and the video of what happened in President MacNault's office is not public knowledge. And it won't be for a while, if ever. So, for now, your secret's safe with us, but we want you to know how happy we are for you, Dillon. It's not what anyone expected–not even you two it seems–but I think it's wonderful. And your mother is just ecstatic."

Malcolm reached over with his glass, so Dillon clinked his against it and they both took sips. "I'm trying to decide whether I should finish my degree first," Dillon said.

His father waved off the thought. "I wouldn't worry about that. If things with the Kwaagi are as dire as I'm hearing, you two are going to be busy upgrading all their fighters, and you're going to be ridiculously rich afterwards."

"She already is," Dillon commented.

"Well, so much the better. And you'll have your choice of worlds to live on. Here, Kiandar, probably even Kwaaganarr if everything turns out all right. So, don't worry about the degree,

Dillon. If you finish it, finish it because you want to, not because you think you owe it to your mother and I."

"Thanks, Dad."

The father-son talk came to an end as the women approached from the kitchen.

CHAPTER 12

HOME AWAY FROM HOME

SHERISZA CAME into the sitting room with Dillon's mother, and both women had smiles on their faces. Malcolm got up and poured them drinks, handing Sherisza a brandy like the one Dillon had. She accepted the glass with thanks but set it down without taking a sip. After a few moments, she strode over and sat on Dillon's lap, leaning into him. He grunted dramatically, and his parents both laughed at the little display.

"She's a big girl," he said with false strain in his voice.

"You *are* very athletic looking," Sasha commented. "Were you in sports before the tragedy that befell your people?"

"Nothing organized or professional, but I had my children young at sixteen. They kept me on my toes even when my work became more pedestrian," Sherisza said.

"And how are things on the *Malshekt?*" Malcolm asked.

"They are well. I have made significant progress on the new device I have been working on thanks to Dillon's help. If I can pick up some supplies from the port or the military bases, I may be able to complete it within the next month."

"Can you tell us what it is?"

She smiled shyly. "A modified type of cloaking device. That

is as much as I want to say for now, though. It is still largely theoretical and the type of thing that would draw nearly as much attention as the Daevol Drive if word were to get out."

"I told you she's brilliant. You know what her IQ is?" Dillon asked.

"Dillon!" Sherisza gasped. "Please do not start with that."

"A hundred and fifty-five!"

Malcolm and Sasha both gasped. "Wow, that is impressive," Dillon's mother said, but she read the Kiandarian's embarrassment well. "So, why don't we get to discussing the Kwaagi?"

"Parts of a whole, Dillon," Sherisza said, her eyes stern.

"Sorry," he offered, and she kissed his forehead.

"The Kwaagi haven't told us much yet, but what we've heard isn't good," Malcolm said. "The imperial war minister spoke with the Joint Senates about sending aid, but even then, there wasn't much detail. The emperor seemed convinced that merely the threat of the Kwaagi Empire falling and this trouble coming through to the rest of us would be enough to secure help. Well, it turns out he's right, but it's not that simple. It was suggested that I ask you two to get the Joint Senates more information than the Kwaagi are giving us."

"Reconnaissance?" Sherisza asked.

"Yes. We obviously don't want you getting involved in the fighting. Your ship is amazing, but it's not a warship, everyone knows that. Even after what you did to that Arkorr destroyer that attacked you the last time you left Earth," Dillon's father continued with a little chuckle. "The Joint Senates are planning to send help, but they need to know what they're dealing with. We can't just send ships to be destroyed, and if these invaders are giving the Kwaagi trouble, they are obviously powerful."

"Yes, we saw firsthand what they were able to do to one of the Kwaagi mobile outposts."

"That's where we picked up Azi, the Kwaagi woman you

saw with us," Dillon put in, his parents' brows rising. "We rescued her from the wreckage; she was the only survivor."

"You two are going to have quite a standing in the Kwaagi Empire at this rate," Sasha said.

"If there's anything left of it."

Malcolm sighed. "True enough."

"I am willing to aid in the Kwaagi war effort for scouting and espionage," Sherisza said. "I just hesitate to delay bringing my people back home for any reason."

"We could always help with that," Sasha said. "If you just told us where they've been hiding all this time, I'm sure the Joint Senates would send caravans and military escorts to get them home to Kiandar safely."

"It is not that simple. I thank you for your desire to help, but I cannot let anyone else aid me in this. It is something I must do myself, though not because I do not trust you."

Dillon's parents were obviously curious but waved off her explanation. "Don't worry about it, then," Malcolm said. "I'll send a message to the Joint Senates before we go to church in the morning and let them know you're willing to help. Once the Kwaagi know you're going to be involved, they may open communication a bit more so they can utilize you but keep you safe. We'll see what they say."

"How's everything else going?" Dillon asked.

"Everyone's doing well. Your cousin Jacob is headed to college in the fall on a full academic and athletic scholarship. Not much else new is going on that you won't hear about tomorrow. May as well let everyone tell you in person," his father said.

"I can't wait."

Sherisza let forth a wistful sigh. "Neither can I. It has been so long since I have been to this sort of occasion. I... I cannot even tell you how much it means to me that you have welcomed me into your lives," she said, a few tears running loose. Dillon pulled her down into an embrace. "I have been alone for so long... yet this year, I have felt so much of the Goddess' blessing upon me. You three are all a blessing to me."

"Oh, sweetie... it's been so wonderful getting to know you," Sasha said, fighting off tears of her own. "I won't lie, it wasn't what we expected, but it's more than we could've hoped for. I want you to know that."

"Thank you," Sherisza whispered breathlessly.

"You don't have to come to church in the morning if you don't want to," Malcolm said.

"No, I would like to," she said, sitting up straight again, her tail thumping the chair once. "Dillon is such a good listener when I speak of my people's theology. The least I can do is listen to some of his, even if it is from another speaker."

"It's fun," Dillon said. "If you look at church like something you *have* to do, it's boring, but if you go there to have fun and learn about God, you'll have fun and learn about God. That's all there is to it, really."

"Our temples to the Goddess were different, I think, but that is a story for another time. Or, perhaps something you will get to see for yourselves if the repopulation of Kiandar goes as I hope it does," Sherisza said.

"Oh, I would *love* to see your home world," Sasha said.

"You two are welcome to come at any time. Just know that it is what you would call a *ghost town* for the time being. It will take a long time for my people to thrive again."

"We're always willing to help," Malcolm offered.

"Something to think about after we help the Kwaagi win their war," Dillon said, and there was a silent agreement.

They chatted for a little while longer, but as the hour grew late, Dillon's parents bid them goodnight and went to their room. Dillon gestured for Sherisza to be patient and sit with him for a while longer. They shared their drinks and some kisses, but once he figured his parents were asleep or close to it, he led Sherisza quietly to the bathroom. Soon, they were in the shower, silently enjoying the leadup to their coming passions.

———

Getting ready to go to church put some strange thoughts in Dillon's head. He was having sex with someone he wasn't married to, she wasn't human, and he wasn't sure how many of the Lord's rules he was breaking in the process. It didn't change how he felt about Sherisza; not one bit. But he did resolve to try to do things the right way in the near future. He began laying the plans in his head but hid it behind a smile while he got dressed up beside Sherisza in front of the bedroom's mirrored closet doors.

Sherisza dressed in a nice outfit she hadn't worn before. It was a white sleeveless blouse with an open tan vest and blue capris-type pants. She looked dead sexy, but then she always did to his eyes. It was nice to see her relaxed and content, not dressed to kill with blasters on her thighs like their usual trips off the *Malshekt*. She wiggled her clawed toes in the carpet and glanced at him in the mirror, her tail lashing a couple of times.

"You look amazing," he said to her unspoken question.

"You look quite handsome as well," she said to his button-up shirt, tie, and dress slacks.

He wasn't wearing a full suit, but he did want to look sharp when attending church for the first time in months. He turned to Sherisza and they shared a deep kiss. He was still cradling her face, lost in the depths of those golden eyes when his mother peeked in through the slightly open door. She just stared, though, not saying anything, and Dillon assumed she was seeing the same thing his father had the night before.

"You two about ready? We don't want to be late," she finally said.

"Yeah, are we walking?" Dillon asked.

"It's a beautiful day for it."

They left the house and walked north along the road toward the neighborhood church. Many of their neighbors had also gotten the idea to walk, and it was almost like a block party gathering as the families strolled together. While everyone took an interest in Sherisza, most were mindful not to stare or intrude, and she smiled when Dillon squeezed her hand. Not a word was said about the two of them walking hand-in-hand, whether positive or negative. Dillon was just fine with that.

It wasn't far to the little white steepled church building. Reverend Warner was out on the front steps as usual, impeccably dressed, greeting everyone as they arrived. "Oh, young Dillon!" he said when they approached. "So good to see you again, son. And who is this lovely woman you've brought with you?"

"This is Captain Sherisza Rousilarru of the *Malshekt*," Dillon said. "I've been apprenticed to her for the last few months, that's why I haven't been around."

"Oh sure, sure. Blame the lady for skipping out on God," the reverend said, flashing a toothy grin at Sherisza. She laughed and nodded politely as she shook the man's hand. "Well, it's nice to have you here, ma'am. I hope you enjoy the service."

"Thank you, sir. I look forward to hearing your songs and words," Sherisza said.

"Oh, I don't do the singing, darling. Nobody wants to hear that!"

Dillon led Sherisza inside as the others on the steps laughed. They found a row of seats with space for all four of them, and Sherisza sat between Dillon and his mother. It wasn't long before the service got started, and the choir and band went up front to play and sing. The congregation got into the music, swaying or dancing and clapping, and Sherisza clung to Dillon's side. It was a lot different than Kiandarian music, but she seemed to be enjoying the atmosphere if not the songs themselves.

The reverend's sermon featured two different stories that tied into a single theme. He drew on the story of the Good Samaritan, but also the Samaritan woman Jesus met at the well. It wasn't hard for Dillon to figure out the man had changed his message on the fly to say something positive that related somewhat to his unexpected guest. Sherisza didn't seem to understand what he was saying, but then she was brilliant; it was possible she was playing clueless. Either way, she held Dillon's hand throughout the service, though she refrained from making too much of a public display by laying her head on his shoulder or anything.

She didn't partake of the communion service, but other than that, Sherisza paid attention to the entire affair. Dillon offered special prayer requests for the Kwaagi and the Kiandarians, and the reverend offered them up along with everyone else's requests. By the time the final songs and choir presentation were done, Sherisza was leaning into Dillon a little bit as they rocked back and forth. Best yet, when the service ended, so many of the other congregants turned and welcomed her to Earth. She graced every one of them with her little smile and bow of the head.

"Dillon, can I speak to you for a minute?" the reverend asked when Dillon and Sherisza were about to leave their row.

"Of course," Dillon answered.

Sherisza stopped by his side, but Reverend Warner smiled and gestured for her to go with Dillon's parents. "Won't be but a minute, ma'am, and I promise to give him right back."

She laughed and went outside with Dillon's parents, and

Dillon turned back to the reverend for the chastisement he was sure was coming.

"Dillon, son, are you fornicating?" he asked predictably. Dillon sighed, but he didn't get a chance to answer before the reverend laid a hand on his shoulder. "I'm not judging you, son, I just want to make sure you understand. The Lord doesn't have these rules to keep you from enjoying yourself or your time with a woman. It's so you don't dishonor her or yourself and either end up in a loveless relationship or with a life-long hatred between you. I'd have to be blind to not see the connection between you two; there's clearly something there. All I'll say is if she means something to you, son, do the right thing, for her and yourself. As unto the Lord."

"As unto the Lord," Dillon repeated. "You're right, Reverend. And I have been thinking about it. It's just... her customs are a little different, and I didn't want to pressure her."

"I understand. You're a good man, Dillon."

"Thanks. You don't think... I mean, is this weird or wrong to God?"

The reverend laughed. "I don't know what she believes, son, but I know what I teach and what you believe. Do you think God didn't create her, too? He's got a plan for you, and if He brought that woman into your life, who am I to say it's not right? You do what feels right to you. Just do it the right way, that's all I can tell you. Trust in Him. And if you two decide to get married, know I'll be more than happy to perform the ceremony."

It clicked in Dillon's mind, then, the last of his doubts and questions. Of course the Lord would be the creator of her people as well, if He truly was the only god. And if humans and Kiandarians could interbreed, it had to mean He'd planned for it. It did still leave questions about what she believed and where that faith had come from, but that was something for them to discover over their life together. It was like a light finally being unveiled in that last dark recess of Dillon's mind.

"Thanks, Reverend. It was good to hear you teach again," he said.

"Come on, let's not keep your little lady waiting," Reverend Warner said, leading Dillon out the front doors. He was smiling broadly, and Dillon found it contagious, so Sherisza didn't look too suspicious when they emerged.

"Always so good to see you," the reverend said to Dillon's parents. "Such a fine young man you two raised."

"We'll see you again soon," Malcolm said.

They began walking home, and Sherisza squeezed Dillon's hand, prompting him to look at her. There was a question in her eyes, but he wiped it away with a smile, leaning in to kiss her. She clearly had an inkling of what the reverend had wanted, but Dillon suspected she probably though it was her species that was the issue. The corners of her mouth turned up a little at the kiss, but he could still see the trepidation in her eyes.

So then, in the middle of the street, surrounded by friends and neighbors, Dillon stopped, took her face in his hands, and kissed her fully. There was no trepidation in the way her fingers came up to trace his jawline. There were some *whoops* and some claps, but Dillon didn't pay them any mind. He let Sherisza know she was his, and he didn't care what anyone else thought.

Dillon's parents weren't exactly smiling, but it wasn't a look of shock or disgust. It was a look of complete realization, of understanding what their son and Sherisza felt was real. Sasha and Malcolm had their own fingers interlaced, and Dillon could see the trace of tears in his mother's eyes. His parents didn't say anything, just smiled encouragingly when Dillon and Sherisza turned to continue walking, but their expressions said everything. Dillon was nearly certain Sherisza saw and sensed it as well.

They arrived back at the house, and Dillon took a couple of minutes to get changed into something more comfortable. He didn't want to look unkempt at his grandmother's birthday party, but he suspected he'd end up playing ball with his cousins or something. He put on a sport shirt and a light pullover with casual pants. He knew his grandmother would understand, and Sherisza had no complaints when he came back out of the room.

"We'll be taking Dad's shuttle," he told Sherisza. "It's a long walk to Grandma's."

"Do you have any idea how much I love you?" she said.

Dillon couldn't help but notice the way his parents both turned to them at that. He cradled Sherisza's head and then pulled her in for a hug. She smelled good and she was warm. He knew it was going to be a wonderful day, doubly so since there was no one he would've rather shared it with than this Kiandarian woman.

"Hey, you two, look at the camera," his mother said, holding up the little fob that dangled from her purse strap.

Dillon held Sherisza, and she turned her face against his chest just enough to smile for the photograph. "You usually don't like having your picture taken," he commented.

"I usually do not like the reason they are taken," she countered. "This is a moment I should like to remember for the rest of my days."

"I'll forward the photo to your ship," Sasha said. "See you two in the shuttle."

She and Malcolm left them alone then, and Dillon and Sherisza shared another long, deep, passionate kiss before they followed.

CHAPTER 13

A DAY TO REMEMBER

IT WAS ONLY a short jaunt over to Grandma Malinda's estate house from Dillon's parents' place using their shuttle. It was like one of those old southern estate homes, large and almost cubic with numerous rooms and columned porches the whole way around. It was a massive house even before one took the property into account, the life's work of Dillon's grandfather and his father before him to provide a big home for their many children and grandchildren.

There were several shuttles already parked on the drive, most of Dillon's family having come straight from church. He recognized most of the vehicles. It looked as though nearly the entire family was there. Only Uncle Amos' and Aunt Jacey's shuttles were obviously missing, but that wasn't such a surprise. Amos was a disaster response engineer, and he was usually on call to go respond to problems all over the world. Dillon knew it had to have been something dire to keep Amos from coming to his mother's birthday. And Jacey was a nurse, constantly on call, so she never knew when she'd have free time.

Sherisza was trembling slightly as she saw all the shuttles, but Dillon kept her hand tightly in his and gave it a squeeze.

Despite her nerves, she smiled at him before she laid her head on his shoulder. Dillon didn't have to see his parents in the front seats to know they were smiling, too. It seemed everyone in the shuttle was at that moment.

Malcolm brought their shuttle in beside the others in the drive, and soon the doors were all open. The four stepped out and into the bright early-afternoon sunshine, and they could already hear the sounds of music and laughter even from the front of the house. Better than that, the smells of firepits getting up to temperature was in the air, and it brought to mind all the other birthday barbecues Dillon had ever attended. He could scarcely remember details, but it all blended into feelings of warmth, happiness, and the bonds of family. Despite the many different lives his parents, aunts, and uncles had pursued, the family was close and strong.

Grandma Malinda had a lot to do with that, as did Ruth, Dillon's paternal grandmother. Though both of his grandfathers had died fairly young, his grandmothers were the glue that kept their large family together. Ruth's birthday was in the winter and generally celebrated around the same time as Christmas, but Malinda's was in the height of summer and perfect for a backyard bash. Dillon loved both women and their birthday celebrations, and each for different reasons. They were the kind of events that seemed to instill joy until the next one arrived.

"Oh my," Sherisza said as they made their way into the home's impressive foyer and she got a first look at its twin staircases and all the photos that lined them. The house had only been in the family for a couple of generations, but Grandpa Charlie and Malinda had kept the memoirs of their own parents and grandparents on the walls. It looked like it had been in the family for far longer than the truth, which was half the point.

Dillon showed Sherisza some of the photos and other keepsakes. They didn't have anything so far back as their ancestors memorialized on the monuments in the city, but there was a lot of history here. Dillon thought of all the photos and trinkets Sherisza had on the *Malshekt*, the reminders of her family and people who'd been wiped out, and he watched her take in all the memories of his family.

Holding her hand in his again, he gestured toward all of it. "It's yours now, too," he said, and she turned a curious gaze his way. "It might take the family a little time to all accept it, but then again, maybe not. But you and I are together, Sherisza. You're part of this family now. All this history is yours now, too. And everything that happened to you, your family, and your people... it happened to *us* now. Everything this family can do to help, they will."

Sherisza closed her eyes, spilling tears down her furry cheeks. "This has been like a dream," she said. "I had always held out hope you might be willing to help me, Dillon, but I honestly never expected you could love me. I thought our differences would be too great. That you love me, and your family has accepted me... there aren't enough thanks that can be given, either to all of you or the All-Mother herself. You have given me new life."

They shared a kiss but kept it brief when they heard other voices in the house. A trio of teenagers came into the foyer, their brows rising in surprise before they came over to greet Dillon. They were his cousins, and though they were shocked by the presence of a Kiandarian, they were glad to see Dillon again. He introduced Sherisza and they were polite, but after asking Dillon if he'd be playing football with them later, they headed deeper into the house.

"Those are my aunt Rita's boys," Dillon explained. "Jacob's the oldest, the one going to college like my father mentioned. The twins are Isaac and Jeremiah. They're probably all going to pursue sciences like you and Daevol did. Smart boys."

"That seems to run in your family," she said.

"Mostly good work ethic passed down from my grandparents and before," he agreed. "If you're willing to work hard, it can make up for shortcomings where smarts are concerned, but not always the other way around. Anyway, they're probably all waiting for us out back."

Sherisza took a deep breath but didn't pull her hand from his as he led her down the central hallway to the kitchen and dining area. Uncle Bart was there, and Dillon couldn't help but smile and laugh when he saw him. While Dillon's father *looked* like he could've played professional contact sports, Uncle Bart actually did. He was bigger than his brother and heavier, a nose tackle for the local football team. His hug was bone crushing when Dillon went to greet him. He was a lot more delicate in his greeting of Sherisza, though in the back of his mind, Dillon thought she would've handled the hug a lot better.

They kept the greeting short, though, letting him get back to loading his arms with meat for the grills. Dillon continued with Sherisza through the beautiful French doors and out onto the patio. Most of the family was there, congregating around barrels of ice that held innumerable beers and other cold drinks. Around the edges of the patio were the firepits and grills, where the food would soon be cooking for a day's worth of festivities. It all looked and smelled the way Dillon could remember from the last eighteen years of his life.

"Here they are," Dillon's mother said, and most of the conversations went quiet as every eye turned toward Dillon and Sherisza.

"Oh my God," more than one person said, and Sherisza gripped Dillon's arm a little tighter, pressing close to him. She seemed to relax a little when she overheard several people whisper, "My God, she's beautiful."

"Hey everyone," Dillon said, being greeted in chorus in

return. "I'd like to introduce you all to Sherisza Rousilarru, captain of the *Malshekt*, my boss, and also my girlfriend."

Everyone stayed where they were, letting Dillon lead Sherisza around for handshakes or hugs where they were offered. There were many introductions, but Dillon's family understood she wouldn't remember any of their names until they chatted more extensively. It truly did seem like everyone but Uncle Amos and Aunt Jacey was there, even some of Grandma Malinda's neighbors and friends from church. Dillon had expected twenty-five or so people, but it seemed closer to forty even without the teenagers and younger children off causing trouble elsewhere.

Eventually, Dillon led Sherisza to a corner of the patio beneath a wide, shady umbrella where there was a pair of large, comfortable padded chairs. Dillon's grandmothers were sitting side by side chatting, no doubt about the same memories these parties always brought to Dillon's mind, though over a much longer period. They both looked up when Dillon and Sherisza came before them, eyes wide though they both smiled after the briefest delay.

"Happy birthday, Grandma Malinda," Dillon said, leaning down to give her a kiss. She gave him her trademark hug, and he let her hold him as long as she wanted to. Once she let him go, he turned to his other grandmother and gave her a kiss as well. "Hi Grandma Ruth, so good to see you again."

"You're getting so big and handsome," Ruth said.

"*Getting?*" Dillon quipped.

"And who is this?" Malinda asked.

Dillon took Sherisza's hand again. "This is Sherisza Rousilarru, my girlfriend."

"Your *girlfriend?* Oh my goodness, this lovely little thing?" Malinda practically gushed. "Oh, come here, sweetheart, let me see you. Don't you worry, I don't bite. Not as hard as you probably can, anyway."

Sherisza chuckled, her muzzle dipped in her blushing pose. She offered a hand to Malinda, but then knelt before her rather than loom over the seated women. Grandma Malinda adjusted her glasses and took Sherisza's face in her hands. Dillon was sure Sherisza would recognize the warmth in the woman's smile.

"I had heard Kiandarians were lovely, but you are a true beauty," she said at length. "I'm so happy to welcome you to my home. I'm sure I don't need to tell you Dillon is a special young man in a family full of exceptional men."

"You do not; I have seen so much of it firsthand," Sherisza said. "Thank you for welcoming me to your home, ma'am. It is an honor to meet both of you."

"Isn't she the prettiest little thing?" Malinda said to Ruth.

"Gorgeous," the other woman agreed.

"You have a beautiful family as well. It is amazing how our perspectives change when we gain more firsthand experience," Sherisza said. "I had once thought humans looked mostly alike, but I am amazed at how much variety there is just in this gathering. I can only assure you that there is similar variety among my own people–or there was, at one point. There will be again, though. I assure you, we do not all look like the same lioness."

Malinda and Ruth both chuckled. "Well don't you fret over us, go get yourself a cold drink and let Dillon show you around. There might be a lot of names to take in all at once, but if anyone doesn't make you feel welcome, you just let me know whose ear to yank."

Sherisza smiled. "Thank you," she said, rising up to take Dillon's hand.

"We'll be back to talk to you soon," Dillon said.

He showed Sherisza around the yard a bit, reminiscing

about the old tire swing, the rose trellis that he and his cousins used to climb, and the remnant of a railroad deep in the woods. She smiled at each and every memory, stopping to admire his grandmother's rose gardens and the vegetable garden his aunt Rita had planted. The huge oak in the center of the yard had a new tire swing, but it still brought a smile to Dillon's face when he pushed it. At least until he saw the look on Sherisza's face.

He wrapped an arm around her and she closed her eyes, taking in a deep breath through her nose. It took her a few moments, but she did manage to smile when she opened her eyes again. She reached for the rope and ran her fingers down it, and Dillon knew she was thinking of the photo of her brother and children riding the one at her home on Kiandar. They were gone now, but they were yet a beautiful, pleasant memory to her, and Dillon wrapped his hand around hers as she held onto the rope.

"We'll build one for our children," he said quietly.

Sherisza's head dipped as though she was blushing. "Dillon," she whispered. "You make me feel so beautiful."

"No, you *are* beautiful," he said. "I just point out the obvious."

They shared a kiss but broke it up laughing as there were some whoops and wolf whistles from the north side of the yard. Several of Dillon's family were already there, warming up to either just throw the football around or perhaps play a touch game. Nobody wanted to play tackle ball when Uncle Bart was around, after all. Dillon kept hold of Sherisza's hand and led her over to his cousins and uncles and made quick introductions. It was a lot of names for Sherisza to try to take in all at once.

"You gonna play a game with us?" Jacob asked.

Dillon looked at Sherisza and she smiled encouragingly. "Oh, have fun with your family," she said. "I will be content to watch. I have not seen so much as an amateur sport in so long."

"You should play with us," Jeremiah said. "You look like you could knock Dillon on his ass without any trouble."

"Hey, now," Dillon protested. His indignation just made the laughter louder. "Yeah, I'll join in. I haven't thrown a ball in a while, though, so don't ask me to quarterback. When are you guys going to get started?"

"About fifteen minutes or so," Uncle Jackson said.

"All right, we'll be back," Dillon said.

He continued the tour of the property with Sherisza. She was fascinated that his aunt and uncle kept an apiary. She mentioned the insects they had on Kiandar that were similar to bees, but said they were much more dangerous and couldn't be kept so easily. To find that Dillon's family did so many things the old-fashioned way was a delight for her, and she seemed excited by each new thing he showed her. He could understand it, too; considering he was now learning how to build warp drives and more, old-fashioned things had a nicer sheen to them.

They made only one more stop so Dillon could show her where the lavatories were in the house, all the better to spare her any embarrassment of having to ask. There were more hugs and handshakes as they exited the house again. On the patio, the food was starting to cook now, and Dillon took Sherisza over to explain what was there. Steaks, chicken, ribs, frankfurters, burgers, kabobs of all kinds, shrimp, fish, and clams were on the grills. There was also a pair of massive steel pots cooking jambalaya and chowder, and more clams were baking in the brick oven.

"What, no pizza?" Sherisza asked, drawing a lot of looks before she laughed.

Dillon laughed with her. "We'll get some of that in a couple of days."

"I hope I have not misspoken," she said to the numerous stares she received.

"I think everyone's just surprised you like pizza," he said, wrapping an arm around her to lead her back over toward the open field.

Uncle Bart was chasing Jeremiah, but though the big man was terrifying in a bull rush, he couldn't catch his wiry nephew. With all of Dillon's cousins, most of his uncles, and a few of the neighbors' kids, they had enough for an eight-on-eight game. Dillon didn't trust his arm after being away from sports for so long, but he could still run, so he played receiver or cornerback as his team swapped from offense to defense. All the while, Sherisza stood off to the side, clueless to how the game was played but happy to watch Dillon with his family.

Dillon had just caught a pass and run out of bounds when he saw his aunts talking to Sherisza on the other side of the field. Soon, Sherisza went with them back toward the patio, and Dillon suffered a lot of taunts for having the wrong head in the game. He threw the ball at Jeremiah to shut him up, but his cousin simply caught it. Sherisza looked back over her shoulder and waved at him, so Dillon returned the gesture and went back to the game.

They played for a while, and it felt so good to get some real exercise again. Dillon worked out with Sherisza in the engineering section, beating the heavy bag or lifting simple weights to keep in shape, but there was no substitute for afternoons of physical activity. Running felt good, as much as he enjoyed living and working on the *Malshekt*. He didn't think he had the height or the build for most sports, but he'd always been fairly athletic, and he loved these football games with his cousins and uncles at the holiday parties.

Uncle Bart brought over a couple of cases of sodas and beers after the game was finished. Just as his father had asked, Dillon refrained from having any alcohol for the sake of his cousins. He took a soda and found he'd missed those as well, drinking mostly water or various Kiandarian teas while on the ship. They stood around talking about this or that; the monotony of their jobs, state of the senate, and whatever other minor things came to mind, but Dillon knew what they all really wanted to ask.

After a few minutes to cool down, he gestured toward his uncles and cousins. "Go ahead, hit me with your questions," he said. Before anyone could, though, he looked back toward the patio. Sherisza was sitting in a chair near Dillon's grandmothers, getting her hair braided by his aunt Rita and Bart's wife, Dominique. *That* made him smile more fully, and he turned back to see what his family had to say when Sherisza wasn't around.

They asked a lot of questions, but they were general for the most part. How had he ended up apprenticed to her? How did he end up falling in love with her? Had they tried sex yet? Was it any different? Were they planning to tie the knot? Dillon answered everything honestly, though with his limited experience with human women, he didn't have much to say to some of the questions. He only left out the more sensitive things like the killing of MacNault, the troubles in Kwaagi space, or the black ship. The last thing he wanted was for them to worry about him.

He could see they found his relationship with a Kiandarian odd or at least curious, but no one barbed him until Jeremiah asked, "So, do we call you Lion Tamer now?"

"Don't be disrespectful," Dillon said with surprising calm. It was actually his uncles who gave Jeremiah more of an earful for it, and Uncle Jackson even cuffed him on the back of the neck. "Remember what you said before the game? If she belts you, nobody's going to jump to your defense. And I might just hit you after."

He chuckled to take the edge off of it, but he meant it. The family was being respectful and understanding so far, but Dillon had made up his mind. If it came down to it, Sherisza was his choice. His family could either accept it or accept not seeing them much, if ever. Fortunately, it didn't seem like there was any of that judgment from anyone else, not really even Jeremiah when it came down to it. He was teasing, just disrespectfully as teenagers do. Dillon pushed it down and tried not to think about it too much.

Dillon excused himself to go see how Sherisza was doing, but when he turned around, she wasn't on the patio anymore. He headed over to his grandmothers. "Is she inside?" he asked, trying to be discreet.

"I think she went out front with your aunts Rita and Dominique," Grandma Malinda said. "You've got to see her with those braids! Lord, she looks even more gorgeous than she did. Where ever did you meet that sweet girl?"

"I'll tell you all about it in a bit," Dillon said, excusing himself. He couldn't think of why anyone would've taken Sherisza out front unless it was to say something rude. He didn't expect that would be the case with Rita or Dominque, but the more he thought about it, the more speed it put in his steps as he made his way through the house. He practically burst out the front door and whipped his gaze around until he found them.

Dillon stood in slack-jawed wonder for a minute before he could move his feet. When he finally found the wherewithal, he walked around the side of the parked shuttles. There he found the three women chatting lightly... while Sherisza repaired one of the shuttles. Dominique and Rita looked up at Dillon and smiled at his approach.

"This woman is amazing," Rita said. "I just mentioned my shuttle was making a funny noise, and out she comes to fix it."

"It is a bad relay pairing, nothing more," Sherisza said, looking out from under the hood. "Dillon, would you get me a laser torch?"

His aunts started laughing, and when he realized Sherisza

was joking, he joined in. "I can't believe you're out here fixing a shuttle engine when we're at a party," he said.

"Sweet Goddess, Dillon, look what they did with my mane!" Sherisza countered. "This is the least I can do in return."

Dillon just stood and stared. He liked the way Sherisza looked with the dreadlocks she did up for work, but with the braids... His grandmother hadn't been kidding. She looked positively gorgeous, and he hadn't thought she *could* look any better to him. He gawked for a couple of minutes until his aunts both tilted their heads in unison. Laughing, he approached and ducked his own head under the hood.

"Ah, yeah, the cohesion relay got overloaded," he said. "Simple enough fix. Heck, she's almost done already."

Sherisza finished the job in only a couple more minutes, then closed the hood. "We will test it later before I leave, but it should give you no more trouble."

"Thanks, sweetie," Aunt Rita said, giving her a hug.

"Come on, let's go get some food," Dillon said, taking Sherisza by the hand, and his aunts followed them through the house to the patio again. They didn't even have to say anything or make any sounds when Dillon and Sherisza exchanged a kiss. He could practically feel their excitement, alien though his girlfriend was.

CHAPTER 14

A NIGHT TO NEVER FORGET

DINNER WAS an incredible assortment of various meats, and there was plenty for Sherisza to choose from without worrying too much about spices. She passed on the jambalaya, but she did try the clam chowder and some of the seafood. At worst, she was trying to be a good guest and not make a fuss, but Dillon got the feeling she truly enjoyed all of it. She even tried a few different beers until she found one she liked, though she refrained from offering Dillon any or getting anywhere near intoxicated.

They ate lightly at first, as Dillon's cousins set up a volley-ball net. Many of the women joined in for that game, and Dillon got to watch Sherisza put on a clinic. She wasn't just muscular, but she had incredible spring in her legs and her spikes were deadly. Dillon wasn't sure, but he suspected Sherisza had over-heard some comments and was repaying his cousins with hard-hit shots to the face or gut. She laid more than one of them out, but whether out of stubbornness or just not wanting to be outshone by a girl, they kept their mouths shut. Whatever the case, she became the toast of all the other women there, helping lead them to some one-sided victories along with Dillon's athletic Aunt Raquel.

After the games, they ate more fully, the afternoon slipping toward evening. Once everyone had eaten their fill, people started bringing their gifts over for Malinda. She had dozens to open, from the small and practical to the large and impractical. She laughed and cried and blushed her way through the entire assortment, and the sound of her laughter cemented so much of the day in Dillon's heart. Sherisza looked at Dillon and her mouth tightened when it became obvious they were the only ones with no gift to give.

She rose to her feet. "Forgive me, Grandma Malinda. Dillon and I have been working in Kwaagi space, so I did not give him the proper time to find a gift for you. This is my fault."

"Oh, sweetheart," Malinda said. "Don't be ridiculous. At my age, it's peoples' *presence* that counts, far more than their *presents*. I'm just so happy to meet you and see Dillon's found himself a wonderful woman. Don't you get your tail in a tizzy."

Sherisza chuckled at the expression, though she had her head dipped in a blush. Dillon got up and stood beside her, taking her hand. "Actually, we did get you something," he said. "I had Jacob grab it for me in advance since I knew we weren't going to have time before the party."

"Oh, Dillon, you didn't have to spend your money on me," his grandmother protested.

"You got it, Jake?" Dillon asked, and his cousin came and handed him a little cubic box in a bag. They shared a quick handshake. "Thanks, man."

He had the eyes of everyone on him now, the last of the gift-givers, but Dillon gave Sherisza a quick peck on the side of her muzzle first. "I've got to apologize too, though, Grandma, since this gift is... indirect?"

"Oh? What did you go and do?" she asked.

Dillon reached into the bag and slipped the little box out, and then he dropped down to one knee before Sherisza. There were intakes of breath all around them, pretty much all the women sucking in their lips in anticipation. Dillon could only imagine the look on his mother's face at that moment. He hadn't let anyone know this was coming; only Jacob would've had any inkling if he'd figured out what the ring was for. But all those reactions were inconsequential and paled before the one he was waiting, hoping, and praying for.

Sherisza put a hand to the end of her muzzle, eyes wide, ears back. "Dillon…"

"I told you the other day that my parents were your parents now. And when we arrived here and you were looking at all the old photos, I told you my family would be your family. I was already thinking about this, Sherisza, but I wasn't sure when the right moment would come. Then I talked to Reverend Warner this morning and he gave me that last little push I needed. I know it's only been a few months we've been together, but it's felt like years, and the best ones of my life at that. So, I want to spend the rest of them with you."

"Dillon," she whispered again, tears rolling from her eyes. She wasn't the only one.

"I know your customs are different, but this is how I bring you into my family. Sherisza Rousilarru, will you marry me?" he asked.

She fell to her knees and threw her arms around him, sobbing lightly over his shoulder. "You have been there for me again and again," she said. "You have become my heart and my soul, Dillon Mackey. I already consider you my mate, but if this is how your people go about things, then yes, I will marry you."

Finally, the cheers and applause could erupt, and they did. Dillon wasn't sure if everyone was as happy with his choice as they made out, but it wasn't worth worrying about. He held Sherisza as she clung to him. When she finally let go to look in his eyes, he took her hand and slipped the ring onto the third finger. It wasn't much, just a white gold band with a single golden gem that reminded him of her eyes. But she marveled at it for a moment before those eyes came up to meet his, searching.

"I had a little help from Daevol," he said. Just the mention of her brother's name made her mouth tighten even though he was talking about the AI.

"You are so wonderful," she said.

"And don't worry, I know this doesn't mean you're not my boss anymore," he joked. That finally made Sherisza laugh.

"Oh, come here you two before I run out of tears," Grandma Malinda said. Dillon helped Sherisza to her feet and led her over to *their* grandmother. She wrapped them both in her trademark hug. "You've always had such an eye for gifts, Dillon, but this is the best one you've given me. It's one of the best I've ever gotten. Thank you both, and congratulations."

"Oh, baby," Dillon's mother said, coming over for a hug as well soon after. "Do you have a date in mind?"

"I was thinking we just have the reverend marry us in a little ceremony before we leave," Dillon said. "Not that I don't want a big party, but we have things we need to go do for the Kwaagi, and we can't really keep them waiting."

"Oh, nonsense," Aunt Rita said. "Don't you have the fastest ship in the galaxy?"

Sherisza dipped her head. "The *known* galaxy," she said modestly.

Among the laughter, Sasha said, "We can plan something for you, and you can come when you have a couple of days. Surely even the Kwaagi can't keep you busy forever."

"Yes, we'll put everything together," Rita added. "You just let us know when you want to have it done, and we'll take care of the rest."

"And you can have it right here, save everyone a lot of time and money," Malinda finished.

Sherisza laid her head on Dillon's shoulder again, eyes closed. "We really appreciate it, everyone," he said. "Mom, we'll work out the details with you, but probably not until we're on our way back to Kwaagi space."

"All right, baby," Sasha said.

"This is like a dream," Sherisza whispered.

Malcolm came over and handed Dillon a glass of something. Then he held his own up in toast. "Dillon, I'm amazed at the man you've become just in these last few months. I can see all the lessons your mother and I and the rest of the family taught you really starting to shine in everything you do. And now you've brought this lovely woman into the family.

"Look around you, Son. This is what it's all about. This is what we fight so hard for. Whether it's Kwaagi fighter pilots patrolling their space, your mother and I arguing before the senates, your Uncle Amos working on weather deterrents in different parts of the world, or whatever else. This is what it's all about: love, home, family, and neighbors. You've already realized that at not even twenty years old, and if you keep your focus on that, you're sure to live a wonderful life.

"So, a toast to Dillon and Sherisza. May the Lord shine His light on your life and your commitment to each other."

"To Dillon and Sherisza," everyone echoed, sipping their drinks in toast.

Dillon tapped his glass against Sherisza's, and they both took sips as well. "I will love you 'til my dying breath," he said, hoping it didn't sound lame.

"And beyond," she answered, kissing his cheek.

The birthday cake was brought out then, and despite the usual joke from Jeremiah about setting off the fire suppression with too many candles, it was another precious moment.

Sherisza watched all the proceedings with wonder, squeezing Dillon's hand every so often. It was quite the crash course on human birthdays and weddings she was getting, but she was taking it all in stride and seemed to love every minute of it. Dillon couldn't stop smiling, either, and as the cake was dished out, he thought of something.

"Grandma, have you ever been on a spaceship?" he asked.

"What would I be doing on a spaceship?" she giggled. "Of course not."

"Well, with the captain's permission, maybe you can come see the *Malshekt*. That can be our birthday present to you if you like and she says yes."

"Of course, the answer is yes," Sherisza said. "You are all welcome to come see my ship before we leave port. It is not very large, but it is home to me, and Dillon as well now."

"I'd love to, that's very sweet. Ruth and I can go see it in the morning," Malinda said.

"That sounds like fun," Dillon's other grandmother agreed.

"And anyone else who would like to come may as well," Sherisza said. "Let us plan for around midmorning, and then–"

"Almost everyone will be at work. What about around dinner time?" Dillon put in.

There was an accord, and then everyone went to eating their cake. Dillon wiped a little dollop of whipped cream on the end of Sherisza's nose. She glowered at him playfully, but the laughs got a little louder when she licked it off. And then the laughs turned to whoops when the two shared a kiss.

It was hard to leave. The day had been so enjoyable, and with the sun staying up until nearly eight o'clock, the party had lasted well into the night. Everyone was welcome to find a place to sleep in the grand old house, but most of the guests either had to work the next day or were at least gracious enough to find their way home and leave the extra bedrooms to out of town visitors. Dillon had only had the one drink when his father toasted his proposal, so he was good to fly the shuttle back home.

Once Sherisza ran her final test on Aunt Rita's shuttle, Dillon got his parents home safely and they shuffled off to their room. It was well after their usual self-appointed bedtime, and Dillon simply hoped there would be no emergency calls regarding the Kwaagi or anyone else. It was going to be a rough morning for the two of them as it was. He was sure they'd consider it worth it in the end, but that didn't mitigate the day that was coming for both of them.

Alone in the sitting room, Sherisza wrapped her arms around Dillon's neck, and they shared another of those wonderful, long kisses. She hadn't drunk much alcohol over the course of the day, and her eyes were bright and loving when he met her gaze again. She ran her fingers along his jaw, then took him by the hand and led him to the lavatory. They undressed, and Dillon got in the shower when Sherisza sat on the commode. He hadn't thought she was *that* comfortable with him, but it made him snicker and grin a little anyway.

She joined him in the shower shortly, and they began kissing again under the warm spray of the showerheads. It still wasn't as nice as the *Malshekt*'s shower, but with Sherisza in his arms, the place didn't matter much to Dillon. They may not have exchanged vows yet, but she had accepted his proposal. He considered her his wife already. Despite the reverend's words that morning, Dillon didn't feel bad about being here with her now. They were together by her customs, and they were together in his heart. That was enough for him.

He ran his hands down her back, loving every trace of her curves, and she laid her clawed hands on his chest and her head on his shoulder. She began to purr as Dillon's hands wandered down to her muscular rump, caressing the base of her tail and more. He kept his touches small and slow, teasing her to excitement but content to wait until they went to the bedroom to truly get the romance started. At least, that's what he'd thought was going to happen.

Sherisza pushed him back against the wall, a bit of predator showing in those golden eyes, but she was smiling nonetheless. "I hope you are not planning to get much sleep tonight," she said.

"If you keep me up all night, I don't think I'll complain," he managed as the air got thin.

She clearly had plans that involved the bedroom, so she was content now with little loving touches but left it at that. It was enough to set his heart racing. He still could hardly believe all of it was real, that he was so involved with this lovely lioness woman. She hugged him tightly, then they shared another long kiss. Sherisza drew off the kiss to muzzle rub him on both sides, all the way to the ear despite being in the shower. She was letting him know he was hers, and he loved every second of it.

When she turned away from him, he admired the braids his aunts had given her while he scrubbed her back. They got washed and then out without wasting too much more time. It did take several minutes to get her sufficiently dried off, but they even enjoyed that time together. Every time their eyes met, he could see the stars in her depths, and her little smiles set his heart on fire again and again. They shared one last kiss, and then, after checking to make sure Dillon's parents weren't out of their bedroom, they snuck naked down the hall into their own.

By the time they closed the door and fell into the bed together, they were giggling like schoolchildren. Dillon could scarcely breathe in anticipation of what she'd told him was going to be a long and entertaining night. He was glad she wasn't nervous about being open with him, confident that he wouldn't be offended by any differences in their species. He loved everything about her and let her know without a word, and she demonstrated her gratitude with the rumble of her purr.

Soon enough, he'd begun to make love to her for the first time as her fiancé. He considered himself her husband now, but there was a ceremony and vows to go through, he knew. Still, it was even more special than all the previous times except, perhaps, for the first. Dillon made love to her slowly and sensually, determined to make it last after her comment in the shower. He concentrated on her, taking his cues from her, kissing her, and even nibbling lightly on the edge of one of her furry ears.

She began purring incessantly and looked as though she wanted to scream, though she kept it held in. Nevertheless, she opened her mouth wide in a silent roar, and Dillon got quite the up-close view of those impressive fangs. There was a hungry gleam in her eyes when they met his again, but she just pulled him close for another kiss. There still weren't any fangs in it, and it didn't feel rough or bestial despite the look she'd given him.

"I must warn you of something," she whispered in his ear, and he met her eyes in the dim light of his room's digital displays. "My time is coming, Dillon. I know it is summer here on Terra Prime, but back home, autumn will be setting in. If you wish to wait until your studies are complete to have children, we should use some type of protection for a while."

He ran a hand along the side of her muzzle, his thoughts excited yet conflicted. "Are we ready for this?"

"I am ready, Dillon. I leave this choice completely in your hands and will be happy with whatever decision you make."

"I just worry it'll be a bother to you when we're dealing with the Kwaagi or that stupid little black ship," he said, wanting everything on the table. "I'm not worried about the studies. I can do that whenever, there's plenty of time for that."

"It will not be a bother," she assured him. "Never a bother, Dillon."

Dillon stroked the side of her muzzle. The thought of fatherhood filled his stomach with butterflies, but it didn't terrify him the way he would've expected at his age. Sherisza had already been a mother before, and he trusted her to know if the time was right. She clutched at him, and in the feel of that and the way she kissed him, he realized grief and happiness were battling in her heart. But she didn't cry, and when her kisses became more passionate, Dillon figured happiness was winning the war.

He fell asleep to the sound of her purring, but as promised, it wasn't to be a full night's sleep. She woke him up an hour later. Dillon left her in control, but though she clearly enjoyed herself, she wasn't going for pleasure now. She wanted to be a mother again, and that seemed her sole focus. This time, she laid her head on his chest, purring beside his heart to lull him back to sleep.

He remembered a third time, and possibly a fourth, but he hardly woke up for the former and wasn't sure if the latter had truly happened at all.

CHAPTER 15

CONSIDERATIONS

DILLON WOKE up groggy and still tired. The digital display on the wall said it was almost eleven in the morning, though, and he groaned, throwing the blankets off. Sherisza was long gone from the bed, not even a trace of warmth where she had slept–or at least lain. He swung his legs off the bed and sat up, feeling like he'd been in a fight, not an hours-long lovemaking session. It still brought a smile to his face though.

He pursed his lips as reality began to sink in. There were probably children in his future now. While he'd been excited at the prospects of getting married and having kids with Sherisza, the reality felt different as it crashed into his mind. Would he be a good father? Were they really ready for this? What would their children look like, and how would they be received by either culture? There was so much to consider before he even took the troubles with the black ship or the invaders in Kwaagi space into account.

He shook off the thoughts and got marginally dressed, then stumbled his way to the lavatory. His parents had to be long since at work by now, but he wondered what Sherisza was up to. When he left his room, he could hear her in the kitchen cooking. He continued to the shower and got washed up, then he went to see what she'd made.

There was a pile of eggs, bacon, ham, and biscuits on the dining room table. Sherisza was still in the kitchen, humming some tune he didn't recognize, her expression one of contentment while she washed the pans she'd used. She dried her hands off and came right over to him, though, wrapping her arms and even a leg around him as she kissed him deeply. A part of Dillon wanted to take advantage of her passionate mood, but the rest of him was still crying for mercy.

"I warned you not to plan on getting much sleep last night," she said with a little smirk.

"God, how many times did we have sex?" he yawned.

"Five."

"*Five?*"

Sherisza shrugged. "You were mostly asleep for the last two. I know I took a lot out of you last night, that is why I made you such a large breakfast. Sit, eat, and get your energy back. We still have most of a day to go out and see the city, and perhaps visit that little restaurant with the excellent pizza again."

"Five times?" Dillon blurted again as he sat at the table. He shook his head as he served himself a bunch of food. Sherisza sat beside him, and he cast a doubtful look her way. "Tell me that's not a frequent thing for your people..."

"Only when the season first comes upon us," she said. "It is vital to make sure everything is stimulated the first night. We should continue to mate once or twice per day for the next few days to be sure, but not to that extent. Unless, of course, you have changed your mind."

"I haven't," he said quickly, reaching to lay his hand on hers. She didn't look concerned at all, and her smile broadened as she patted his hand. "That was just a lot, even for a nineteen-year-old human guy."

"I understand. I would have given you warning, but I lost track of the time myself. Time does not have the same meaning in space as it does on our worlds... or to a time traveler," she said with a pensive shrug. "Do not worry, Dillon. I will make it more than worth your while."

He wasn't sure what she meant by that, but Dillon loved seeing her in such high spirits. He knew she'd been thinking about her lost children when they'd been making love, some lingering grief over "betraying" them or trying to replace them. She seemed at peace with it now, though, and if she had any of the same doubts or butterflies in her stomach that Dillon did, it didn't show. She looked ready for this adventure, no hesitation or doubt on her beautiful leonine countenance. And when those golden eyes met his again and she smiled more broadly, his heart nearly melted.

We can do this, he thought. *Like anything else in life. One step at a time, get up every time something knocks you down.*

"When did you want to head back to Kwaagi space?" he asked.

"Tomorrow. We cannot wait too long; they need our help. But I want to let your family come see the ship you live on now and get used to me a little more. I put in a requisition for the parts I need for our phase-cloaking device, and they should be delivered to the *Malshekt* by the time we leave. Other than that, there is no work to be done, so we can enjoy the day, walk the city, visit that pizzeria..."

"You either love pizza or you just don't like mine as much," he joked.

"I do enjoy it quite a bit, but I want to bask in the memories of that day again, Dillon. That is half the reason I want to see the memorials again and then go to that shop."

"All right, then," he agreed.

There were messages waiting for him, and Dillon brought

up a little holodisplay from the dining table while they ate. They were mostly from family and friends planning to meet them at the *Malshekt* around half-past-five for a tour. Dillon sent confirmations to all of them and then dismissed the holodisplay. He was looking forward to showing off the ship to his friends and family, but at the same time, it was a reminder that he and Sherisza had to leave soon.

What he wanted to do was take her back to Kiandar. To sweep out the ghosts in her old home and get it ready for her coming children, then help her people build their new world. They had no business getting involved in a war, not when they were trying to start a family. And every trip they took toward Kwaagi space risked seeing that black ship again, not to mention tangling with any of the unknown invaders. It was too much risk, and Dillon didn't want to put his wife or their coming children in harm's way.

But the Kwaagi were their friends now, and friends didn't walk away when they could help. He only had to think of the way all the separate governments had essentially ignored Kiandar and Sherisza herself to put things in perspective. To turn their backs on the Kwaagi would be no better, and it would be something he looked back on with shame and regret for the rest of his life. As much as the risks made him nervous, he didn't want that hanging over them when they were raising children.

And if the Kwaagi fall, no place might be safe anyway, he thought.

It wasn't an easy decision for a nineteen-year-old, but Dillon made the resolution in his heart. They had to help their friends, and in the process, they'd be working to protect the galaxy for their coming children to live in. The only other choice was to abandon everyone, hide in the streams of time somewhere, lost and adrift and alone for God only knew how long. And while they might be alive, that wasn't a life. Not one anyone should want to live, anyway.

"I wonder how the Kwaagi are holding up," he mused aloud.

"We will receive no news here on Terra Prime, so there is little reason to worry about it for now. Let us enjoy the day; there will be plenty of time to consider the trouble ahead."

She was right, of course, and Dillon chuckled as he tried to remember if Reverend Warner had said that during the prior day's service. He supposed it was general wisdom across many races and theologies. They shouldn't be ignorant of what tomorrow would bring, but they had to enjoy each day for what it was. He squeezed her hand again and then made it a point to finish breakfast quickly. She was already done and took her plate to the kitchen to wash.

"I'm betting Jeremiah has some lovely bruises from getting hit with spikes yesterday," he said, and she laughed from the kitchen. "You never mentioned you played volleyball."

"Something close to it," she said, coming back out to the dining room. "I did not always have my head in books or machines, Dillon. Nor was I always a mother."

"Just shows how much more there is to learn about each other," he said.

She came and sat in his lap and they shared a brief kiss, but then she got up and gestured for him to finish. "The day is already passing us by, do not take too long."

"I'm hurrying, I'm hurrying," he said around a mouthful of bacon.

He had hardly shoveled the last of it into his mouth before she took his plate and cutlery and shooed him to go get dressed. Dillon put on a light but socially acceptable outfit, and Sherisza was wearing the same capris and sleeveless shirt she'd had on the day before. As they headed for the front door, though, he took note of the other thing she was wearing that made the entire outfit so much more special: The engagement ring.

———

They walked the city for a few hours, passing by the war memorials again at Sherisza's request. She obviously didn't know any of the people named on the Vietnam Memorial, but by the way she ran her fingertips over many of them, Dillon guessed she was imagining her own people, so long dead. He wasn't the only one to notice, either, many of the other tourists and pedestrians taking note of the Kiandarian paying her respects. No matter how long ago the war had taken place, it still reverberated, the constant reminder of the cost, and it was something every race in the known galaxy had dealt with at some point.

They visited the Lincoln Memorial again, and the way Sherisza just stood and stared at it made Dillon wonder what similar incidents may have taken place on Kiandar. It was the nature of man to romanticize everyone else, to expect they were so much more enlightened and had never dealt with things like slavery or racism. Most people probably assumed—and Dillon had been one of them until Sherisza's comment at the party—that all Kiandarians were leonine. The fact that they weren't or hadn't been raised many questions about their culture and their history.

And considering how little of his own people's history Dillon knew, it was a staggering thing to consider the histories of so many worlds and peoples.

That brought the Kwaagi Empire to mind briefly. Dillon remembered Azilija saying that Kwaagi didn't mate with non-Kwaagi. The way she'd said it sounded more like a law than a rule of thumb. Just how many non-Kwaagi races were there in their empire, and how were they viewed and treated? It helped cement something Dillon had already believed, as enamored as he was with space travel and all the various races out there. Everyone had problems, and usually the same ones.

When they stood in the iconic space where Dr. Martin Luther King Jr had made his speech, Sherisza went pensive, looking about the plazas at all the people. She, too, had viewed humans as being mostly uniform, homogenous, cardboard cutouts of each other. Sherisza was waking up to the same reality Dillon had been considering for the past couple of hours, and he laced his fingers with hers and gave a squeeze. She glanced at him sidelong, and he could see she was coming to terms with her own cluelessness, no longer safely shielded by the façade of being afraid of humanity.

"I had a dream," she said quietly. "A dream that I could save my people, and that I would not always be alone in the universe until the All-Mother took me home. You have woken me up to realize it is not a dream, but a reality. Thank you for that, Dillon."

"And that's part of Dr. King's legacy," he returned. "That we can see your people the same way he taught us to see our own."

She leaned in and kissed him, and Dillon was acutely aware of the many stares their act of passion in public received. Some people snapped photos, but there were plenty who just didn't know how to react. Was Sherisza putting his words to the test? It didn't seem like it, as when she pulled away, her eyes were solely on him, running her hand down his jaw, smiling broadly.

"Come, let us go find that little pizzeria," she said.

Dillon took her hand in his and began to lead her toward downtown. He had to bite his lip to keep from chortling when a man asked, "Hey, where can I get one of those?" The humor of it died a moment later when the man was whacked by his woman. He tried to assure her he was just kidding, but that just seemed to infuriate her further and she started screaming at him. Dillon and Sherisza hustled their footsteps to get away from the brewing fight.

"Someone's going to be sleeping on the couch for a few days," Dillon commented once they were a good distance away.

"Why is that?" she asked, her brow furrowed.

"That's where you sleep when you make your woman mad."

"You slept on the couch when I stayed that first night..."

Dillon chuckled. "Yeah, but that was different. You were a guest, and I didn't want to be presumptuous or rude or get in any trouble with my parents. But the couch is usually where the man ends up when he makes his woman angry, at least among many of our people. Can't leave him there too long, though, because as the saying goes, *Woman who put man in doghouse soon find him in cathouse.*"

Sherisza blinked. "I have no idea what that means."

He was glad for that when he considered he'd made a *cat* comment to a lioness while trying to be funny. "It's probably better if you don't," he chuckled, mostly at himself.

They walked by the river, and Dillon stopped to watch some of the ducks and geese down below. Sherisza was content to spend the peaceful time with him, and he loved being with her, even out in public under what he knew was probably a lot of subtle scrutiny. They went to the pizzeria, stopped by a jewelry store so Sherisza could look at the many styles of earrings, and then passed through the downtown to the park.

They stared hand-in-hand as they watched children play in the park. Neither had to speak a word to the other, the tenderness of the moment implicitly understood. She laced her fingers with his and gave a squeeze, and even the curious stares of other people in the park didn't ruin the moment. In fact, after a few minutes, a number of children came to see Sherisza, excited to see a "lion lady from another world."

She took the blunt nature of the children in stride, and her smile remained broad and friendly as the children touched her fur or asked to see her teeth. Dillon savored the moment with her. It was only the beginning of their life, but it already felt like they'd been together for years. Now there were children in their future, and things would just get better and better, he was sure. This was yet another day that Dillon didn't want to end except for one reason: to see what the future would bring them.

Eventually, though, they had to take a public shuttle to the spaceport. Some of the family was already in the terminal waiting for their tour of the *Malshekt*. There were so many warm, loving greetings, Sherisza receiving mostly hugs but some smiling handshakes as well. It only seemed to lift her spirits higher, and Dillon watched her as if in a dream, seeing his family hug and chat with his future wife. His friends, too, were cordial, though Dillon wasn't sure any of them understood just how far his relationship had progressed.

Sherisza led everyone onboard, and thankfully, Daevol kept his humor to himself. She showed them around, even letting everyone peek inside the guest cabins and engineering. She didn't explain what everything was, trying to be vague about the things she normally kept secret. Of more interest to everyone was the flight deck, where she sat and showed them a lot of the controls. Dillon sat beside her while she pointed out the combat controls, demonstrated how the HUD worked, and even gave them a quick rundown of the weapons systems. Of course, she made sure to talk about them as defensive measures.

"Who's that?" Aunt Rita asked, pointing to the photo clipped to Sherisza's console.

Dillon had to swallow his heart, but Sherisza actually smiled. "That is my brother, Daevol, and my children, Eesha and Maduu," she said, not bothering to go into how Kiandarian couples worked. She unclipped the picture and handed it to Dillon's aunt. Rita seemed to recognize what it meant, and she sucked her lip in. "They are safely home in the bosom of the Goddess."

"Such a beautiful little family. I'm so sorry," Rita said.

"You've got a new family, sweetie," Grandma Malinda said. "We can't ever replace them, but you're a part of our family now."

"And I am grateful for being welcomed into it," Sherisza said, rising to give Malinda a hug.

"How long do you two want to stay? You can always stay at my house, I won't bug you as much as my daughter and her husband," Malinda quipped, making everyone giggle.

"We must leave tomorrow, I fear," Sherisza said. "As much as I would love to stay here, there are those who need our help, my recovering people not the least of them. But we will be back for the next big family get-together, I promise you."

"Isn't that going to be your wedding?" Dillon's mother asked.

Sherisza glanced at Dillon, and he wrapped an arm around her and pulled her close. "We'll talk about it," he said.

"And one day, we will take you to my home world for a visit," Sherisza added.

That certainly prompted a lot of excited chatter. The family left after a last round of hugs and handshakes, and Dillon and Sherisza stood alone on the flight deck.

"I guess we may as well stay at the house one more night," Dillon said. "Our stuff's still there. No sense going to pick it up and then coming back to sleep here."

"That is fine," Sherisza said. "We will be back with you tomorrow, Daevol."

<I look forward to it, Captain.>

"Have we gotten any messages from Kwaagi space or Kiandar?" Dillon asked.

<Negative, Commander. All quiet, though I do not know if this is good or bad.>

"Like you said, no sense worrying about it for now," he said to Sherisza. After bidding the AI farewell, they caught up with Dillon's parents to head back to their house.

CHAPTER 16

SHADES OF CONFLICT

IT WAS a serene egress from Earth. There were no inquiries or statements from the Joint Senates about the issues with the Quarran Dominion. On the other hand, some of the family that had stayed at Grandma Malinda's house sent a signal to wish Dillon and Sherisza a safe trip before they'd left orbit. It was just one more bow of love wrapped around Sherisza's heart, and the way she was smiling when the transmission ended, Dillon appreciated the gesture almost as much as she did.

But there was work to be done. It was nice to see everyone back home living mostly quiet lives; it served as a reminder of why Dillon and Sherisza were going to help the Kwaagi. Now came the hard work though. It made Dillon think of his uncle Amos, putting in long hours in unforgiving elements to safeguard lives, and he was glad to have something in common with the man. Dillon hadn't dreamed an apprenticeship with Sherisza would lead to becoming something of a war hero, but it was becoming a little truer every day.

Sherisza set the coordinates for the Kwaagi Empire, Outer Dock Seven. She wanted to pick up Azilija now that they would be working in Kwaagi space again. There was the question of whether the woman had managed to decipher any more of the odd messages, of course. But it would also help to have a Kwaagi woman on board when dealing with their armada, which was on high alert and probably rather touchy.

The weapons were primed just in case they received an unwelcome visit in the time stream, and then Sherisza engaged the Chrono Drive and sent them hurtling across space. Dillon swore he could feel everything he'd eaten in the last three days make a reappearance in his roiling gut, but the feeling passed. He focused on the stars through the viewport, the HUD, and the various holodisplays showing views in every direction. If the black ship was there, he was determined to spot it before it could cause trouble.

After ten minutes, they were satisfied that the black ship wasn't there and likely wasn't coming at all. Had their enemy given up? Did the trip to Earth throw off their ability to track where the *Malshekt* would be next? Or were they giving Sherisza time to decide to destroy her life's work? There were so many questions and so few answers. Dillon was looking forward to speaking with Azi again and maybe finally getting some clues.

They took a detour to make love, keeping to her requested schedule, and then Sherisza led Dillon back to engineering. She quizzed him on a number of things, and even after a few days where work had been light years from his mind, he answered them all without trouble. Conventional thrusters, weaponry issues, shielding power loss, relays and couplings, and even taking apart the casing of the Chrono Drive were all within his grasp now. Dillon knew Sherisza was in love with him, but the way she looked at him after her quizzing was something else.

There was pride in her eyes, and all he could think was that he'd exceeded her expectations. How much had she truly anticipated from some human teenager when she took him on as her apprentice? Had she expected he would become a good engi neer and mechanic like she was, or had she just hoped he would have children with her and then part ways? He couldn't really say, but it also occurred to him that she may have expected he would slack off now that they were mated, married, or however they wanted to call it. Perhaps she'd figured he would try to become the dominant of the pair once they were having a sexual relationship.

But Dillon meant what he'd said at his grandmother's house. She had asked him to promise that their relationship would not change their working dynamic, and he'd agreed. He'd further promised that getting married wouldn't change it, that he still considered her the boss, and that he knew his apprenticeship still had a long way to go. Despite everything he already knew how to do, it was a drop in the bucket compared to what she could do and, more importantly, what she could teach him. Even if they never went their separate ways, he wanted to learn everything and be, as she'd said, the other half of her.

The same way Daevol was, but maybe more so, he thought.

"I think soon, when time allows, we will build a warp drive together," she said at last. "It will not hurt to have a redundant system in place, perhaps even beneficial should we ever find we have trouble with someone else in the time stream again. It will be the precursor to showing you how to build a Chrono Drive, and also help familiarize you with non-conventional propulsion systems. For now, let me introduce you to the impulse engine."

"Now we're talking," Dillon said, leaning back against a railing.

It felt good to be working again. Dillon loved Sherisza, but at the same time, working with her let him confirm that it wasn't just lust or young love. As his father had said, they had to have a relationship outside the bedroom, and the fact that he loved being with her even when they weren't making love was a good sign. That working with her was one of his favorite parts of the day truly drove the point home, but he recognized there wasn't anything he didn't like doing with this woman.

The reflection of the Chrono Drive's blue light off her engagement ring caught his eye, and she looked at it and smiled when she noticed his attention. She stayed on topic, though, going through the basics of the impulse engines and how they differed from warp or chrono drives. If anything, though, her focus made Dillon smile wider.

Sherisza didn't beat him over the head with too much information, but she did ask questions to see how much he'd retained. As expected, he didn't remember all of it, but she was happy with how much he could answer after only one discussion. They didn't get into the technical yet; she'd want him to be able to explain it verbally before she moved to hands-on demonstrations. Instead, she told him to check on his studies while she made him something to eat.

The thought of studies was less appealing than it had been. As he thought about it, though, Dillon concluded it'd be easier now than when there were cubs on the ship with them.

Grinning like a young fool in love, he went to his old cabin.

———

Outer Dock Seven had some blast marks on it but was otherwise none the worse for wear when they arrived. It looked as though it'd been attacked, but there were Kwaagi fighters flying about on patrol, and there was no structural damage to the station that Dillon could see. From his vantage point, it didn't look like any of the Kwaagi fighters were docked at the moment. After a brief conversation with the flight director, Sherisza was able to land the *Malshekt* in the main hangar rather than docking on the outside, and she and Dillon exchanged a knowing look.

There was no missing Azilija when they spotted her in the

hangar, her blue scales and orange stripes distinctive enough before they took her colorful plumage into account. By the time Sherisza had landed the ship and opened the hatch, the Kwaagi woman was standing at the base of the steps. She had her hands folded before her nervously, but at the same time, her feathers stood straight up in excitement. And then there was the *click-click-clack* of her large inner talons tapping on the hangar floor.

"Captain Rousilarru, Dillon; it is so good to see you both again," Azilija said with a polite bow of the head.

"It is good to see you again, too, Azi," Sherisza said, she and Dillon returning the gesture.

"How have things been? Or can you not talk about them?" Dillon asked.

The Kwaagi woman nodded. "There is only so much I can say, but you no doubt saw the damage to the station on your way in. We were attacked by a small reinforcement group that came to our border, but thanks to your modifications, they were destroyed. I will let the brigadier or someone of higher rank tell you how the war progresses within our borders, but we have thus far held the line here–again, thanks to you."

"That is good to hear," Sherisza said. "We are honored to have been of service. We will not be here long; we are headed to Outer Dock Eight next to do the same modifications to their wing. Have you made progress on your translations, and would you like to accompany us?"

"I will request permission from the brigadier," Azi said. "As for the translations, I think that is best discussed in private, or once we are safely away in the *Malshekt*."

"Does the station need any repairs we could help with?" Dillon asked.

"No. We are quite sufficiently able to defend ourselves now. Come. Once our Visitations Clerk notes your arrival, I will escort you to see the brigadier."

"Lead the way," Sherisza prompted.

They were checked in by the visitation clerk, the *Malshekt* not officially scheduled for a stop. She offered them accommodations, but as they were only there to pick up Azilija, Sherisza declined. Soon, they were on their way to see the brigadier.

The trip up the lift was a lot less tense than the last one. Fortunately, now they knew the rules and protocols and followed them while on the Kwaagi station. Arriving in the brigadier's office, they each bowed their heads politely and waited to be beckoned forward. The Kwaagi general took Azi in with interest but then gestured for her and their guests to approach.

"Administrator, what is the meaning of this?" he asked.

"Sir, I have come to request permission to accompany Captain Rousilarru to Outer Dock Eight and beyond," she said.

He stood up at that and bowed deeply toward Sherisza. "Captain, you have the thanks of the emperor himself and thus all of the Kwaagi Empire for your help. Your modifications to our wing proved invaluable in repulsing the latest incursion by our enemies. The emperor would like you to continue with your work on our wings, and he has decreed that our forces stationed at Kiandar will not be withdrawn to aid in the war effort here. We will keep our promise to defend your people."

"Thank you, General," Sherisza answered. "I hope that our mutual aid leads to a long and lasting friendship between Kiandar and the Empire."

"I have little doubt it will. Administrator, permission granted to accompany the captain and her second," the brigadier said. "Anything you can do to aid her in aiding us will be considered service to the empire."

"Thank you, sir," Azi answered with a bow.

"Brigadier, can we inquire about the state of the war?" Dillon asked.

The brigadier let out a bit of a scent, but it wasn't anger. It was strong but gave Dillon the impression of anxiety, just shy of fear. "The invaders are powerful; I will give them that. They continue to harry our forces and have threatened Kwaaganarr at times. We are slowly wearing them down, and our stations holding the line here are instrumental to ending their invasion. That is as much as I can say, but at the same time, our need for your services should say plenty more without a word being spoken."

"We understand, General. Thank you. We will proceed directly to Outer Dock Eight now, that they are prepared to help you hold the line," Sherisza said.

He gestured them away after a gracious bow of the head, and Sherisza, Dillon, and Azi made their way back to the *Malshekt*. There was a Kwaagi male coming off the ship when they got back to the hangar. Dillon wasn't sure if he was more surprised that someone had entered without permission and survived or that the Kwaagi wasn't arguing with the AI.

"I left some fuel cells for your conventional thrusters by the flight deck," the dock worker said with the typical Kwaagi gesture of respect. "Your replicator has also been resupplied."

"Thank you," Sherisza said, mounting the steps as the worker went back to his duties. When all three of them were up on the ship, the Kiandarian added, "I am surprised you let him on board without a good deal of harassment, at least."

<I knew Azilija would be joining us, so I made certain the replicator would not run out of power or supplies.>

"Jesus, Daevol, she hasn't even put her bag in her cabin yet," Dillon laughed.

<I have not argued with anyone for some time. It is nice to have you back, Azilija.>

"And it is good to be back, you glorified oven timer," the Kwaagi woman shot back.

<Please put your things directly into the escape pod, it will make it easier for me to eject you and them into the nearest nebula.>

"Daevol, enough," Sherisza said sternly, though she had a little smirk on her face.

<She started it. I was trying to be nice.>

"*Maqua*," the Kiandarian said. "Begin departure protocols. I want to travel to Outer Dock Eight as quickly as we can."

<Confirmed, Captain.>

"Do not take too much offense at our banter, Captain," Azi said semi-apologetically. "It is a welcome change for me from the typical stiffness of my people, particularly aboard one of our border stations."

"I understand, but I do not want him getting in the habit of speaking to guests that way," she replied. "Stow your things, and when we are underway, you can tell us what you have managed to figure out since we last saw you."

"Aye, Captain."

Sherisza glanced at Dillon once Azi went in her cabin, and he chortled. "Glorified oven timer, that's a good one. Why didn't I ever think of that?"

<Good taste?>

That got a laugh out of Sherisza, and she took her seat on the flight deck as the hangar doors opened. Dillon grabbed the fuel cells and headed back to engineering to secure them.

Azi came back out of her cabin after nearly fifteen minutes, and Dillon wondered if she and Daevol had been trading barbs behind the closed door. She brought up a holodisplay once she was standing behind and between Dillon's and Sherisza's chairs. She read through something, then gripped both seats tightly as she prepared for the Chrono Drive to be engaged. Soon, they were fast on their way to Outer Dock Eight, and Azi recovered from the momentary discomfort.

"Captain, bear in mind that what I tell you is not absolute," she said, Sherisza nodding. "I have only a small subset of their vocabulary to work with; however, this is a clue. Whoever this mystery pilot is, they have a limited vocabulary; the messages are simple, with many of the same words repeated across them. That is why I was able to answer them and at least entreat them to give us time to see to their request."

"It's amazing that you can even do that," Dillon commented.

"Thank you. As I said, it is simpler thanks to the limited vocabulary the pilot used. I was able to deduce tone and inflection easily, and the urgent nature of the messages pointed to a request, not a demand or declaration of hostility. But now I am completely sure they are telling you not to use something on this ship, and I suspect, given that you meet them in the... time stream, they want you to stop using your drive."

"Which I will not do until they give me some reason why," Sherisza said. "The Chrono Drive is the only means I have of saving my people, and unless there is some galaxy-threatening reason to stop, I will not do so."

"I understand, Captain. Perhaps, if we meet that ship again, I will be able to converse with them and find the reason for their request. I regret that I cannot deduce it from what I already have access to," Azi said.

"Does it match any of the transmissions–assuming your empire has received any–made by the invaders from the reaches?" Sherisza asked.

"We have not received any transmissions, but we have intercepted some. It is not the same. The language used by your mystery attacker is almost guttural, lacking complexity or niceties. It could simply be a matter of their desperation, but I suspect the species is not terribly advanced despite piloting a ship like the *Malshekt*."

"That is weird," Dillon said. "Pretty sure they taught us in school that complexity of language comes with technological advances, so you can tell a lot about a species from either one or the other."

"This is usually true, but not always," Azi said.

"You're the expert," Dillon said without sarcasm.

"Well, we may be headed for a breakthrough where that is concerned," Sherisza said.

"Why is that, Captain?" Azi asked.

Sherisza brought up the main HUD, and there was no need of further questions. Their mystery black ship was back. Though it approached at breakneck speed even for being in the time stream, it came up alongside the *Malshekt* and flew off her port side wing.

And then that garbled message came across the hailing frequency.

CHAPTER 17

TRIAGE

"*OM-CUBWE!*" Azi called over the hailing frequency. "*Daetoo nosh tayga tenar.*"

There was a long delay, but the black ship made no move to attack the *Malshekt*. Sherisza had her hand on the combat controls regardless, watching out the port side of the viewport. If that black ship attacked again, Dillon figured there was a good chance one or the other would be destroyed. Everyone was getting fed up with this game, but no one more than Sherisza.

A long, garbled message came back over the frequency after a few minutes. Azi tried to work quickly on translating, but it didn't matter. Sherisza brought them out of the time stream and into normal space as soon as the black ship stopped transmitting. They weren't too far from Outer Dock Eight, and they could arrive there in a couple of hours just under the impulse engines. Once they were on their way again, the Kiandarian turned to her Kwaagi guest.

"Azi, work as quickly as you can on that. The next time we enter the time stream, I either need an answer that gets rid of them, or we are going to have to destroy them," Sherisza said. "They have already proven capable of disabling us, and if we refuse their request, I imagine they may do more than that soon."

"Understood, Captain," the Kwaagi woman said, dismissing the holodisplay and moving into her quarters for some quiet.

"What if it's not the Chrono Drive?" Dillon mused when Azi was away.

"What do you mean?" Sherisza asked, turning to him.

He looked into her eyes. "What if it's Daevol's notes and schematics? It's the only other thing I can think of that the black ship might be talking about. Maybe there's something in Daevol's work that they're afraid you might build."

"I suppose there is a good possibility you are correct," she said, rubbing a finger across her chin. "Even still, I will not destroy my brother's life's work. I have already lost him; I will not give up the remainder of what he wanted to create for our people."

"Well, hopefully Azi can communicate with them and ask them what's so dangerous. Maybe we'd only have to get rid of a certain thing. Hard to say what, or why, though."

"I would rather get rid of that ship. If that ship turns out to be from the future and my brother's theories are true, it is trying to change history, which cannot happen. So, the only other thing that makes sense is that it is some rival trying to keep this technology from my people for whatever reason."

"Or Daevol's theory about changing history is wrong," Dillon offered, shrugging when she fixed him with a wide-eyed stare. "The man was a genius, Sherisza, but that doesn't mean he was right about everything. Nobody knows everything."

"Or perhaps they are not changing history at all. Perhaps they know they succeed in getting us to do what they wish, because history already recorded it," she whispered.

"Right. There's all kinds of possibilities. And we could be wrong about everything we think they might be talking about.

Maybe they just don't want Azi on board with us; they didn't react well to hearing her talk that first time. It's possible they're only talking to her because she's the only one who can understand them at all."

"More questions without answers," Sherisza sighed. "Well, regardless, we will be at Outer Dock Eight in a little while. Let us get our things together in preparation. We will be staying in quarters there as usual."

"Yes, ma'am," he said, giving her a peck on the side of the muzzle when they both got up.

———

Sherisza was consumed. She and Dillon worked separately on the Kwaagi wing as had become their usual routine. At night, when they were finished, though, Sherisza began going through her brother's notes that Dillon had taken from Kiandar. She started with the handwritten notes first, as she didn't want to have to interface with the Kwaagi computers to read the digital ones. By the same token, she didn't want to spend too much time on the *Malshekt* and look like she was up to something.

The Kwaagi were guileless and straightforward, as she'd explained, and so they viewed everyone else with a bit of skepticism and suspicion.

Dillon reclined against the backrest, watching another goofy classic martial arts movie while Sherisza lay beside him, reading a notebook. He looked at her every so often, fascinated by the way her mind worked. Daevol had supposedly been quite a bit smarter than Sherisza, but she was brilliant by any standard, and she was working through his scattered thoughts and ideas as best she could. There might be some clue what the black ship wanted in those books, or at the least, there might be some new inventions that could help Kiandar—and the rest of the galaxy.

He couldn't make heads or tails of any of it, thanks largely to the fact that all of it was written in Kiandese. Dillon thought perhaps he should learn Sherisza's native language at some point, especially considering how quickly Azilija had or continued to do so. Nevertheless, he was astonished by some of the designs and sketches Daevol had left in his notebooks. Dillon didn't have to be able to read Kiandese to see the man's mind had operated on numerous levels, theorizing about energy sources and dimensional breaches among other things. There was a sketch of the galactic core with a bunch of notes beside it; what had he been thinking?

Maybe that's the Doorstep of the Goddess he mentioned, Dillon thought. *I have to ask Daevol if he's made any progress figuring out what his namesake was talking about.*

Dillon turned back to the holodisplay as someone got kicked in the jaw, and he laughed. Sherisza ran her hand along his thigh, chuckling lightly through her nose at his silly movie. He wrapped an arm around her, and she leaned into him, but she didn't stop going through her brother's notes. Soon, though, she reached the end of the notebook, closed it, and set it aside.

"We should make love again," she said, leaning her head on his chest.

"Of course. Do you mind waiting until the movie's done?" he asked.

She didn't answer for a moment. "You are not becoming bored with me, are you?"

"Huh? No, of course not," Dillon assured her, brushing her braids back from her face. "It's just... well, if I'm being honest, doing it because you have to isn't the same as doing it for fun."

"Oh," she said. "I am sorry, Dillon. I have not meant to pressure you..."

"No, no, it's fine. I'm trying to keep my focus on the goal.

We'll be back to making love for the fun of it soon enough, right?"

"If I have not conceived by now, I am probably not going to this year," she said. "And as I told you, Dillon, I will make all this worth your while, I promise."

"Like how? You'll start having sex with me?" he teased.

She lifted her head to meet his gaze. "You will just have to wait and see," she teased back with a narrow-eyed smirk.

"How was the reading? Find anything interesting?"

Sherisza sat up and shook her head. "He has theories for so many things, Dillon. Infinite energy sources using gravity, new geothermal energy designs, ideas about crossing into parallel dimensions in similar fashion to our phase-cloaking device..."

"See? You're just as smart as he was. You just work too hard."

She kissed and then muzzle rubbed his cheek, then laid her head on his chest again. "How much longer is this silly *karate* movie of yours?"

"It's almost over," he answered. She slipped the covers off him and began kissing his chest and then down his belly. Dillon dismissed the holodisplay. "Yeah, never mind, it's over..."

Sherisza took his words to heart and tried to make their love less mechanical and required. They enjoyed the time in each other's arms, getting back to remembering that it was as much to bond as to make children in this instance. Part of her was desperate to be a mother again, he knew, but as much as he was looking forward to children, too, he saw her first as his wife. Or his wife-to-be, anyway. He wanted to love every minute with her, and when they made love like this, he truly did.

She cuddled up against him when they were done, purring beside his heart as she always did, but she didn't fall asleep. "What exactly does a human wedding entail?" she asked.

"Well, we get dressed up really nice, make vows before

Reverend Warner and God—or your goddess, if you prefer—and then we have a big party that may put Grandma's birthday to shame," Dillon answered, eyes closed, running his fingers through her braided hair.

"What sort of vows?"

"That I'll love you forever and never leave you," he whispered, trying not to fall asleep when she was asking questions.

"I have made this vow to you already," she said.

"I know. The ceremony is as much legal as theological. Honestly, in our case, it's going to be more for the family than for us. But it's still something I want to do with you, Sherisza. I want to tell God and the whole world that you're my wife, and nothing will ever change that."

He felt her smile against his chest, her rumbling purring easing him off to sleep.

———

The modification work went smoothly over a couple of days. Dillon almost felt like he'd been born to work on Kwaagi craft. Of course, he didn't know a thing about their ships aside from what he was modifying. Their weapon systems were something few outside the empire knew anything about, and he suspected most of their technology, while similar to Earth's or the *Malshekt's*, was unique in some ways. He was hoping to learn more about all of it at some point in the future, though even Sherisza had never fiddled with their disruptors to figure out how they worked—yet.

Sherisza continued spending the evenings going through Daevol's notes, and she and Dillon took a break from her rigorous lovemaking schedule. He was just as happy when they fell asleep in each other's arms, and he could smell her fur and feel her purr against his chest. The woman was so driven on everything she put her mind to, so Dillon was happy to enforce a rest. How she would "make it worth his while," he wasn't sure, but he was looking forward to finding out.

Azi, too, was consumed with her work, trying to piece together what the mystery pilot had been saying. She stopped by to let Sherisza know of her progress from time to time, but the Kwaagi woman seemed hypersensitive to her employers' relationship. She kept her distance unless there was something to report, and despite all her work, there wasn't much yet. Dillon and Sherisza were confident Azi would make a breakthrough, but they didn't pressure her. Too much pressure forced people to make mistakes and begin hating their work.

It was something Dillon hadn't had to worry about at all under Sherisza, though he realized it was a large part of his issue with the law studies.

When half the wing was finished, they were diverted from going to the mess hall for supper, escorted to the brigadier's office by a clerk. Like the one on its nearby sister station, the brigadier's office was simple and sterile, the Kwaagi officer seated behind a metal desk. He had his clawed hands steepled before him as he dismissed the clerk with his eyes, and once they were alone with him, Dillon and Sherisza approached and bowed their heads politely.

The Kwaagi general's voice was a low hiss as he spoke. "First, allow me to thank you for the work you have done and continue to do for our empire. On behalf of the emperor, we owe you a great debt that our contract hardly compensates you for."

"The friendship of the empire is payment enough for me," Sherisza said.

The brigadier stood up, and Dillon marveled at the size of this Kwaagi male. He was at least a foot taller than Dillon and quite muscular despite his uniform's attempt to hide it. His dark plumage stood up as he saluted Sherisza, touching his right fist to the opposite shoulder. "That is now well-known to the emperor, and that is why he has asked a great favor of you, Captain Rousilarru. Please understand that what I am about to tell you is considered top secret, and cannot be shared with anyone, whether inside or outside the empire."

"We will keep your secrets," she assured him.

"You have my word," Dillon added.

The brigadier nodded. "Our enemies from the beyond have reached Kwaaganarr. Thus far they have not attacked the planet, but they are planning something large. Escape or retreat do not seem to be among their goals; they are there for a suicide mission at best. The emperor has therefore made this request of you, Captain Rousilarru: He would ask that you go to Kwaaganarr and take his family to a safe location that will be disclosed personally by them."

"He believes the *Malshekt* can slip past your enemies?" she asked.

The Kwaagi general nodded. "Yes, and your ship's speed and capabilities are well-known to him and all the empire. Know that he would not make this request if he did not trust you fully and completely and consider you a friend to the empire."

"We will be happy to help," Sherisza said. "Should we go immediately, or do we have time to finish our modifications on your wing?"

"Half of our wing is now complete; that will suffice for now. We would ask that you go to our home world immediately and take the emperor's family to safety."

"Then please let the emperor know we are on our way and have your clerks prepare the *Malshekt* for immediate departure," Sherisza said.

"Is there anything else we can do to help?" Dillon asked.

"No, young human. We will speak with the Joint Senates when the emperor deems the time is right. For now, we ask that you respect our communications block," the brigadier said.

"Of course," Dillon and Sherisza agreed.

"Go, and may the Scale Father guide you to victory," the brigadier said with a dismissive gesture before he sat back down.

"Brigadier," Sherisza said before she turned away. "May we take Azilija with us again? Or is this mission too secretive for her to be present?"

He considered the request for a minute. "She will remain here. The location of the imperial family must be a secret even from those within the empire."

"Understood. Farewell, sir," she said, and she led Dillon to the lift after being dismissed with a salute and a wave.

Once the lift was underway and the brigadier's office was out of sight, Dillon said, "This is bad. If they're asking us to evacuate the emperor and his family, they're expecting Kwaaganarr to get hit hard."

"Indeed," Sherisza responded absently. "We have now become embroiled in a war. This is not what I have ever wanted. Even all those fights as MacNault tried to finish the job of wiping out my people will be as nothing compared to this. I am not sure we are ready, Dillon."

"Maybe not, but we've got something to fight for," he answered. He put his hand to her lower belly, and she laid hers atop it. "A couple of somethings, not to mention you and everyone else in the known galaxy."

"I pray we do not encounter the black ship while we have the emperor and his family aboard," she said, still holding his hand. "I would ask that they install a standard warp drive so we can avoid going into the time stream altogether, but that would raise a lot of questions. I still do not feel ready to even let anyone else know we have a time-bending device, much less share it with them. I do not think they are ready."

"No, I think it's something we need to keep to ourselves for a while yet," he agreed. "I just hope Azi never mentions it by accident."

"As do I."

They made their way to their quarters and packed their things hastily. Soon they were on their way to the *Malshekt* and found the hangar crew waiting for them. Most of the crew here was military despite being tradesmen, and Sherisza and Dillon walked to their ship to a number of salutes and bows of the head. They returned the latter gesture graciously and approached Azi, who stood at the base of the boarding steps.

"I fear I may not go with you, Captain," she said.

"I know. I would appreciate any further work you can put in deciphering our messages, Azi. If you come to a conclusion, please obtain the brigadier's permission to contact us while we are within your space and let me know. If you can create and send a recorded response, that may be the most helpful thing to avoid further attacks."

"As you wish, Captain," the Kwaagi woman said, bowing her head.

"Hope to see you soon," Dillon said, holding out his hand.

Azilija stared at his hand for a moment, then tried to approximate a human smile, unable to keep from releasing her pleased scent. She shook Dillon's hand to the surprise of many of the hangar crew. "Thank you, Dillon. Be well in your journeys. I look forward to your return."

"Be safe, and if any more of those bastards come to your border, give them hell," he said.

"Oh, we will. Worry not about that," she returned, showing her teeth.

Dillon and Sherisza mounted the steps to the *Malshekt*, and the hatch closed behind them. Once they stowed their things in their cabin, they took their seats on the flight deck and Sherisza got them underway. Though the common workers on the station may not have known where they were going and why, there was little mystery that they were going to do something dire if they were leaving in the middle of a job.

With a final farewell to the flight director, Sherisza took the *Malshekt* out of the hangar and to a safe distance. She set coordinates for the planet of Kwaaganarr with Daevol's help, and then she engaged the Chrono Drive.

They looked for their mysterious pursuer vigilantly, but all remained calm for now.

NOT SURPRISINGLY, Kwaaganarr was located near the center of their empire, all the better to keep it well fortified and protected. It may not have amounted to much in their current situation, but against any other government in the known galaxy, Dillon figured it would seem nearly impregnable. By the same token, though, it meant help had much farther to go when needed. As it stood, the *Malshekt* cruised along at a hurried but inconspicuous speed, Sherisza desperate to get to the planet and aid the emperor but not at the cost of her secrets.

While they traveled, Daevol kept an overlay on the HUD showing their relative position in the empire. There were locations marked of where the enemy fleet was currently. The Kwaagi still didn't offer much in the way of news, but the *Malshekt* couldn't receive it while in the time stream anyway. Dillon expected the Kwaagi were fighting what felt like a losing battle, but that they were whittling down their enemy. The reinforcements getting stopped at the border would make a big difference in the days to come.

The *Malshekt* wasn't a fighter ship, but she was far from

helpless. The goal wouldn't be to engage enemy ships while the emperor's family was on board, but if they had to, Sherisza's ship could defend herself well. It was entirely possible a few well-placed shots with the ion cannon could change the trajectory of the battle, if not the war. But those were considerations for *if*, not *when*. The primary goal was to avoid trouble and save the emperor's family first.

Their course took them around the enemy fleet, coming at Kwaaganarr from the far side. Sherisza was able to use that and some shielding modifications to effectively cloak the *Malshekt* from their approach angle. She brought the ship out of the time stream with the star behind them and Kwaaganarr between them and the enemy fleet. Regardless, Daevol began scanning for any scout ships or other signs they had been detected.

<Nothing yet, Captain.>

"Keep scanning," she ordered. "If any scout ships detect us, we will have to destroy them."

<Understood.>

They kept on their approach vector and encountered no issues, though, and Dillon took his first good look at the Kwaagi home world. Where Earth was a great big ball of yellow, green, blue, and white, Kwaaganarr was mostly green at first sight. It had a massive supercontinent and many smaller islands, but most of it was green, as though the majority of the planet were jungle or rainforest. Its ice caps remained white and there were some wild weather patterns that were impressive from orbit, but its greater oceans must've been out of view.

<Receiving transmission. Permission granted to land in the imperial capital city of Aeliksi. Coordinates translated to the HUD. Radio silence requested.>

"Do not even confirm, keep all outgoing transmissions silenced," Sherisza said, bringing the *Malshekt* down toward the planet.

A pair of Kwaagi fighter ships escorted them when they reached the atmosphere. These were larger and more heavily armed than the ones Dillon and Sherisza had been working on. It looked as though they could take apart the *Malshekt* with little trouble, and Dillon hoped that meant they'd be a sufficient last line of defense if the enemy attacked Kwaaganarr directly. There had to be a lot of defenders here, protecting their emperor from any and all threats.

Daevol pointed out all the gun emplacements on the surface as well as high-altitude launch platforms for further fighter wings. The planet had plenty of defense, but Dillon appreciated that they weren't taking any chances with their leader. Still, he wasn't sure he was ready to meet and escort an emperor to safety. It didn't help that he was human and his people had insulted the Kwaagi on their first meeting—and, he got the feeling, several more times since then. How much more scrutiny would he be under when meeting the emperor or his family? Might they do or say something to truly put him to the test?

"Not sure I'm ready for this," he commented as they approached the capital city.

"Why is that?" Sherisza asked.

Dillon didn't answer for a moment, amazed by the way the golden city seemed to come out of the jungle on their approach. It was massive, but there were still so many trees and plants in the city itself, it wasn't like the more urban cities on other worlds. There was a spaceport, and Dillon could see a massive pyramidal building that had to be either the palace or a temple of some kind. It wasn't all steel and glass like most of the cities back home, but it was impressive. Dillon couldn't help but recall his earlier thoughts about worlds and their histories; how much more would a race as old as the Kwaagi have?

"We're going to meet the emperor," he said finally. "It's intimidating."

"Why? He is simply a hereditary *president* of this empire. Do not let the title confuse your perceptions. Just continue to be the same polite, respectful man you have always been, and I trust this meeting will go well."

"I sure hope so."

<Dress lightly, Captain. Sensors indicate the average temperature is roughly fifty *capreks*.>

"What's that in Fahrenheit?" Dillon asked.

"A little over one hundred and five," Sherisza calculated absently before the AI could answer. "I hope they do not mind me panting."

"Maybe it's cooler inside. The stations were never too hot that I noticed," Dillon said.

"Balmy, but no, not too hot. I will deal with it. We should not be here long."

<The spaceport has indicated where we should land. Would you like me to handle it?>

"Go right ahead," Sherisza said. "Daevol, I know you and Azilija had fun teasing each other when she was on the ship; however, you cannot behave that way with the imperial family. Any teasing or joking could be taken as a grave insult. I must implore you to be respectful and accommodating at all times."

<Acknowledged. I will be on my best behavior, Captain.>

"For all that's worth," Dillon quipped.

<Commander, I had a surprise installed for you.>

Dillon raised an eyebrow and glanced at Sherisza, who was smirking despite shaking her head. "I'm afraid to ask. What was it?" he prompted.

<A couch.>

Sherisza chuckled, and Dillon put his hand over his face. "Listening in on our conversations again, were you?"

<Of course. I had the couch installed in the escape pod to

facilitate ejecting you into the nearest nebula if you annoy the captain enough to be banished there.>

"You're such a dickhead," Dillon laughed.

<I love you too. Taking the *Malshekt* down to the indicated slip. Docking procedures are already engaged. Prepare to disembark.>

"Do we need our bags?" Dillon asked.

"For now, I am going to assume we do not," Sherisza answered. She did, however, get her blasters and strap them to her thighs. Dillon followed suit, strapping on his personal defense blaster, and then they headed for the hatch.

———

Kwaaganarr wasn't just a hot world, it was exceedingly humid as well. It was a nasty combination for Dillon to deal with, but he actually felt sorry for the Kwaagi. After all the embarrassment that had surrounded that first contact between Kwaagi and humans, now their emperor and his family would have to deal with a sweaty teenager and a panting Kiandarian. He was concerned it might be more off-putting than the fact that he was human in the first place.

As he'd suspected, it wasn't quite as hot within the buildings, but the Kwaagi seemed to appreciate the way the humidity felt on their scales. There was little relief to be had outside or in the spaceport, though the pilot of the transport shuttle that took them to the palace did adjust the climate control for his passengers. Dillon and Sherisza enjoyed the cooler, drier air for as long as they could. Dillon hoped he didn't end up smelling worse after the sweat dried up a bit.

They arrived at the palace, and the pilot took the shuttle directly inside a narrow hangar in one of the upper tiers of the pyramid. Once out of the sun, Dillon and Sherisza got even more relief, and when the door of the shuttle opened, they were both pleased to find the palace wasn't marked by a jungle atmosphere. It wasn't quite as nice as the shuttle's climate-controlled air, but it was far better than the spaceport, so they acclimated to it quickly.

Dillon was starting to get used to the particulars of Kwaagi customs. They were met in the hangar by a Kwaagi female with an electronic clipboard, just as on the stations. She wasn't as colorful as many of the other females, more officious and even stuffy looking, if such a thing was possible on their reptilian visages. Her outfit was modest and efficient, and Dillon couldn't help but think all she was missing to make the look complete was a pocket protector and some glasses. He wondered if any of the Kwaagi needed bother with the latter but kept such pointless questions to himself.

"Greetings, Captain Rousilarru and Dillon Mackey. On behalf of His Imperial Majesty, I welcome you to the world of Kwaaganarr and the imperial palace," the clerk said with stiffer diction than Dillon had heard from her people, even before the translator did its work. "I am First Imperial Administrator Selanjja, and I will escort you to see His Imperial Majesty in just a few minutes. While we do appreciate shows of strength, I must first ask you to surrender your weapons before we go to see him."

"Of course," Sherisza said, unbuckling her weapons belt and handing it over.

Dillon did the same, adding, "Nice to meet you, First Administrator."

"It is a pleasure to meet you as well, Dillon Mackey. Now we need you to pass through a bio-scanner to ensure you do not carry any communicable diseases or biological weapons into the emperor's presence. It is merely a formality; please do not take offense."

"No offense taken. We can appreciate your efforts to safe-guard the emperor, and we look forward to meeting him," Sherisza said.

Even the administrator passed through the scanner, and Dillon felt only the slightest tingle as whatever waves they used passed over him. He was admitted into the palace proper, and he wondered how deeply it scanned for diseases and other ailments. It was always nice to get a clean bill of health no matter the occasion.

They were escorted down a couple of hallways and then up a rampway that took the place of normal stairs. They headed deeper into the heart of the palace, and soon came to a grand room that took Dillon's breath away completely. He had seen the grand hall of the senate building back on Earth, and he had been amazed at the smaller but no less magnificent office of President MacNault on the Eye of Chronon-Er. This, though, was something else entirely.

There were shades of ancient Terran civilizations in the architecture and the golden leaf on just about everything. It was as grand an audience chamber as Dillon could imagine, including a stately throne set twenty-one steps up to overlook the floor. He could only imagine the respect the emperor received when seated up there, looking down to pass judgment or pronouncements over his people. When he thought of villains in the old stories fighting to try to rule the world, it's what he imagined they had in mind the entire time.

But the emperor wasn't seated on his throne. He was standing at floor level, speaking with a couple of other Kwaagi males. The First Administrator stopped and gestured for Dillon and Sherisza to wait behind her. Dillon took the time to look around some more, as did Sherisza. They both had slightly opened jaws as they beheld the richness of the chamber, and they started to take in the tapestries and inlaid murals that spoke of some of the imperial line's past. Just as Dillon had mused, there was so much history here, enough to keep someone busy for years trying to study or chronicle it all for outsiders.

At last, the emperor looked their way and gave the slightest nod. The First Administrator led Dillon and Sherisza over to him, and without even being prompted, they both bowed deeply. He bowed his head respectfully, and the other two males moved away to take position on either side of the steps leading up to the throne.

"Captain Rousilarru, it is an honor to welcome you to my home," the emperor said. He turned to Dillon then. "And you, young Mister Mackey, I have heard many good things about you from my brigadiers and from my imperial war minister. He was quite impressed with the way you held yourself when he met you at the Joint Senates. Allow me to introduce myself. I am Emperor Malshii Denexxtu of the Kwaagi."

To Dillon's amazement, the emperor reached for a handshake. He shook with the man with no delay, and then the emperor shook with Sherisza as well.

"It is an honor to be welcomed to Kwaaganarr, and much more so to your home," Sherisza said with another deferential bow of the head.

"Your service to the empire has been exceptional, and though I hesitated to ask you to put yourself in the middle of our conflict, there is no outsider I would trust more," the emperor said. "With your agreement, tomorrow, I would like you to take my family to safety, that they will be out of harm's way should these invaders strike here."

"We will be happy to," the Kiandarian said. "How many will be in the party?"

"My mate and our three children," he answered. He glanced at the Kwaagi woman still standing attentively nearby and released a scent; Dillon recognized it as amusement. "My many administrators and generals wish me to go with them, but for now, I have decided to stay. That may change, but I expect not. My family has never been one to shy away from fighting for our empire, and I do not expect to be the exception to that. I would much rather stay and defend my home. However, they yet have time to convince me to leave."

"If I may be so bold, Your Majesty, I think your people will fight harder knowing you and your family are safe," Dillon offered.

Emperor Malshii met Dillon's eyes. "I know. But that's not who I am."

Dillon noted the slip in his speech and wondered. "Whatever you decide, we'll be happy to help and have your family aboard."

"Well said," Sherisza agreed. "My ship is not equipped with a cloaking device; however, we do have other technology that should allow us to spirit you and your family away without your enemies' knowledge. Merely tell us when, and where we are going to, and we will get you there safely."

The emperor's feathers bobbed at that. "Thank you. First Administrator, take word to the dining hall that I will be bringing our guests for food soon."

"As you wish, Your Majesty," she said, bowing before she departed out the far side door.

When they were alone but for the guards at the steps, the emperor looked at the soldiers over his shoulder before turning back. "I can't tell you how exciting the prospect of flying aboard the *Malshekt* is to me," he said. "I spent nearly a decade as a fighter pilot, and to be honest, I miss it quite a bit. If I go with you, you must promise to let me try flying your ship, Captain."

I thought so, Dillon thought. There'd been something about the stiffness of the man's speech that seemed forced. When he'd slipped, Dillon heard the other personality clearly. The man had adopted a certain persona to fit the office of emperor, but he was a fighter pilot and, if Dillon's instincts were good, an everyman at heart.

"If it convinces you to come to safety, consider it a promise," Sherisza said.

"Since I suspect no one can tell you not to talk, Your Majesty, can I ask if the situation is as bad as it seems?" Dillon ventured.

The Kwaagi emperor sighed. "It's not as bad as it seems; we're whittling away at the enemy forces and, so far as my brigadiers report, no reinforcements are coming. However, there's a good chance they launch an attack on Kwaaganarr. I wish to stand and fight with my people. My people prefer I get to safety. I have little doubt we'll win in the short term, at least, but where all this will lead, I don't know."

"What precipitated all this?" Sherisza asked. "Was it truly just a colonization that they took offense at?"

Emperor Malshii nodded. "Yes. The system was dead; there were no colonies or outposts of any kind in it. We're not sure why they attacked and continue to attack us so vehemently. A simple discussion could've prevented so many losses on both sides. If it was their system, I would've ceded it back to them without a fight. We were exploring, not invading."

"Whole lot of people with a *shoot first and ask questions later* mentality lately," Dillon said.

"Indeed," the emperor said. "You two seem a little ill at ease here. Kwaaganarr isn't the most hospitable planet to non-reptilian peoples. After dinner, I will have you escorted to the pools to wash and keep cool until you're ready to retire for the night. Tomorrow, either you'll take my family to safety, or you'll take us all to safety. Either way, you will have the eternal gratitude of this empire as well as myself, my friends."

Dillon and Sherisza both smiled and bowed. Emperor

Malshii gestured for them to follow. "Come, let me introduce you to my family, and we will share a meal. It is one of the highest honors my people bestow on guests."

"As it is with mine," Sherisza said, and neither Dillon nor Malshii missed the tense of her sentence.

CHAPTER 19

COMPLICATIONS

DINNER HAD BEEN an exceptional blend of meats, fruits, and greens, like the biggest salad Dillon had ever seen. The pools were an even lovelier treat. Sherisza and Dillon were able to wash and relax in the waters, cooling down a little after the extremes of the day. Kwaaganarr cooled off quite a bit once the sun went down, but not to the extent Dillon would've liked. The Kwaagi enjoyed it hot and humid, and they rarely had visitors, so there was virtually nothing in the way of climate control in the city. It led to a fairly uncomfortable night where Dillon and Sherisza kept their distance so they could stay cool.

Dillon didn't quite understand it. He'd expected Sherisza's people would like it warmer, too, if a bit drier, based on where lions liked to live on Earth. He reminded himself, though, that she wasn't really a lioness, and any such comments or questions would almost surely come across as extremely insulting. She was a person, and she regulated her body heat differently than the great cat she resembled. And, as he thought about it, he remembered lions spent most of the day sleeping, so there was that.

I'm gonna end up on the couch thinking like this, he thought, trying to get back to sleep. It was tough when it was so humid, and the temperature stayed on the wrong side of comfortable. Wanting to laugh as he thought of Daevol ejecting him, couch and all, into a nebula didn't help his efforts to get some rest.

Dillon had just dozed off when something woke him. It felt like a deep vibration that he felt through the floor and sleeping pallet. He waited for the sound to repeat or for other similar sounds, but nothing came. The palace remained quiet, and he silently cursed whatever idiot had dropped something heavy in the middle of the night. His mouth twisted in a wry smile when he considered they might get an earful from the emperor or his administrators.

He was just starting to fall asleep again when Daevol's voice woke him.

<Captain, wake up. Something is wrong.>

Sherisza sat bolt upright, and Dillon rose beside her. "What is it?" she barked.

<There have been attacks on Kwaaganarr, however, I believe these to be diversions. Enemy ground forces have infiltrated the palace itself.>

"How the hell did they manage that?" Dillon asked around a yawn.

<Unknown. Cloaked transport shuttles perhaps. Get back to the ship immediately.>

"We cannot do that," Sherisza said. "We are here to safeguard the emperor's family. Dillon, get dressed, quickly."

Dillon didn't need to be told twice. He regretted not having his defense blaster now, and he wondered if the Kwaagi would reconsider taking their guests' weapons away. He hoped that wouldn't need to be the case. Once he and Sherisza were dressed, they opened the door of their chamber and scanned the halls nearby. Everything was empty and quiet in the guest wing, and they slipped out of their chamber and headed back the way they'd come.

When they reached the end of the hallway, a patrolling guard stopped them. "Halt! What are you doing out of your chambers, skulking about?" he asked, bringing his blaster rifle up. He didn't point it at them, but his tone was clear before they took his flattened feathers into account.

"There are invaders in the palace," Sherisza said. "We must get to the emperor quickly and make sure he and his family are safe."

"Invaders in the palace?" he echoed. "What nonsense is this? Not a single alarm has been raised. Do you think us so foolish?"

"My ship is monitoring the situation and assures me there is an attacking force already inside. Has the city not come under attack?" Sherisza demanded.

"Not that I am aware of," the guard returned.

"Aware of? Didn't you hear that boom? Man, just take us to the emperor and let's be sure, will you?" Dillon said.

"Mind your tone, human. You are a—"

The guard went silent, letting out a couple of grunts as he was struck by two blaster bolts. He fell to his side, his eyes wide and the pupils dilated, a last gasp escaping his body.

Sherisza grabbed the blaster rifle from the corpse and ducked back behind the corner with Dillon. She peeked around the corner, just getting behind cover again as bolts struck the walls. "I need to start carrying grenades if we are going to be involved in this sort of conflict," she growled. "Be ready to run with me, Dillon."

He nodded, and she turned up the power on the rifle. When the sound of light footsteps began to creep up the hall, she leaned out and shot the wall twice. There was an explosion of bricks and masonry, clouding the air with dust, and she took off the other way up the hall. Dillon fell into step behind her, crouched even as they ran, trying to present as small a target as possible for the trailing fire that would come.

And come it did. They were narrowly missed a few times, but Sherisza shot another section of the wall behind them before she ducked into a side passage. Dillon stayed close on her tail, almost literally. He hated to see them have to damage the palace to escape, but there was little other choice. They were neither armed nor trained for a stand-up fight with invading soldiers.

"Daevol, guide me to the emperor's chambers if you can," Sherisza said.

<Affirmative. Giving you silent directions, Captain.>

Dillon remembered how Daevol had been able to show him where all the miniscule hull breaches were when they'd rescued the ship *Crooked Talon*. He must've been doing the same for Sherisza now, because she began leading Dillon through the hallways with purpose. There was still pursuit behind them, but the attackers were being methodical, taking their time, most likely to check for other flanking forces or their true targets.

Another patrolling guard turned into the hall they were running down, and Sherisza pointed her rifle at the floor, finger off the trigger. She only slowed a little bit, though.

"Halt! What are you about?" the guard said, aiming his own weapon at them.

"Invaders in the palace!" Sherisza yelled back. "You must protect the emperor at once. Call for help and lock down the palace and its corridors."

"Invaders in the palace?" the guard repeated, his feathers standing up. He was convinced a moment later when shots came up the hallway from around the far corner. "Scales of the Father! Captain, there are invaders in the palace attacking. Initiate full lockdown, get the emperor and his family to safety. The emperor's guests are with me; I will lead them to shelter."

"Understood. Initiating lockdown," came the voice of the guard captain over the soldier's personal comms.

"Holy crap," Dillon blurted as a bunch of grit hit the side of his face, debris from a blaster bolt that had come far too close. He was hurt before he'd even registered the heat of the nearby energy bolt.

The guard waved for them to stay with him and then took up the rear, firing some deterrent shots back at their pursuers. "Where are you going?" he asked when Sherisza didn't wait for him to suggest a course.

"To the emperor's chambers. My ship's computer is assisting me with a path of least resistance," she said. "Follow with us, you can protect us and your emperor at the same time."

"Yes, ma'am," he said.

As the hallway stretched out before them, Sherisza paused and took a knee, aiming back the way they'd come. She and their guard escort let off some suppressing fire, destroying a portion of wall to buy them time to clear the hallway. Shots were coming in return, but they were firing blind through dust and debris. Nevertheless, Dillon stayed low as he ran between Sherisza and the guard. He hated to use someone else as a shield, but that was the guard's function and, in this instance, his choice. There was no sense arguing the point to try to be noble.

They cleared the hallway and into the next, and Sherisza led them up a ramp. It was an arduous flight, and despite Dillon's athleticism, his heart was pounding and his breath was heavy when they reached the top of the ramp. Sherisza seemed little worse for the wear thus far, and she led them down another corridor. The path to the emperor's chamber was a crisscross of intersecting corridors, probably for exactly this reason. It felt like they were buying him time, if nothing else, by keeping the attackers on guard.

There were more sentries up here, holding positions at the corners and sweeping the hallways with their gazes and blaster rifles. Sherisza pulled up short and raised her hands, and their escort came up and led them through the defensive line. No words were exchanged, the guards keeping on their vigil to protect the emperor.

"Stay with your comrades, I know the way to the emperor's quarters," Sherisza said. She surrendered the blaster rifle to the guards, not wanting to show up at the emperor's chambers with a rifle in hand. Then she led Dillon along with the help of Daevol's navigation.

"I'm gonna have to stop for a minute soon," Dillon huffed.

"We are almost there. Stay with me, darling," she said, a tone of pleading in her voice. She was scared. She didn't have to secrete a scent like the Kwaagi for Dillon to recognize it.

Turning a final corner, they found a quartet of guards outside a stately double door. There was no doubt they'd found the emperor's quarters. After showing their hands and the fact that they weren't armed, Dillon and Sherisza were waved forward. These guards, too, remained silent, the smell of their anxiety all about them in the air. One of them knocked a specific pattern on the door, but other than that, they didn't interact with their visitors at all.

The door opened a crack, a slit-pupiled golden eye looking through. First Administrator Selanjja opened the door wide enough for Sherisza and Dillon to slip through, then shut it behind them quietly. She leaned her weight against it when she turned back to them.

"Captain Rousilarru, thank the Scale Father," she said, only the third theological words Dillon could remember hearing from the Kwaagi. "The emperor and his family are in the escape tunnels. You must follow them, quickly. However, listen closely. The tunnels lead out of the palace and to an empty, unused transport shuttle depot. Can you have your ship meet you there to pick all of you up?"

"I can. The *Malshekt* can pilot itself as needed," Sherisza said.

"Excellent. Please, proceed down the tunnels and protect the emperor as best you can. Get him and his family off world, I beg of you. What happens to us is of no consequence if His Imperial Majesty survives."

The first administrator indicated their weapons on the emperor's desk, and Dillon and Sherisza went and strapped them on. Selanjja then walked to a sconce on the wall and turned it left, then right, then left again at specific angles. It was like something out of an old book or movie, a secret door opening over the headboard of the impressive bed. Dillon and Sherisza climbed up and into the cramped passage, and Dillon turned back to see the first administrator straightening out the bed to remove any evidence of their passing.

"Shut the door behind you and go with the Scale Father's blessing," she said, taking up a blaster rifle of her own.

"Be safe," Dillon said as he shut the secret hatch.

The passageway was dark, no power sources present that would give away its location. But Sherisza could apparently see, as she started forward. She paused after a moment, though, and put her tail in Dillon's hands. "Just do not yank on it," she said with no humor.

He followed her blindly for what felt like miles before the passageway started to lighten around a corner ahead. Sherisza stopped and her ears flicked this way and that. "Your Majesty, it is Captain Rousilarru and Dillon," she whispered sharply.

There was the sound of a blaster rifle powering down. "Come, we will wait for you," the emperor called back in a similar whisper.

Dillon let go of Sherisza's tail now that he had some light to see by. They walked in a crouch around the corner to find the Kwaagi emperor and his family in the tunnel ahead. There was a haggard-looking female and three young children with him, looking much different in this situation than they had at dinner. The emperor himself was leaning against the wall, a blaster rifle in hand though it was pointed safely down. He beckoned for them to come, but he didn't stay, shoving his family along before him.

"Allow me to take the lead," Sherisza said. "The *Malshekt* is going to meet us at the end of this escape route and take us off world. It will not be a risk-free escape, though."

"How did they get into the palace?" Dillon asked.

"Some sort of technology we are not familiar with," the emperor said. "We are fortunate to have kept so many decoys to throw them off, or my family and I might be dead already."

"Hard to believe this all started over an uninhabited rock," Dillon muttered.

"Tell me about it," Emperor Malshii grunted.

"*Maqua!*" Sherisza spat from up ahead. "The way is blocked. Daevol, find us an alternate route that leads back to this tunnel."

<Calculating. Captain, I am not the only one scanning for you. Our enemies, too, are using scans to try to locate the imperial family. This collapsed passage is not a coincidence.>

"They are cornering us," Sherisza said. "Daevol, get us out of here."

<Go through the south wall and have the imperial family lead you to the upper kitchens.>

"Understood," Malshii said aloud. "Watch out, Captain."

Sherisza crawled back and let the emperor take the shot at the wall with his rifle. He blew a hole in it wide enough to get through, but it'd be a tight squeeze. Sherisza gestured for the family to let her go first with Dillon to make sure it was safe. She slipped through with little trouble, and thanks to his lankier build, Dillon followed soon after. They emerged into a small study that was dark and didn't look to have seen much use.

The imperial family came after them, the three children first. A blast rocked the palace, and the sound of collapsing brickwork reverberated and rumbled through the floor. The empress hissed and lost her purchase on the stones, so Dillon took her hand to help her out of the secret passageway.

"How dare you!" she spat, swiping at Dillon with her clawed hand and drawing three angry lines of blood on his upper arm. "Unhand me, you filthy mongrel."

"Ow! Shit, sorry," Dillon blurted, backing away from the angry woman.

"Kwinaja, he is just trying to help, not challenge our mated bond," came the emperor's voice from behind her. "Remember, he's human, not Kwaagi."

"All the more reason he should not touch me," she insisted, dusting herself off as she got to her feet, tapping her inner claws on the floor in irritation.

"Wife, please," Malshii sighed before letting forth a pained grunt.

Dillon crouched to help him out of the passage and saw the tunnel light up with blaster fire. "Your Majesty, come on!" Dillon shouted, reaching through the hole.

He took a hit to the hand, and Dillon pulled his arm back, clutching this newest wound tightly to his side. First debris from a wall had scraped up his face, then he'd taken claw slashes from an angry Kwaagi woman, and now there were blaster burns on the back of his right hand. It was shaping up to be a lousy day, and the sun hadn't even risen yet. There was another grunt from in the tunnel, and the emperor spat something that Dillon's chip couldn't even translate. Pushing down his fear, Dillon reached his other hand through the hole.

Emperor Malshii came through with Dillon's help, but there were blaster burns on his left arm and ribs. His breathing was labored, and his wife and children cried out, but he waved for Sherisza to get them all clear of the hole. He pulled a small black cylinder from his belt and pressed a button on the top. Then he reached back through the hole and threw it up the tunnel. A few seconds later, there was a deafening explosion, and the palace shook again.

"Assholes," the emperor muttered, and Dillon's chip had no issue with that. "Come, we should not be far from the upper kitchens."

Malshii was walking slowly now, in obviously considerable pain from two blaster shots that would have felled a lesser man. It cemented the toughness of the former soldier turned emperor in Dillon's mind. He kept those thoughts and words to himself, though, clutching his own wounds as he followed the rest of the party. Sherisza dropped back to check on him and the concern on her face was impossible to miss. She shoved him ahead as she took up the rear.

The palace was a mess in this area, but the invaders clearly hadn't expected to find the emperor of the Kwaagi hiding in a kitchen. Malshii led them into the deserted cooking chamber and indicted the far wall. "That is the outer wall of the palace. Stay clear in case the *Malshekt* is doing what I think it is doing," he said.

<Captain, this will be a most stressful rescue. Stand back

and allow me to destroy the outer wall. Be prepared to board as quickly as possible.>

"Understood, Daevol. Get us out of here," Sherisza answered.

There was a long, tense silence as they waited. Emperor Malshii was staring at the door to the kitchen, though his blaster rifle hung loosely with his arm injured. His wife kept looking at him, but she was huddled in a corner with their children. No look of apology came Dillon's way as he cradled his own wounds, but he hardly expected her to care about him when her husband was hurt and her children were in danger. After some deliberation, Sherisza turned a table on its side and took up position behind it with her blasters. Malshii moved behind it with her, and Dillon turned over another prep table for the empress and the children to hide behind.

<I am almost to you, Captain.>

"Take your time if it means you do not bring company," Sherisza said through her teeth. There were bootsteps in the hall now, and Dillon was sure her sharp leonine ears had heard them well before he did.

The door burst open followed by a flurry of blind blaster shots. Sherisza and Malshii took cover and returned fire when they had the opportunity. They dropped one of their attackers, and Dillon finally got a glimpse of black and red uniforms. He certainly wasn't impressed by the cliché colors, but he wasn't going to heckle them when they were already firing at him. He kept down and out of the way, his good hand useless to fire his defense blaster. Instead, he looked over at the empress and her children, then at the outer wall when he heard a roar.

Four *thumps* sounded against the outer wall before it disintegrated into sand and dust. There was a brief second of air pressures balancing, and then he could see the *Malshekt* hovering outside, its boarding tunnel extended.

"Get on the ship, quickly!" he shouted to the empress.

She started to usher the children toward the breach in the palace wall, shielding her children with her own body. In similar fashion, Malshii rose and let forth a barrage of blaster fire while he kept himself between his wife and children. Sherisza couldn't pull him down in time, though, and the emperor took yet another hit, this one high in the gut. He grunted but his eyes were closed before he even hit the ground.

"Shit!" Dillon shouted, scrambling forward. Sherisza took a number of blind shots over the top of the table, trying to lay suppressing fire so they could all escape. Dillon thought better of it, pulling another grenade off the emperor's belt. He pressed the button and then lobbed it toward the doorway, leery of it ricocheting off the walls or even an enemy soldier.

The resulting explosion pushed the table into Sherisza hard enough to knock her down, but she shook her head and grabbed up her blasters again. Dillon threw a second grenade, then he hooked the emperor under the arms and dragged him to the breach. No more blaster fire came after that second blast, and by the ringing in his ears, Dillon could understand why. The empress and children had gotten on the *Malshekt*, and Dillon followed them with the emperor's body. Sherisza brought up the rear and closed the tunnel and hatch as soon as she was on board.

She spared the emperor and his family only a glance before she slid into the pilot's seat. She set a course, then punched the throttle, reaching escape velocity before anyone had time to grab hold of anything. Dillon caught the children and they clung to him, which allowed him to grab a hold of the emperor's body as well. The empress rolled up the corridor of the *Malshekt* a bit, spluttering oaths the whole way. She finally got hold of a seam on the bulkhead, and when her eyes fixed on Dillon, he could swear he finally saw gratitude in them. He bowed his head politely but didn't expect much more.

Three ships gave chase as they exited the atmosphere, but Sherisza immediately engaged the Chrono Drive. The empress and the children passed out, but Dillon held onto Sherisza's seat, the emperor's body, the children, and consciousness as they hurtled into the time stream.

God, don't let that black ship be there, he prayed, holding Malshii's limp, clawed hand.

IF THERE WAS one positive that came of their hectic escape, it was that having to grab the children and the emperor proved Dillon's hand hadn't been burned too badly. It still hurt like hell, and he curled and flexed it a few times once the *Malshekt* had leveled out and began to cruise in the time stream. It seemed the blaster bolt had only glanced the flesh, but that hardly made it hurt any less. Dillon could hear Sherisza's ragged breathing even over his own, the silence of the *Malshekt*'s normal flight amplifying both. Even worse than theirs, though, was the shuddering, shallow breathing of the emperor.

Emperor Malshii had been hit by at least three blaster shots that Dillon knew of. It was as selfless a thing as Dillon had ever witnessed. Logic and decorum would've said the emperor, the most important man in the entire Kwaagi Empire, should've been the first to get to safety. Yet like what Dillon considered a real man, he had put himself between his wife and children and the danger more than once. The pride Dillon felt for him was only dampened by the fact that the man lay dying now.

The empress and her children stirred from their unconsciousness, and the youngsters ran to their mother when they got their bearings. She held tight to them, but her eyes were on the body of her husband. She kept her distance, and Dillon understood why. He rushed to the galley to get the medical kit, and the empress said nothing either time he passed her.

"Daevol, can you tell me what to do?" Dillon asked.

<There is nothing you can do, Commander. The emperor's organs are shutting down.>

"What should I do?" he asked again, looking to the empress.

"Do nothing. Leave him be," she said, wrapping her children up in her arms.

"Are we clear, Daevol?" Sherisza asked, still looking in every direction out the viewport and on the holodisplays.

<Affirmative. No sign of hostile or unknown vessels, Captain.>

She got out of her seat at that, spinning to take in the emperor lying motionless at Dillon's knees. When she saw the state Dillon was in, her mouth tightened, and he could tell she was just barely keeping her emotions from exploding in a fit of crying. She crouched and laid a hand on the emperor's chest, but then she turned her attention to Dillon. She stared at the scratches on his face that were stinging like crazy with his sweat, the claw marks across his upper arm, and then she took his hand in hers to examine the blaster burn.

"Dillon," she whispered, her voice quivering.

"I'm all right," he said, trying to sound it as much as say it. It wasn't the truth, but he wasn't the worst one off here. "Show the empress and the children to one of the guest cabins. I'll get a blanket and stay with the emperor."

Sherisza ignored his suggestion. She opened the medical kit and pulled out the regenerative gel in its tube. Her clawed fingers were gentle as she rubbed some of it into his facial wounds, and the pain receded a bit. Her eyes were glistening, but she remained businesslike, trying not to cry in front of their guests and exacerbate things. She rubbed more of the gel into the claw wounds on his upper arm, not bothering to ask where they'd come from. Those hurt far worse than the little scrapes on his face, and he was glad for the numbing of the gel.

She sprayed the blaster burn with something that was cold and stung badly. It, too, numbed the pain, though, and Dillon flexed his hand a few more times. She rubbed in the regenerative solution on that wound as well, but then she grabbed him and pulled him to her bosom, finally crying. She held him tightly, and Dillon rubbed her back to try to comfort her.

"I'm all right," he said.

"I cannot lose you too," she sobbed.

"You won't. I promise. I'm not going anywhere," Dillon said. They looked at the emperor as a final breath shuddered out of him. "But we failed."

<No, Commander, you have not.>

Dillon glanced at the empress, now the ruler of the Kwaagi empire unless there was some other facet to succession he didn't know about. "We failed to save *him*, though," he corrected.

<Commander, the emperor's life signs are returning.>

"What?" Sherisza blurted. She looked down at the emperor's body and her eyes widened as he sucked in a shuddering breath, though he remained unconscious. "Is he... is he healing from these blaster burns?"

"We heal quickly," the empress said. "And my mate is the chosen of the Scale Father."

"Holy crap," Dillon said, leaning in close to watch the burns flake away, revealing tender flesh that was already healing and trying to grow new scales. Did that mean the soldiers who'd apparently been killed in the palace might still be alive as well?

"Thank the Goddess," Sherisza said, taking up one of Malshii's hands in her own.

His breathing steadied after a couple of minutes. The

wounds didn't mend all the way, not that quickly, but the charred bits of him had fallen away to allow for healing. Dillon tried to scoop the man up in his arms, amazed at how much lighter the emperor was than his size and muscular build may have indicated. Malshii wasn't exactly light, but Dillon had expected to embarrass himself trying to lift the man. With the emperor cradled in his arms, Dillon made his way to one of the guest cabins.

"Come, let us get you situated, Empress," Sherisza said. "It has been a terrible morning for you and your children, so come and rest."

The family followed Dillon and Sherisza into the guest cabin. Sherisza pulled out the second bunk from below the main bed. It would be a tight fit for three children, but they could make do, and Dillon was sure the empress wouldn't want them far from her. Dillon laid the emperor on the main bed and then backed away so the empress could get to him.

She grasped Dillon by his uninjured upper arm when they passed, though it wasn't a threatening display. She had her head tilted slightly down, but not all the way in submission. "Forgive me, human. I should not have struck you."

"It's all right, Your Majesty," Dillon said. "It was a scary moment, and I *had* been warned about putting my hands on Kwaagi women without permission. I didn't realize it was considered a challenge to your marriage. So, I'm sorry, too."

"Thank you both for saving us. I hope my behavior has not made you regret helping."

"Of course not. We are glad to have been of service to you and the empire. Should I set up a fluid drip or such for your husband or do you expect he will wake up soon?" Sherisza asked.

The empress crawled up into the bed beside her husband, and the children huddled on their lower bunk. "I am not sure if he will wake soon. He was badly injured. I believe nutritional fluids would be of benefit, though, thank you."

"I will take care of that," Sherisza said. "Do you know where we were to take you?"

Empress Kwinaja looked up and met the Kiandarian's eyes. "Under the shadow of Outer Dock Seventeen."

"You want us to take you to Kiandar?" Sherisza blurted.

"If you do not object, it will put us close to one of our mobile docks that has ships modified by your work. It is also a good distance from our space and safely neutral, for the time being."

Sherisza looked at Dillon, and he nodded and put a hand on her shoulder. "Consider it done," she said to the empress with a bow of her head. After Dillon repeated the gesture, they left the imperial family to themselves.

Once the door to the guest cabin closed, Sherisza pulled Dillon into her arms again, cradling his head and holding him tightly. "Are you all right?" she asked him again.

"I'm fine," he insisted. "These should be gone in a few days with the help of that gel."

"I was not sure Daevol was going to get to us in time. I was so frightened."

"Me too," Dillon agreed. "But you didn't show it. You didn't let it slow you down, and your quick thinking saved all of us. Come on, let's get that IV set up for the emperor, and then we can go change our course to Kiandar."

———

Later, Dillon returned from the lavatory to find Sherisza napping in the pilot's seat. He would've liked to carry her to their cabin and put her in bed, but he didn't want to risk waking her. He may have been the one injured, but she'd been through an emotional hell, and that after a short and fitful night of sleep.

He was just as tired, but he took his seat on the flight deck and kept watch out the viewport as if Daevol might need his help to fly them to Kiandar.

The wounds were nicely numb. They were healing a little faster than usual, but not being painful was enough of a blessing for now. Dillon had suffered his share of injuries in his life, usually playing sports or getting into hijinks with his friends, but nothing like this. He'd been *shot*, and nearly multiple times. In truth, it didn't hurt as badly as he'd expected, but then he'd only taken a glancing hit to the hand. Reflecting on the numerous wounds he'd been dealt, he still marveled at how tough the Kwaagi emperor was to take three blaster shots to put down. Most people would've succumbed to a single blast if it hit them in the torso.

He figured it was better if he didn't tell his parents and family about *this* adventure, or at least not about its side effects. Doubtless he and Sherisza would be lauded as heroes again when the Kwaagi finally let the news spread to other governments. But that didn't mean anyone had to know what kind of life-threatening situations or injuries they'd suffered. Sherisza was already nervous about being rejected by Dillon's family; she didn't need the anxiety of them finding out about him getting wounded in a firefight to exacerbate it.

That brought up the subject of the wedding in his thoughts, and Dillon relaxed in his seat with a smile. He'd only been to a couple of weddings in his life, and as he thought about it, he realized he'd been too young to really appreciate them. They'd been parties with lots to eat, fun music, and dancing, but they hadn't ever meant much beyond that. Granted, this was his own wedding he was considering, but as the meaning of it began to sink in, he realized he truly was becoming a man like his father had said.

Oh Dad, are you ever going to have your hands full if you

need to negotiate with these people who've invaded Kwaagi space, he thought.

And that was an important thing to remember, he knew. They had attacked the Kwaagi, nearly assassinated the emperor, and had injured and harried Dillon and Sherisza, but the invaders were still people. Anger and vindictiveness had to be framed by that basic fact, all the better to allow cooler heads to prevail and perhaps peace to blossom. Dillon's parents had been an integral part of bringing the Jiskkan civil war to an end and mitigating their anger over Earth's interference. If they could manage that, they could start talks with these invaders.

Whether or not the Kwaagi would be interested in talking was another matter, but Dillon had a feeling the emperor would be agreeable to it. For all his military background and position of power, Malshii seemed a level-headed man. They'd have to wait and see what his thoughts were when he woke up from his near-death experience.

Whichever way things went, Dillon just hoped war wasn't the mode of travel and that he and Sherisza didn't get caught in it if it was. He wasn't a soldier, and neither was Sherisza, and for all its technological wonders, the *Malshekt* was not a fighter craft. There were people that needed their help, and though in this instance that had involved stepping into a war zone, Dillon wanted to get back to rescuing Kiandarians and stranded travelers. That was what he and his wife-to-be were best suited for, and it was less risky for them as parents-to-be.

Dillon dozed off in his seat, too, but was awakened by the weight of a muscular Kiandarian woman sitting in his lap a while later. He had hardly opened his eyes before Sherisza was kissing him, and though she longed to run her fingers down his jaw, they hovered just above his wounded skin. She gripped his shoulders instead, impressing her fear and her joy together in the powerful yet intimate touch. Dillon ran his hands down her back, maintaining their kiss for as long as she wanted to.

She leaned back and slipped her shirt off, and Dillon's eyes widened. "They are asleep," she whispered, leaning in for more kisses. "Daevol will monitor them."

"We could always just go to our bed," Dillon chuckled.

"We could," she said, finally silencing him with a kiss. She made no move to leave his lap.

The co-pilot's chair wasn't exactly made with intimacy in mind, and accordingly, it wasn't comfortable. Dillon didn't complain, though. He recognized this was fearful sex, that she was still grasping at anything to convince herself she hadn't lost him, and he was happy to play along and ease her tensions. He continued kissing her until she began to purr, and then they gradually moved on to other things.

Dillon caressed her as much as he could, but the chair made things awkward at best. "You are right, we should take this to the bedroom," she said, cradling his head gently.

Dillon grabbed her shirt and then stood with her still in his lap. She was surprised at first, but she wrapped her legs around him to make herself a little easier to carry. She was a hefty woman, but Dillon got his feet under him and carried her over to their cabin. When they tried to enter, though, the security protocols were engaged. It was standard procedure when they had guests on board, after all.

"Oh, just open the door for the Goddess' sake, Daevol," Sherisza whispered sharply.

The door opened, and Dillon could swear he heard the AI laughing in the back of his mind. He carried Sherisza over to the bed and sat her on its edge. They both got undressed and then he joined her up on the bed. They shared another deep kiss, and when they broke apart, Dillon ran his fingers down her arm and her side.

"You're so beautiful," he said, and she tilted her head down as she smiled.

She encouraged him to try a new position and muzzled rubbed him even at the awkward angle, purring as they satisfied their lusts, their fears, and their anxieties together. With their intimate touches, each told the other without words that they were one, and they never wanted anything–not family, not friends, not war–to get in the way of that. When they were satisfied, Dillon turned Sherisza on her side and lay behind her, wrapping her in his arms.

For a while, he was able to forget that he'd even been torn up by the maw of war.

———

They woke up after a little nap and kissed for a few minutes before they got dressed and headed back out to the flight deck. They found Emperor Malshii standing between their chairs, staring out at the endless expanse of space. He had his clawed hands folded behind him, standing somewhat at attention though his expression was pensive. If he had any thoughts on what they had been doing behind closed doors, he had the graciousness to keep them to himself. He offered only the approximation of a smile and raised his white feathers in greeting.

"I may be an emperor, but I wouldn't deign to sit at the controls of this ship without your express permission, Captain," he said.

"Your Majesty, I am glad to see you are feeling better," Sherisza said, clasping his offered hand. "We feared we had lost you when your organs began to shut down."

He tilted his head as he gave a half-shrug, a decidedly human-looking gesture. "Well, it will yet take time for the wounds to fully heal, but I'm on my feet, at least. We can be a strange species to outsiders at times. Our bodies shut down to a degree after trauma to allow our brains a rest to figure out what has happened. Then, our regeneration will kick in after everything starts up again. At times, it also allows our soldiers to feign death, only to *resurrect* themselves and attack the enemy as they pass."

"I'm amazed you can heal blaster burns so easily... Your Majesty," Dillon said.

Malshii waved off his words. "When I'm on your ship, you don't need to bother with all the *Your Majesty* nonsense," he said. "My wife may disagree, but I have your respect and your friendship, and that means more to me than some title. So, humor her as you must, but don't feel like you need to fawn over me. As for healing from blaster burns, well... why do you think my people invented disruptors?"

Dillon shuddered. "I'd rather not think about it."

"I don't blame you."

"Is everyone well and feeling safe?" Sherisza asked.

"Yes. You have our eternal gratitude, Captain. I didn't want to flee but dying would only have served our enemies' purpose and, in honesty, been foolish. I hope our request to hide on Kiandar doesn't create issues for you."

"Nothing we cannot account for," she assured him. "Now, may I invite you to sit at the helm with me?"

Malshii looked at Dillon, who gestured toward his seat, suddenly thankful that he and Sherisza hadn't gone too far in it. "By all means, sit in my chair, sir," Dillon said.

The emperor grinned and sat at the copilot's console of the *Malshekt*, making the best of its lack of accommodation for his tail. He looked over every button, switch, throttle lever, and control stick. "Magnificent!" he said. "Is it true you built this entire ship by hand?"

"Aside from the metal fabrication, yes," Sherisza answered. "Many of its features were based on the work of my brother, but I crafted and put together all of it myself. The only part of this ship that is not of my own design and implementation are the disruptors that were a gift from your people."

"Incredible," he said with a shake of his head. "So many rumors surround this ship... that it can cross dimensions, travel through time, that its power core is a concentrated singularity..." Sherisza kept a poker face as he went through the list. "Oh, I don't expect you'll spill all your secrets to me, Captain, but I didn't offer you half of our entire home world economy for nothing. I would seek to use this ship toward similar ends as yourself... to defend my people, whereas in your case you're bringing them back from the brink of extinction. I'd like to have that same failsafe in place for just such occasions as this war."

"I understand," Sherisza said. "A time may come when I feel ready to share the technology my brother and I invented with the rest of our friends and allies. For now, I am still trying to ascertain the limitations of its uses."

Malshii bobbed his head, his feathers laying flatter. "A good engineer considers the uses of their creations as much as the thrill of having made them. Well, I won't bother asking to fly us about when we're set on a course, but perhaps you could let me land her on Kiandar?"

"Of course," Sherisza said. "If I may ask, is there anything else you can tell us about the invaders?"

The emperor sat back and sighed. "We don't know much about them. Those we've killed have been destroyed in space battles, leaving nothing to study. I suspect that may have changed after this recent attack, though. We know their offensive capabilities aren't nearly as advanced as some of their utilitarian ones. They have cloaks, they have powerful deflectors and shields, and they apparently have some sort of transportation that we couldn't detect when they arrived at the palace. We've also deduced that they're carbon-based mammals that breathe oxygen. Not much beyond that."

"Well, it tells us we probably have what we need to kill them. Talking to them might be another matter altogether," Dillon said.

"True, but once we can put an end to the immediate hostilities, that may be where the Joint Senates–and your father in particular–can become quite useful to all," Malshii told him.

"I sure hope so. Looks like we should arrive at Kiandar by tomorrow. Are you and your family hungry? I can show you the replicators and get you fed while the captain showers," he replied.

"Oh, certainly. Don't let us get in your way, Captain," the emperor said. He bowed his head in response to her gesture, then got up and followed Dillon toward the galley. They brought the empress and the children from their quarters on the way, and Dillon got them settled with food.

DESPITE THEIR UNPLEASANT INTRODUCTION, Dillon found the empress almost as easy to manage as her husband. She didn't fuss over what she'd done to Dillon, but she had apologized, so he considered the matter closed. Sherisza was probably the most miffed of all of them over what had happened, but she kept her feelings to herself as well. Dillon was mending quickly, and that was good enough for both of them.

The children were a bit of a handful, but Dillon treated them like the Kiandarian children for the most part. He set up games and learning modules for them in his old cabin, and they were happy to stay there for most of the days during the journey to Kiandar. When he had time, Dillon made sure to school them on *Galactic Command*, but for their part, they were thrilled that the game took Kwaagi technology into account. Once again it made Dillon happy that the game's creators hadn't targeted any of the known races as the "bad guys" in it.

The emperor was equal parts curious and deductive, nosing around the *Malshekt* as he was allowed and asking tons of questions. Sherisza was concerned he was going to figure out that the Chrono Drive was just that and be more insistent on its purchase. He was inquisitive, but he never got too persistent about things she asked him not to speak of. Nevertheless, Dillon got the impression the man was as familiar with mechanics as Sherisza despite his station, and he was figuring a lot of things out with little information.

The rest of the trip to Kiandar was pleasant, with no sightings of the mystery ship and nothing else bothering them along the way. They came out of the time stream a respectful distance from Outer Dock Seventeen, and Dillon surrendered his copilot's seat to Malshii. The Kwaagi emperor slid in beside Sherisza with a toothy grin and took stock of the control sticks, throttle levers, and foot pedals again.

"Greetings, Captain Rousilarru," the station's flight director said. "It is good to see you and the *Malshekt* again. Will you be stopping here for supplies or heading straight to the surface?"

"We will be heading straight for the surface, thank you Outer Dock Seventeen," Sherisza answered. "Has all been well down on Kiandar?"

"Yes, Captain. To my knowledge, some of our wing fighters have been helping your people move photovoltaic equipment and wind power turbines to the neighborhood to expand their electrical grid now that it is back online. Things seem to be proceeding well, though I am not the best person to ask for news, I'm afraid."

Dillon didn't miss the pleased scent the emperor released on listening to one of his people chat cordially with their Kiandarian benefactor.

"Thank you, sir," Sherisza said. "Are there still Dominion warships in the area?"

"No, ma'am. All clear for the time being. Enjoy your visit."

Sherisza closed the communication channel. "I did not want to mention that we had you aboard or ask of any news, but you are welcome to re-hail them and do both."

The emperor thought about it for a moment, then bobbed his head. "I should let my people know we are safe. The mission needed to be secret, but Kiandar is far enough from our enemies that I can risk it."

She opened the hailing frequency again, being greeted with another, "Yes, Captain?"

"Flight Director, this is Emperor Malshii Denexxtu aboard the *Malshekt*," he answered, and Sherisza established a video feed so there would be no doubt.

The Kwaagi on the other end was silent for a few moments before he started spluttering. He finally got his tongue and his brain to align and said, "By the Scale Father, he's alive! The emperor is alive and aboard the *Malshekt*! Your Imperial Majesty, it is so good to see you and hear your voice. It is an honor to welcome you here, sir. May... can we help you with anything? Will you be coming aboard the station?"

"I think I will, Flight Director. Captain Rousilarru has things she needs to see to with her people, and I do not wish to impose."

"Is the rest of the imperial family with you, Your Imperial Majesty?"

Dillon smelled a slight trace of impatience from the emperor, probably over the constant use of his title and honorifics. "Yes, the family is with me, and we are all well. We will stay with you on the station for a couple of days before we go down to Kiandar ourselves. Let the brigadier know and tell him he has my permission to share this with the rest of the empire."

"Of course, Your Imperial Majesty. I will have the administrators and clerks prepare for your arrival at once!"

The emperor nodded but then shut off the video feed. He looked as though he was fighting down a sigh, but then he turned his gaze to Sherisza. "Do you trust me to land your ship in the station's hangar?"

"Well, if you damage it, I will hold your empire to financing the construction of a new one," she teased him.

He laughed. "No pressure, then. Good."

He wasn't kidding. He piloted the *Malshekt* with an expert hand, bringing her delicately into the station's hangar before he spun her one hundred and eighty degrees and landed her with barely a tap. Kwaagi faces may not have been all that expressive, but there was no missing the upturn of the corners of his mouth, the high feathers, or the slight narrowing of the eyes. He had enjoyed every second of that, and Dillon could well understand.

"Thank you, Captain. Your ship is almost as remarkable as you are," Malshii said, rising from the copilot's seat.

"You honor me," Sherisza said with a bow of her head.

The rest of the imperial family came up the corridor. It wasn't hard to pack considering they hadn't had time to bring anything with them. The children moved to their father by the hatch, but the empress came and stood before Dillon. She laid her hand delicately on his upper arm where she had scratched him.

"I hope you hold no ill will after what I did to you," she said, not letting him interrupt to say it wasn't a big deal. "You saved my entire family, and I owe you a life debt. If those wounds scar, young man, wear them not as a badge of shame or annoyance, but as a reminder that the Kwaagi Empire owes you its unending friendship."

She held her hand out awkwardly. Dillon assumed she was looking for a handshake, but instead, he took her hand like that of the noblewoman she was, and he kissed it. She seemed bemused by the gesture, but she didn't react poorly. "I'm just glad we were able to get to you in time and bring you to safety.

As my captain has said several times, we're glad to have your friendship and offer ours in turn."

Emperor Malshii shook his hand as well. "Thank you, Dillon. I look forward to meeting your parents at some point. They probably hear it often, but I would like to tell them what a fine and upstanding son they raised, and what a wonderful woman he has chosen as a mate. Captain Rousilarru, thank you once again. I will see you soon, I expect."

"Until we meet again, Your Majesty," Sherisza said, shaking his hand.

He blew the Kwaagi equivalent of a raspberry. "Malshii," he said. "Until I step off this ship, I can be informal, and choose to be so with you, my friends."

With that, Sherisza smiled and opened the hatch, waiting until the imperial family had left the hangar completely before she closed it again. She approached and hugged Dillon tightly, and he let out a long sigh. They had saved the Kwaagi emperor and taken him and his family to safety. Now they were heading to Kiandar with nothing scheduled, no place to go, no one to rush to save other than additional settlers.

All the better to alert the ones here that they couldn't tell Malshii about the Chrono Drive.

Sherisza left Dillon in control of the ship, and he raised the *Malshekt* off the floor and coasted out of the hangar, taking the slight rotation of the station into account. He was getting better and better at piloting the ship, though the ease with which Malshii had handled her on the first try left him feeling a bit green. He got her out of the hangar with no trouble, though, and soon began the descent into the atmosphere.

Daevol overlaid the directions to the settlement on the HUD. Dillon didn't know the way by heart, still learning the lay of the land of Kiandar. He followed the graphical prompts, though, and soon brought the *Malshekt* down in the cul-de-sac where Sherisza's home had been. Several of the houses had been renovated a bit, spruced up by their new residents with the yards converted to gardens and play areas. It was clear even before they'd landed that the Kiandarian settlers were progressing well.

Dillon saw solar panels on all the houses now, and there were windmills set up at the far ends of some of the open fields. That meant their electric utilities would be stable until they got the larger overall grid online and manned. Sherisza had chosen well; by bringing engineers and mechanics as well as farmers and laborers, the town was developing quickly on many fronts. Once they had consistent electrical power, it would simplify a lot of the building and even some of the farming as more power tools and machines became available. It was like a chain reaction, and all its success was thanks to the calculating mind of the woman sitting beside Dillon.

"You're amazing," he said, reaching over to lay his hand on hers once he'd landed.

"Why?" she asked, a bit distracted, and Dillon knew the reason.

"This is only succeeding because of all your hard work. And Daevol's ideas. But mostly your hard work," he explained.

Sherisza leaned over and pulled his face toward her, but not for a kiss just yet. "Dillon, my focus to see this done is mostly thanks to you," she said, then kissed his forehead. "When I tell you that you gave me the will to live again, I am not saying that to stroke your ego. I mean it."

He kissed her back and then got up. "Let's go see the people and let them know more are coming," he said. "While we're here, you can answer one other question for me."

"What is that?" she asked, rising to get her blasters before she followed him to the hatch.

<No, not that one.>

Dillon laughed and pulled her into his arms. "Do you want to have the babies here? If you want to live in your house again and have the children in it, that's more than fine with me. Just let me know what you want to do, and I'll get to work helping to see it through."

"Oh, Dillon," she said, laying her face against his chest and purring happily. "I think I may want to give birth on Terra Prime, actually. But we shall see. We have some months to come to a decision."

He kissed the top of her head and then opened the hatch, and they descended into the late afternoon sunlight to go greet the settlers.

———

Dillon gave the rope swing another push, Sherisza silently lost in her thoughts as she swept back and forth. The neighborhood was quiet, the sun going down and the settler families in their homes preparing for their meal. The windmills were still, set up but not online yet, and there was a tranquility to the world that was a little bit haunting. Dillon didn't get the sense of ghosts or anything unnatural, but billions of people had died here, and that was hard not to think about.

It was heavy on Sherisza's mind, he could tell. She didn't seem sad or depressed, but she was still processing everything. Having put her family to rest hadn't fixed everything, just given her momentary reprieve from her grief. Now, every time she set foot on this world, it returned, but not in the form of crushing despair. Instead, it sharpened her focus, and despite the calm twilight skies and the cool air, Dillon knew she was thinking of the next phase of their rescues.

There would be two more families of four next, but Sherisza was also planning to pick up a couple that hadn't had children yet. Dillon had to remind himself that they would be brother and sister, and so they would have children with another couple or couples that were already here. It was also possible the woman was already pregnant, but he didn't concern himself with that. The Kiandarians could take care of themselves without some human butting into their sex lives.

The plan was to bring at least one hundred people here to recolonize the planet and make sure there was a sufficient gene pool to repopulate the species. The next set would bring them to almost the twenty-five percent mark on that, but Dillon suspected Sherisza would continue to bring more as she combed through the historical archives. The more disappearances she could find that pointed to a visit from her, the better her peoples' chances of thriving again.

Sherisza had mentioned the possibility of cloning to enhance those chances, but she'd also stated that it posed theological issues for her and her people. Dillon could understand that. Cloning was something that had been explored on Earth but had never been allowed for humans. Not legally, anyway; not as a whole. There were always stories about rich elites using it to create decoys and fall guys for their misdeeds, but Dillon never believed it. Clones weren't telepathically linked to the original person, so what would be the point in that case?

She slipped off the rope swing at last, turning to pull Dillon into a hug. She held tightly to him for a few minutes, and he tried to make her feel safe and warm in his arms. Aside from his grandfathers, Dillon hadn't lost any family, so he could only contextualize what Sherisza was feeling so much. But in the end, he hated to see her cry or in pain, and so he felt everything she felt in another sense. She shared her pain, and he shared his strength.

They returned to the house, and the lights came on when they entered. The settlers had done some touchups and repairs to Sherisza's home in thanks for their new lives. Gone were the scorch marks from that Jiskkan assassin, along with any trace of the dead. They hadn't touched any of Sherisza's personal effects, though Dillon had grabbed many of those when they'd first visited. He figured if they were going to have their children on Earth, she might want to bring some of these things there. For now, though, she was content to leave the house as it was.

In confirmation of his thoughts, she moved to the refrigerator and the painting that now hung on its door. It was a finger painting of the house and her family, and Dillon walked up behind her and wrapped her in a hug as she stared at it. Sherisza closed her eyes and reached up to rub the back of Dillon's head, and she let a long sigh out through her leonine nose.

"Safely home," he whispered.

"Dillon," she whispered back, turning to him.

He held her for a few minutes while she cried, but it wasn't pain riddled. She was letting out some more of her pent-up emotions, accepting reality in her heart and trying to make peace with it. Even several years later, the loss was only dulled so much, but Dillon was glad she was proving so strong. She may have lost her children, but she was a mother to her entire race now, the woman who was bringing them back from the brink of extinction.

There was a knock at the door, and Sherisza brought Dillon along by the hand when she went to see who it was. A few of the settlers were outside with plates of food, and Sherisza lost a few more tears at the display. Dillon took the food but stayed back, merely smiling while hugs and thanks were exchanged all around. It was clear the people knew no matter how tumultuous their lives had become, Sherisza had lived through far worse but had still brought them through. Sufficient thanks may never have been possible, but they were giving what they could.

Dillon waved his thanks as the neighbors went back to their

homes, and he half-hugged Sherisza. They took the food back to the kitchen, and when they uncovered it all, Dillon thought it smelled like fresh venison and some vegetables. It wasn't exactly the same as food from Earth, but it was similar enough in look and smell. It wouldn't have much in the way of spices or flavoring, he knew, but he resolved not to complain about the loving gesture.

They shared the meal sitting side by side, and Sherisza kept reaching out to touch Dillon every now and then. He flashed her a smile every time, patting her hand or wrapping an arm around her as seemed appropriate. He expected he knew where the increasing anxiety was coming from, so he stayed close and gave her the support she needed.

After dinner, she headed upstairs, and Dillon followed close behind. As he'd expected, she went to stand in the doorway of her children's room. She leaned her head against the doorframe and let out another long sigh, and Dillon laid his head on her shoulder. He couldn't imagine how much it hurt, but it pained him just to look at. He held tight to her until she found her strength again and strode into the room.

Sherisza looked at some of the wall hangings Dillon had left behind, running her clawed fingers down them affectionately. Each one brought a pained smile to her face; a drawing, an award from school, a photo of the children making goofy faces with their manes all askew. When she'd looked at and touched the last of them, she climbed into their bed and curled around the spot where Dillon had found them. After a brief hesitation, he climbed in behind her and wrapped her in his arms.

"Such a waste," she said quietly. "All for one man's hatred."

"He'll never hurt anyone else," was all Dillon could think to offer. "Your people are here now, and he's gone. You won."

"Goddess, lift this pain from my heart," she said.

Dillon thought of Reverend Warner's words and prayed

that Sherisza would find peace. He rose up on one arm when she sat up, but she kissed him and then climbed out of the bed. She left the room, and Dillon followed her across the way to Daevol's old study.

Sherisza looked around this room wistfully but didn't seem as pained as in the children's room. She began going through his drawers and boxes, but Dillon was sure he'd gotten all the relevant notes and computer cores. At least until Sherisza pushed on a section of wall and it slid away, revealing a safe. She punched in some code she knew by heart, the numbers in Kiandese so Dillon didn't recognize any of it but for the apparent order. And then the safe opened to reveal two more books and a data core.

"Is that the good stuff?" Dillon asked.

Sherisza managed a chuckle. "This is his diary, and this is his schematic book," she said, handing each of them to Dillon in turn. She held up the data core almost reverently. "And this... this is his real work. All the other things you have seen me go through have been theories, hypotheses, dreams, and ideas. This data core has his actual working models, Dillon. We shall see what he was working on."

"I look forward to it."

The emotional toll of looking through everything had taken a lot out of her, and Sherisza led Dillon to her old bedroom. It, like everything else, had been cleaned, and she climbed into the bed she had once shared with her twin brother. Now, she shared it with Dillon, and he curled up with her, her face close to his heart, though she didn't purr.

After everything that had happened to him in recent days, Dillon thought that hurt far more.

CHAPTER 22

PREPARATIONS

DILLON WAS ECSTATIC. Sherisza seemed refreshed the next morning, and rather than mope around the house, she had gotten to work. They'd flown the *Malshekt* to a nearby space-port where the Kwaagi were touching down to take breaks from their patrols. Accordingly, the place had been cleaned up, the dead given their final farewells and burned on ritual pyres. The Kwaagi were using the base, but they left much of it untouched, wary of insulting the Kiandarians by taking too many liberties.

Sherisza had no concerns about that. She'd landed the *Malshekt* near a hangar and, once they'd gotten it open, she began Dillon's newest lesson. They found a mid-sized cruiser ship and Sherisza began taking apart the warp drive to install on the *Malshekt*. Its warp core was compact much like the Chrono Drive, so she was confident they could mount it to the ceiling above the other engine. More than that, though, she wanted to teach Dillon how to handle all of it safely, take it apart, and put it back together.

He couldn't help but think of the booby trap that had been laid for her on Chronon-Er, when someone tampered with the retention field on a warp drive. It took nerves of steel to work on something that could disintegrate you and possibly the entire world you stood on if you made the slightest mistake. He had the nerves in his bloodline, he knew, after his father had told him about his grandfather working on rigs and heavy machinery as a union mechanic. Still, the destructive potential of a warp drive sobered him from his excitement a bit.

Sherisza explained every step in detail before letting Dillon help execute them. She was meticulous to the extreme, and Dillon felt like he'd taken an entire course just on dismounting the drive. Sherisza was respectful of the device, but she seemed far less nervous. She set it on a cart and they wheeled it off the cruiser and toward the *Malshekt*. Dillon stayed beside it the whole way, watching it like a hawk, afraid it might tip over and kill everyone.

The rest of the day involved slicing into the framework of the *Malshekt* to add fail safes and power relays to hook it into the ship's systems. In an amusing twist, Sherisza took care of the majority of the laser torch work, better suited to cutting and welding than Dillon. It was the first time in a while that Dillon had seen her as the mechanic he'd first met. Much of their recent work had involved them working apart, so he'd missed this part of her quite a bit. Seeing her in the black work clothes with the welding goggles on, cutting into her ship to add a new system, was a simple delight to him.

It wasn't all watching and learning for him, though. He got to lay the electrical work, and she was beside him every step, supervising but not micromanaging. It was tiring work with his arms above his head or laying on his back up on a scaffold for much of the day, but he received a lot of encouragement from Daevol as well as Sherisza. It had never occurred to him, but though the AI couldn't feel pain, it had to be the computer equivalent of nerve-wracking to have such work done.

Especially by the apprentice and not the master, he mused with a lopsided smile.

Once Sherisza was satisfied he knew what he was doing, she began welding the metal back together in his wake. She left a lot of open spots where she'd be putting access panels, but her welding was amazing. Dillon didn't remember Daevol mentioning her being an ironworker, but he guessed maybe it fell under mechanical sciences in the old Kiandarian schools. She had a tool which, when used in conjunction with the welding lasers, left the metal looking almost pristine.

She called it quits an hour before her usual supper time. They stood and admired the work they'd gotten done in one day. The warp drive was still deactivated and had yet to be attached to the ceiling, but that was too delicate to do in bits and pieces. Sherisza wanted to get back to rescuing some of her people, but she also wanted to be safe while doing so. Having a standard warp drive would, in theory, eliminate the threat of the mystery black ship until Azi or someone else made a breakthrough in communications.

Done for the day, they shared a shower and more beyond that. Dillon enjoyed making love to her in the shower, and it was nice to unwind and bond after being so focused on work all through the day. He'd honestly gotten a little tired of her rigorous schedule when she'd been trying to conceive, but now it was fun again. He found his enjoyment of the sex and their relationship as a whole increasing more and more even in light of his looming fatherhood.

Once they got out, dried off, and dressed, she fixed supper. There was a certain tension to her work while she cooked, though, and Dillon wrapped his arms around her waist from behind.

"Is everything okay?" he asked.

"I expect our neighbors will have tried to serve us food," she said quietly.

Dillon pursed his lips. "But you didn't want to stay in the house again," he guessed.

"I needed some time away," she confirmed.

"Sherisza," he said, and she glanced at him over her shoulder. He turned her around and took her fully in his arms. "Sherisza, are we having babies?"

She smiled, and it was wondrous, the stars reflected in her eyes despite them being inside and the sun still being up. "Yes," she breathed, and she laid her head on his shoulder as he pulled her in tight.

"I know they can never replace your other children, but I hope they bring you joy again."

Sherisza let forth what sounded like a sob, but she drew away and took his face in her hands. "*You* bring me joy, Dillon. In everything we do together, whether work, play, or making love. You have brought joy back to my life, and this adventure we have embarked upon... it means everything to me. I know my pain brings you pain, but I will be happy again, I promise you."

Dillon slid down to his knees, and Sherisza let out a little joyful cry when he kissed her furry lower belly. He put his ear to it as if he might be able to hear something so early in the process, but it didn't matter that he couldn't. He was smiling, and he knew she was smiling without even having to look up at her face. Her tail was going back and forth along with her emotions.

Dillon got to his feet and looked into her eyes. "I love you," he said.

"The Goddess only knows how much I love you," she returned.

"Hmmm, if we're going to use the warp drive to go out to

our usual spot in the reaches, we can talk to my mother a bit about wedding plans," he said.

"I would like that very much."

"And are we picking up Azilija again if they'll let us take her along?" Dillon asked.

Sherisza sighed and went back to her cooking. "It would be the safest option, since we will have to enter the time stream again to make the next rescue. I meant what I said before, though, Dillon. If she cannot help us make significant communication, and that black ship attacks me and my cubs, I will destroy it."

"Not if I blow it up first," he said. "No one threatens my girl... or my cubs."

It was weird to say it, but the way the word *cubs* split her face in a smile made it feel right. Just what would their children look like? He couldn't wait to find out. On a hunch, he excused himself and made his way into their cabin where he could have a moment's privacy.

After a brief chat with Daevol, Dillon gathered the things he was looking for and returned to the galley. He put a pair of candles on the table and lit them, then set the table while Sherisza worked. When she turned around, she paused in surprise.

Daevol dimmed the lights, letting them enjoy a candlelight dinner, and they romanced like the young lovers they were.

———

They spent the next couple of days installing the warp drive. While Sherisza didn't go into the functions of the drive, she had to partially take it apart to properly mount it. She showed Dillon its basic structure and how to dismantle everything but the core and retention fields. It was both fascinating and terrifying, but he enjoyed even the trill of the latter. In the end, he felt safe having her there to save the day if anything went wrong.

Emperor Malshii and his family came down to Kiandar on the third day, and Sherisza bade them stay in her old home for the time being. She had no plans to return there for a while, it had active electrical, and it was close to the settlers. She introduced the Kwaagi to her people, but they left off the fact that he was the emperor for now. The people were bemused to have a Kwaagi living near them, but just as Dillon had expected, they were polite and accommodating anyway. It seemed a common trait for Kiandarians.

The emperor would be about as safe as could be expected. Few outside the empire knew where he was, there was a mobile station orbiting Kiandar above his location, and the local wing of fighter craft had been modified by Sherisza's work. On top of all that, he insisted that Sherisza not fawn over or worry about him and instead focus on continuing to rescue her people. It was just one more flower among the blooming friendship between Kiandar and Kwaaganarr.

Dillon and Sherisza finished installing the new warp drive, and after some testing, she was satisfied taking the *Malshekt* off-world to try out its actual function. After giving their farewells to the settlers and the imperial family, Dillon and Sherisza took off for space again. They checked in with Outer Dock Seventeen and gave an approximate timetable for their return, and then set a course for Outer Dock Eight to pick up Azilija.

"Well, let us see how our installation went," Sherisza said. She engaged the warp drive, and the *Malshekt* reached speed in little time with no issues.

Not that Dillon had expected any differently.

Sherisza went to the galley and came back with two glasses of Ulian brandy, handing one to Dillon before she sat. "My last drink for some time to come," she said, clinking her glass with his. "To my family and yours, to our friends and allies, and to the All-Mother and your Father, for all they have done for us to bring us to this point."

"Cheers," Dillon said, clinking their glasses again before he took a sip.

"And now that we are alone and underway, I can get back to work," Sherisza said, setting down her glass as she called up the schematic of the phase-cloaking device. Beside it appeared another holodisplay, this one with more of Daevol Rousilarru's notes in Kiandese.

"Find something good in the data core?" Dillon asked.

"The rest of what I was missing," she said. "Your ideas were not far off the mark, Dillon. We visualized the wave almost correctly, and your idea about aiming for nothing rather than the coalescence was good instinct. Daevol's notes have the balance of it, and if I can get just a few more parts from Outer Dock Eight, I believe I can make it work."

"You're so brilliant," he said, leaning over for a kiss.

She met him halfway but let him kiss the side of her muzzle. "Half of a whole," she said.

He ruffled her ear playfully, and she chuckled before going back to her schematic. She hardly touched any of it now, just working through calculations in her head. It was amazing to watch her mind at work, but Dillon left her in peace, taking his drink to engineering to get in a little bit of exercise.

———

The trip to Outer Dock Eight was uneventful, thanks to using a standard warp drive rather than the Chrono Drive. Whatever the case, it was nice to not even have to worry about the black ship. Sherisza completed her work on the phase-cloaking device schematic, and Dillon got in some studying, several games of chess with Daevol, and plenty of exercise. And every night he got to sleep with his bride-to-be and the mother of his coming children. Every moment they got to spend together, but especially alone on the *Malshekt*, was special.

They had talked with Dillon's mother a bit about wedding plans, but not much was concrete yet, not even the date. Sasha was thrilled to know Reverend Warner had already agreed to perform the ceremony, and Sherisza was satisfied with that as well. There would be much to talk about as far as the vows and whether Sherisza wanted her All-Mother included in them, but most of it was left up in the air by the end of their chat. All Dillon could impress upon his mother without mentioning that Sherisza was already pregnant was that everyone was invited, and they wanted to do it soon.

It all felt so surreal to Dillon. He hoped he wouldn't lose the fire he felt for Sherisza, though he wasn't too worried about it. This didn't feel like the same young love he'd shared with Maddie Thomas back in junior high school. That had been fleeting, new, and wonderful because it was the first one. His love for Sherisza transcended all that, even the fact that they weren't the same species. It was different and it was wonderful, and the more he thought about raising kids with her and spending the rest of his life flying the stars, the better it sounded.

He was on an emotional high by the time they had landed in the Kwaagi station, and it only got better when he saw Azilija waiting for them in the hangar. He'd grown to like the Kwaagi quite a bit over the last few months, and he found his nose was accustomed to them now. Their emotion-signaling scents still weren't pleasant, but he recognized most of them, and they didn't assault him the way they once had. The fact that Azi was so courteous even while helping them try to solve the mystery of the black ship just made her that much more likable.

Azi was waiting at the base of the steps when Sherisza and Dillon disembarked. The way her feathers were standing straight up said she was just as happy to see them. She bowed her head graciously. "It is good to see you again, Captain, Dillon. I am sure it goes without saying how thankful we are that you helped rescue our emperor."

"It's good to see you again, Azi," Dillon returned, reaching for a handshake. She obliged, letting out a little waft of her pleased scent.

"We were honored to help," Sherisza said, likewise shaking with the Kwaagi woman.

"Will you be finishing the work on our wing?" Azi asked. "The brigadier would like to see you immediately regardless."

Sherisza sighed but glanced at Dillon. "We should while we are here. Every bit we can do to aid the empire in repulsing the invaders is worth it, even if it delays my plans."

"Yeah, we should," he agreed, laying a hand on her shoulder.

"Come, I will take you to see the brigadier," Azilija said.

The way was familiar to them, as was the greeting when they went into the presence of the brigadier. He didn't keep them long, merely informing them that the last of the invaders had been destroyed, and Kwaaganarr was safe once again. Numerous thanks were given for the work Sherisza and Dillon had put in rescuing the emperor and his family, though no mention was made of the specifics. It was just as well, since Dillon could see Sherisza was reliving those tense hours the same way he was.

This time, when Sherisza requested permission to take Azi with them, it was granted. They returned to the hangar, where Sherisza requisitioned the last of the parts she would need to get the phase-cloaking device working. After stowing the parts on the *Malshekt*, she and Dillon got to work on the Kwaagi fighter wing. They'd already done half the ships, so it would only take a few days to complete the job. It was a few days more than Sherisza wanted to wait to rescue the next group of her people, but she didn't complain.

As with previous visits, Sherisza didn't want to stay on the *Malshekt* and raise any sort of suspicions, so she left the phase-cloaking device for later. Instead, she and Dillon shared dinners in their quarters and their bed and bodies afterwards. For being in the middle of a contract job, it was a wonderful time, and they had so much to look forward to.

WITH YET ANOTHER full wing of Kwaagi fighters modified, it was time to move on. Sherisza promised the brigadier that they'd be back to work on Outer Dock Nine in the future, but she didn't commit to a set schedule. She wanted to bring a good deal of settlers to Kiandar and having to constantly rush to work on other contracts detracted from that. And that was to say nothing of the fact that they kept getting attacked in some fashion, which Dillon knew weighed heavier and heavier on Sherisza's mind.

They boarded the *Malshekt* with Azilija, and the Kwaagi woman looked up at the ceiling expectantly. When no smart remark came, she huffed. "What, do you not like me anymore?"

<I was ordered not to insult the imperial family, and you all look the same.>

"Surely you can do better than that," Azi hissed. "Or did the captain divert too much power to more useful systems?"

<Well, Captain Rousilarru did have to divert quite a bit to the replicator when she found out you would be joining us again.>

"Why don't you tell her about the couch?" Dillon chuckled.

"The three of you are terrible," Sherisza said with a shake of her head, and she went to put her things in their cabin.

<No need, Commander. I already added her biometrics to the escape pod so she could use that as her quarters.>

"I might want to if your humor does not improve," Azi laughed.

"Speaking of improvement," Sherisza said as she reemerged from the cabin, "have you made any progress on the messages? We will be using the Chrono Drive soon to pick up more of my people, and I expect we have not seen the last of that black ship. At some point, we either need to convince them to go away altogether, or I am going to destroy them. There has been a... development since we last saw each other, and I will not take any more risks when it comes to dealing with that ship."

Azi bowed her head. "I understand, Captain. I believe I know a bit of the language now, but as I have said before, the message points to them demanding you stop using something. Given where we meet this ship, I continue to expect it is the Chrono Drive they are referring to."

Sherisza grimaced. "I hesitate to resort to killing them if they have something important to say, but..."

"What new development do you speak of, Captain?" Azi asked.

Dillon smiled when Sherisza looked at him, and she tilted her head down slightly in a blush. "Dillon and I are expecting."

The Kwaagi woman's feathers went back, then stood straight up. "By the... truly? I had no idea such a thing was even possible. My warmest congratulations to you two."

"Thanks," Dillon said. "Why don't you get your things stowed–in your guest cabin, not the escape pod. Then we'll get underway."

"Aye, Commander," Azi said, turning to her quarters. The

door to her cabin wouldn't open even after she scanned her biometrics, though.

"Daevol," Sherisza grumbled, and suddenly the door opened.

<I could not help it.>

Dillon and Sherisza took their seats on the flight deck and began preparing the *Malshekt* to leave the hangar. Azi came out soon after and stood behind and between them. She watched all their preparations curiously, but she refrained from asking any questions until they were done and had gotten the flight director's permission to leave. She watched the hangar doors open and gripped the backs of their chairs a little tighter, and Dillon got the sense that she was where she truly wanted to be.

I know the feeling, he thought, smiling, though he didn't give voice to the thoughts.

"Who are the next group of Kiandarians we will be bringing?" the Kwaagi woman asked as the *Malshekt* lifted off and began to coast out the hangar doors.

"An important group, though this is not to say any of the others have been unimportant. But this time, I have arranged for us to pick up a physician and his sister who is a seamstress. The other couple we will be picking up are a soldier and a mechanic who have two children. Then there is a single woman whose twin was killed; she is a wilderness ranger and may be quite helpful to our settlers dealing with wildlife and regulating their hunting."

"You have put a lot of thought into all this," Azi said. "Most would simply take whoever they could and not consider the needs so thoroughly."

"She puts a lot of thought into everything," Dillon agreed.

"Azi, please keep the news of our coming children quiet until we deem the time right to let Dillon's family and everyone else know," Sherisza said. "There is also a piece of technology I am working on that I need you to keep secret for now."

The Kwaagi woman bowed her head. "Of course, Captain. What wondrous new thing have you been working on?"

"I will tell you once we are on our way through the time stream."

Sherisza took them a safe distance from the mobile station and began to lay in their course. They would have to slip into the time stream three times to rescue all those she had selected. It took a little longer to lay out the courses sequentially, but she got everything prepared ahead of time. Then she began powering up the shields and weapons systems, and she didn't need to tell either of her companions why. With a deep breath and a long, drawn out sigh, Sherisza engaged the Chrono Drive and began their journey.

Azi held on to their seats and consciousness as they slipped into the time stream, and there was the scent of excitement and happiness in the air. Dillon smiled but kept his eyes open for any sign of the black ship. All looked calm and quiet for the moment, and he reached over and laid a hand on Sherisza's arm. She leaned toward him to meet halfway for a kiss, paying no mind to the grinning Kwaagi woman behind them.

After several minutes with no sign of their mystery ship, Sherisza brought up the schematic of her phase-cloaking device. "This is what I have been working on," she said with a gesture toward the holodisplay. She gave Azi a moment to look it over before answering her unspoken question. "This is a modified cloaking device that should allow the *Malshekt* to go out of phase and thus pass detection, harm, or even solid objects."

"Out of phase?" Azi echoed.

"Yes, possibly through an alternate dimension. My brother's notes were unclear on exactly how it works, but his theories aligned with my thoughts and Dillon's observations. I need only make a few more minor technical changes and it should be operational."

"How curious..."

<Captain, another ship has entered the time stream and is in pursuit.>

"*Maqua*," Sherisza muttered. "Is it the same ship as always?"

<Affirmative.>

"Azi, I would recommend you strap yourself into the seat in your cabin."

"Negative, Captain. I want to be here if they try to communicate," the Kwaagi countered.

"Better hang on tight, then," Dillon said.

Sherisza let the black ship gain on them, diverting power to the rear shields in case it made no attempts to communicate. The minutes were tense as the sleeker ship caught up to them in the time stream. All three of them watched its approach in the rear holodisplay. Dillon wasn't sure he had even been breathing until the hailing frequency came alive and he let out a sigh. It was another of the garbled messages as always, but then the black ship opened fire.

"*Om-cubwe! Om-cubwe!*" Azi called across the hailing frequency, hoping to buy them a few minutes to talk.

It was no use. Several more blaster bolts slammed into the *Malshekt*'s rear shields. Already the ion cannon was nearly fully charged, so Sherisza began evasive maneuvers. She executed her corkscrew dive, evading enemy fire and trying to establish distance. The black ship stayed with them, but Dillon saw its blaster fire miss and pass by.

He took hold of the combat stick and flipped its switch, turning the Kwaagi disruptors to fire backward. Daevol overlaid the HUD in the flight deck, and Dillon watched the targeting reticle as it remained a passive yellow. The targeting system was trying to lock, but it was difficult when Sherisza was flying so erratically to evade enemy fire. He squeezed off a few shots in the hope of a random lucky hit, but the black ship was just as evasive even in pursuit.

"What did they say this time?" Sherisza asked through gritted teeth as a couple of blaster shots hit the *Malshekt*. The shields had almost reached their absorption limit; they'd have to fire the ion cannon soon or risk the shields overloading.

"So far as I can tell, *if you will not destroy it, then you must be destroyed,*" Azi answered.

"Lovely," Dillon grunted. "Don't suppose they've mentioned what *it* is?"

"Not that I can understand, no."

"*Maqua,*" Sherisza said again when the *Malshekt* took another hit.

A blinking red light said the shields were getting overwhelmed. They needed to discharge the ion cannon, but she had to either become the pursuer or perform a risky maneuver to try to get the black ship in her sights. As if in answer to Dillon's thoughts, Sherisza leveled out their flight and then spun the ship one hundred and eighty degrees, bringing their pursuer into the line of the ion cannon's firing arc.

Just as she went to squeeze the trigger, though, the black ship swept upwards out of their line of fire. Sherisza pitched the ship back to try to lock on the target, but the *Malshekt* was traveling at a curious angle, limiting her maneuverability. The black ship raked the *Malshekt* with several more shots, and then Dillon watched a salvo of missiles head straight for them. The alarm was going off now, warning of critical energy storage for the ion cannon.

<Captain, the cannon must be discharged, or the shields will...>

"I know!" Sherisza shouted. She throttled them the other

way, blinking as the point-defense lasers destroyed the missiles. The *Malshekt* wasn't even buffeted by the explosions, the Kwaagi PDL system destroying the projectiles at a longer range. Heading in the opposite direction of their enemy, Sherisza bought them some time while the black ship came about to take up pursuit once more.

"Can you not simply discharge the ion cannon at random?" Azilija asked.

"No," the Kiandarian replied. "It is not like blasters or disruptors, designed to dissipate after reaching a maximum range. Its pulse is an energy wave that does not stop until it has struck something. I could disable a ship or kill people on a planet thousands of light years away in the future... or in the past. I cannot take that risk."

"Understood," Azi said, her feathers lying back flat.

The black ship was *fast*. Despite already being in the time stream, it was able to accelerate, and was soon catching up to the *Malshekt* again. Dillon wondered if they could disable it and take some of its technology for their own. Of course, that involved winning first, and he wasn't going to make inane observations when Sherisza was already frazzled.

He took hold of the combat sticks again and fired some deterrent shots with the rear-facing disruptors. One lucky shot hit the black ship and he saw its shields glow as they tried to dissipate the blast. The ship seemed otherwise unharmed, though, and Sherisza began evasive maneuvers as it drew into close combat range again. Sherisza slowed the *Malshekt* suddenly, but the black ship matched her speed, coming up alongside her but not passing and becoming the prey.

Dillon fired two salvos of missiles at the other ship, its own point-defense lasers taking them out. An idea occurred to him, though. "Daevol, set the point-defense lasers to allow for manual fire as well as automatic," he barked.

<Acknowledged.>

He pulled the only other trigger he'd never bothered with and, as hoped, it set off the PDL. The lasers struck the black ship toward the rear, trying to penetrate the shields and disable its engines. The black ship rocked but the shields seemed to hold. Dillon could tell they were barely dissipating the disruptor fire, and in their weakened state, they were being stretched to their limit to deflect the *Malshekt*'s point defense lasers.

"Got you, you bastard," Dillon said. "Sherisza, turn and fire the ion cannon, quickly!"

She didn't hesitate. She spun the *Malshekt* almost a perfect ninety degrees, bringing the black ship into her sights and discharging the ion cannon with no delay. The blast rocked the enemy ship, and as blue and purple lightning danced across its surface, all its lights went out and it powered down. It was hurtling through the time stream, almost end over end after the rocking of the ion cannon's blast. With no power and no artificial gravity, Dillon imagined the pilot was terrified and probably on the verge of getting physically ill.

Sherisza watched the black ship flipping around helplessly, and she turned the *Malshekt* slowly, her finger hovering over the disruptors' trigger. Dillon looked at her hand and then her face, and he reached over and moved her fingers away from the trigger. There was a time and a place to kill, but this didn't feel like it to him. He wanted answers more than revenge for all the trouble this ship and its pilot had caused them.

She looked at Dillon and sighed, but then maneuvered the *Malshekt* so it was flying in the wake of the helpless black ship. "Daevol, align and time this shot for me," she said. "I want the back wall of its engineering bay disintegrated. Then I want its engines disabled. Do not breach either the warp or Chrono Drives, whatever it has."

<Understood, Captain.>

"How many life signs are on board?"

<One, Captain. There is one person with declining vitals and there appears to be a corpse, relatively fresh according to my sensors.>

"What is going on over there?" Sherisza mused.

"Maybe a mutiny?" Dillon suggested.

"I believe there is only one way to find out," Azi said quietly.

"Indeed," Sherisza agreed.

They watched as the black ship continued to hurtle through the time stream, and then Daevol fired off two perfectly timed shots. The rear wall of the black ship disintegrated under the Kwaagi disruptor fire, and then he raked the interior of the engineering bay with the PDL. There was no cataclysmic blast, so Dillon assumed the engines were disabled but not breached. The black ship was now completely helpless for all intents and purposes. Dillon waited to see if the pilot would try to eject in an escape pod. He'd be trapped in the time stream forever if he did and they didn't rescue him.

Sherisza rose above the enemy ship a bit and accelerated to close the distance between them. Using the nose of the *Malshekt*, shielded with energy, she stopped the black ship from flipping over endlessly. The pilot would still be stuck in a state of zero gravity, but at least now he'd have some concept of which way was up. Dillon didn't want to think about what vomit did in zero gravity, but then figured he might be finding out quite soon.

<Captain, the enemy ship's current life support will expire in less than thirty minutes.>

"Understood," Sherisza said absently.

Dillon laid his hand on hers. "Whatever we feel, that's a person over there."

"Yes, it is," she agreed. "We will give them opportunity to explain themselves. Azi, let Dillon and I go first and make sure the enemy ship is secure. Once we have the pilot detained, you can come and try to communicate with them. Understand that if I do not like his answers, I will be killing him. I refuse to look over my shoulder the rest of my life."

"I understand, Captain, and will not question your orders or decisions," the Kwaagi woman said with that stiffness her people were known for.

Sherisza brought the *Malshekt* above the black ship and then gently in front of it, matching its velocity before she began slowing her own ship. Gradually, she brought the *Malshekt* to a stop, the black ship easing to a motionless state against the *Malshekt*'s shields. When both had ceased hurtling through the time stream, Sherisza eased the *Malshekt* forward and positioned her with the maneuvering thrusters so the boarding tunnel could reach the other ship's hatch. The wings would prevent such a thing side-by-side, but with them facing in opposition directions, Sherisza was able to make it work.

Daevol extended the tunnel and the blinking green light and *bongs* said all was ready for them to board the enemy ship. Sherisza and Dillon got their blasters, and Azi took up a position out of the way of any line of fire.

"Let's go get some answers," Dillon said, gesturing toward the hatch.

Sherisza nodded but stepped to the side before opening it. When no fire or sounds of trouble came down the boarding tunnel, she glanced around the corner and then made her way to the enemy ship.

"DAEVOL, extend the shields over the joined ship," Sherisza said.

<Acknowledged. As the Chrono Drive is currently engaged, I should be able to maintain this safety net indefinitely, Captain.>

"Excellent. Dillon, follow me, but stay low and be ready for anything."

They crept across the boarding tunnel. The black ship's hatch was still closed, but even with no power, Dillon was leery of it opening and blaster fire raking him and Sherisza. He knelt a few steps from the door and kept his defensive blaster trained on where he expected an enemy to be when it opened. He nodded to Sherisza, and she took up a similar crossfire position as they waited for Daevol to power the door and open it.

There was a hiss as the other ship's hatch opened, and Dillon and Sherisza tensed, their fingers on the triggers. There was no one there immediately, so Sherisza crept forward against Dillon's protest. She kept her head on a swivel, then glanced both ways inside the hatch before she sat back on her heel. She beckoned Dillon forward, and he went and knelt beside her.

"No sign of anyone on the flight deck, but there is a body in the corridor," she whispered. "Air quality seems fine for now, but the life support systems are not working, obviously. Let us go in and see if we can capture the pilot. I will keep my blasters set to stun as well."

"All right, but will you let me go first? You're the expectant mother."

She cast a dubious gaze at him. "Please do not treat me differently because I am pregnant," she said. "I do not want to lose you to a foolish sense of heroism any more than you want to lose me. We do this together or not at all. I will simply destroy this ship and spend the rest of my life wondering before I let you go to your death alone."

"Sorry," Dillon said, leaning over to give her a quick kiss on the muzzle.

"Come," she said, walking onto the enemy ship in a crouch.

Dillon walked in a slightly higher hunch, keeping aim over Sherisza to cover her. As she'd said, the flight deck was empty as well as dark. Crouching or kneeling started to become a problem as they left the artificial gravity pull of the *Malshekt*. Dillon got only his second real taste of what weightlessness felt like, but he swallowed down the unease and tried to keep close to the walls for maneuvering. Sherisza pushed over to the opposite wall of the corridor and did the same.

The black ship was remarkably similar to the *Malshekt* but not an exact copy. There were no guest cabins, the starboard side all cabinets and lockers that looked like they held weapons. One was open, its door swinging listlessly, revealing an empty blaster rifle port between several other weapons. Sherisza glanced at Dillon and he nodded his understanding.

The flight deck was dark, but Sherisza activated the glow on her work coat to illuminate it all softly. The pilot wasn't hiding anywhere under the consoles, which resembled the *Malshekt* in much of their form. This ship was either a prototype of a smaller *Malshekt* or had at least been based on the original's design. The panel for the electricals was even in the same place, and Dillon moved over toward it.

He pried open the panel and began flipping the switches to see if anything would come back online. If the warp drive and other power sources had been disabled, nothing was going to work, but it didn't hurt to try. It was possible this ship had auxiliary power. After exhausting most of the switches, Sherisza pointed to a smaller panel inside. Opening that, Dillon found the emergency auxiliary power switch and flipped it. It took a minute for the artificial gravity to kick in, but the body in the corridor sank back to the floor with a soft *whump* once it had.

"Do blaster rifles have a stun setting?" Dillon asked.

"They do," Sherisza answered. She left Dillon to go grab one from the locker while she crawled toward the corpse in the corridor.

There was blood all around it, and it became obvious under her vest's glow that it was Kwaagi. Dillon understood her hesitation after the way the emperor had healed. This one's eyes were glazed over though, its heart and lungs perforated and most of its blood on the floor now. If this soldier managed to heal from *those* injuries, Dillon would be beyond impressed. With a blaster rifle in hand and set to stun, he took up a kneeling position, watching up the corridor.

There was a lavatory and a replicator on the starboard side, but no galley like the *Malshekt* had. Dillon understood this wasn't a joyride ship like Sherisza had originally designed the *Malshekt* to be. It was efficient and deadly, more of a warship than its prototype. There was an escape pod on the port side, more storage lockers, and then the wall and door to the engineering section. Dillon glanced at the door and then Sherisza.

She looked up at his attention. "He's got to be in the escape pod or the lavatory," he said, gesturing toward the door to engineering. "Otherwise, he'd have to be outside with a suit."

"Daevol?" Sherisza prompted.

<The pilot is in the escape pod, Captain.>

"Armed?"

<He appears to have a knife. Other than that, no. There are no energy or projectile weapons on the escape pod that I can detect.>

Sherisza looked back at the open weapon locker but didn't comment on the missing rifle. "What species is he?" she asked instead.

There was a long pause while Daevol scanned the escape pod extensively. <Kiandarian.>

"No shit," Dillon blurted.

Sherisza sighed. "Azi, it should be safe for you to come aboard. We will need you."

The Kwaagi woman boarded the ship shortly after. She glanced at the open cabinet with the weapons in it but made no motion to grab one. Instead, she moved to crouch near Sherisza, and her eyes fixed on the Kwaagi corpse on the floor. She crawled toward it and began looking it over, and Dillon didn't need to smell her confusion to sense it.

"I do not recognize these markings or the uniform they adorn," Azilija said. "This man was clearly Kwaagi, but not from our empire."

"From the future, maybe?" Dillon suggested.

"Trying to change the past or keep it from being changed...?" Azi added.

"The past cannot be changed according to my brother's theories," Sherisza said. "From what little I have seen and done, I believe this to be true. However, this person or these people may not be aware of it." She looked at Dillon. "Or my brother could have been wrong."

Sherisza crept a little closer to the door of the escape pod but then stopped. She was looking at the floor, and as Dillon followed her gaze, he saw more blood. There was a trail of it leading into the escape pod. It wasn't so copious that he thought the pilot was in immediate danger, but there had clearly been a fight between the Kwaagi and the Kiandarian. The latter may have won, but he didn't come out unscathed.

"We'd better not leave him in there too long or he'll bleed to death," he said anyway.

Sherisza sighed, then shuffled forward in a crouch and knocked on the door of the escape pod. She backed off to the far side of the corridor immediately, her blasters up though she didn't have her fingers on the triggers yet. She tensed as the door of the escape pod was forced open a little bit and a knife was tossed out in the corridor.

Dillon waited for the door to open the rest of the way, but it didn't. He looked to Sherisza and gestured toward the door with his head, and she nodded in agreement. Kicking the knife safely away, he gripped the edge of the door, half expecting his fingers to get sliced or smashed. No such thing happened, though, and he muscled the door open to reveal a figure in a black suit like a full-body version of Sherisza's, their face obscured by a helmet.

Whoever it was, he had a knife wound under his ribs, and he was leaning to the side to help clench it. He began speaking in that garbled tongue again, though it was muffled even worse now by the powerless helmet. Dillon leaned into the escape pod and looked around for any sign of other weapons, and then he stepped in and to the side.

Sherisza came in his wake, kneeling before the injured pilot. The man reached his fingers toward her but didn't try to actually touch her. Sherisza reached up and unfastened his helmet before pulling it off slowly and gently.

Removing the helmet revealed a Kiandarian with features

like a puma. His battered ears were only the beginning of his scars, his face crisscrossed by battle wounds. His eyes were a magnificent blue, but there was the coldness of lost hope and pain in them even as he looked into Sherisza's golden eyes. A grimace showed broken fangs, and Dillon wondered at what the hell had happened to this man. Why couldn't he speak an intelligible language, or at least a dialect of Kiandese that Sherisza might recognize, even if she couldn't speak it? Where did he come from and when? And what was he so hell-bent on stopping them from doing?

Azi looked into the escape pod and the reaction was immediate. The pilot's hand dropped to his side as though searching for a blaster, but when he realized he was injured and didn't have any weapons left, he slumped further into the corner. Azilija kept her distance, but she tried to ask something of him that he didn't appear to understand. She tried a couple of other things, but her feathers flattened out when he either couldn't or wouldn't answer.

"Does he not understand, or does he just refuse to speak with you?" Sherisza asked. That got another reaction from the pilot, and he said something to Sherisza that was broken up by a deep grunt of pain. "Come to my ship, we can patch you up."

He didn't understand a word she was saying, but Sherisza gestured for him to stand. She took his injured weight and began to escort him back to the *Malshekt*.

Dillon was amazed. Yes, the pilot was a Kiandarian, but he'd harried them for so long and threatened them a number of times. Sherisza seemed to have forgotten all of that now, though, more fixated on who he was, where he was from, and what he could tell them. She half-carried him to one of the guest cabins on the *Malshekt* and laid him on the bed. Dillon followed her and brought the medical kit with him.

"Daevol, analyze my notes and see if you can correct any

errors I may have made logically," Azi said. "If you can upload the cipher to our translation chips, it may greatly simplify our attempts to talk to this pilot."

<Acknowledged. I have not detected any major logical inconsistencies. I am rearranging the vocabulary database and uploading.>

Sherisza had an easy enough time working on one of her people. She cauterized what she could of the wound before sealing it and then coating it with the regenerative gel. There was no guarantee the pilot would survive such a grisly wound, but at least he wouldn't bleed out before he could talk to them. With that done, she started to remove his jacket, and the Kiandarian pilot didn't object. What was revealed, though, made Sherisza suck in a sharp breath.

The scars on his face and the damage to his ears apparently had nothing to do with battle. His chest, upper arms, and back were all likewise crisscrossed by scars, and he had a number branded into the flesh of his inner forearms. It didn't take long for Dillon to recall a similar thing from Earth's history, and he, too, took a deep breath.

"Who are you?" Dillon asked, and suddenly the Kiandarian perked up a little. "Can you understand me now?"

<Our "guest" does not have a translation chip, Commander, but he does have a tracking and biometric chip of some kind. I am attempting to interface with it if I can in order to facilitate communication.>

"What about this, can you understand me?" Azi asked in her tongue. The Kiandarian's ears went back, and he flinched, but then he showed the broken tips of his fangs menacingly. "Now we are getting somewhere. I mean you no harm. Tell us who you are."

The pilot looked from Azi to Sherisza, who nodded encouragingly. "Am *toushu*," he said in that guttural language, though the chips were starting to be able to translate it. "*Toushu* stop black ship. *Toushu* stop *currigu nakka* from using it."

"Using what?" Azi asked. "Show us."

The Kiandarian's mouth tightened. "No use," he said, making a gesture with his hands.

"We don't understand," Azi said. "But keep speaking, I am learning your tongue the more you speak. The more you say, the more I can understand with help from our computer."

The pilot rambled out a whole long thing that Dillon could only understand parts of, but then he made the same gesture with his hands. Dillon's brows went up. "Sherisza," he said. "Look what he's doing with his hands. Azi, tell him to show us again."

When she did so, the Kiandarian pilot made the gesture again and Sherisza gasped. "What is it? Does that mean something to you?" Azi asked.

"Over instead of under..." Dillon said.

"It is not the Chrono Drive at all!" Sherisza cried. "It is the phase-cloaking device he wants us to destroy. But why? Why must we destroy it?"

The Kiandarian didn't seem to understand what she was saying, but he understood her tone and the pleading under it. He turned and pointed at Azilija, then gestured to all the scars across his body and face. "*Omushti Kwaagunu medutuno dinasca*," he said.

<Cipher updated. His mention of the Kwaagi by a similar yet different name has unlocked the work of our Kwaagi interpreter.>

"Well done, both of you," Sherisza said. "Tell us again. Why must we destroy my work?"

The pilot looked at her and repeated himself. "Kwaagi destroy us if not," the translation chips echoed, making some sense of his more guttural speech.

"Sweet Goddess," Sherisza said. "But how? Why? Azi, ask him. Ask him to explain it all to us in detail."

"What did my people do? And how is it related to the captain's device?" Azilija asked in the Kwaagi tongue.

"Will explain... let this one rest first. Destroy device, then destroy other ship, get far before others follow this one," the pilot said.

Sherisza grimaced, but then she nodded. She opened a dropper from the medical kit and had Azi tell the pilot it would help him sleep and numb his pain. He trusted Sherisza, at least, and he swallowed the offered liquid without complaint. It didn't take long to work, and Sherisza laid him down and covered him with a blanket just before his eyes rolled back and he went to sleep.

"What does this all mean?" Azi asked.

"I do not know," Sherisza answered. "But I will not destroy the phase-cloaking device until he explains things. As far as his other request, if someone else does enter the time stream, we are in a precarious position. Come, we will detach the *Malshekt* and destroy the other ship, then continue on our way."

"Sherisza... let's just destroy it," Dillon said, and she turned to him, her brow furrowed. "We have the schematics and the designs. We can always build it again. Maybe we should do what he said... you know, better safe than sorry. If it turns out he's wrong or just a lunatic or something, we can build it again."

Her mouth tightened but then she nodded. "Help me remove it, and then we will eject it and destroy it along with the other ship."

He pulled her into a hug, and she didn't resist. Azi's feathers rose, and she approximated a smile before she left them alone.

———

The pilot slept for several hours. It gave Sherisza time to come to terms with what he'd requested of her while she and Dillon removed it. Since it hadn't been connected to the ship's systems yet, it wasn't difficult to dismantle. She set it on the floor of the other black ship, and then they disengaged the boarding tunnel and got a safe distance away. Sherisza remained silent while they disintegrated all of it with the *Malshekt*'s disruptors.

Azi remained in her cabin working on something to do with the stranger's language. Daevol had managed to program a cipher for their chips based on Azilija's work, but that didn't satisfy the Kwaagi woman. She wanted to truly understand this new language, and though she left the door of her cabin open so she could stay aware, she was engrossed. Daevol was helping her as he could, but Azi seemed to prefer to do it the hard way—through study and practice.

Sherisza got them back underway toward Kiandar in the time stream. "Fortunately, all this ruckus taking place in the time stream has not cost us any actual time."

"What about aging, though?" Dillon asked. "We still age the same way when we spend a lot of time using the Chrono Drive, right?"

"This is true," she said. "It only serves so much purpose to travel through time. It does not buy us additional years of life, unfortunately."

"We'll just have to make the best of what we have," Dillon said, leaning over for a kiss.

"Good answer," Azi commented from her cabin.

Dillon and Sherisza laughed as they split apart.

<Captain, our "guest" is waking up.>

"Thank you, Daevol. No need to restrain him," she answered.

There was the sound of the guest cabin door opening and then a long yawn. Dillon turned to watch the puma-like Kiandarian pilot approach up the corridor. He stopped a respectful distance away, glancing through the door to Azi's cabin with a grimace. Then he turned to the front, and it was clear he was just as amazed to see the *Malshekt* in person as they'd been to find his ship was such a close copy.

"Feeling better?" Dillon asked.

<I have been unable to interface with his identification chip, Commander. I believe this to have been an intentional thing, considering he appears to be–or have been–a slave.>

Azi came out of her cabin, then, and the Kiandarian pilot moved away to the far side of the corridor. She stayed in the doorway to keep her distance. "The Commander asked if you are feeling better," Azi said in her tongue.

"Still in pain. Tired. But this one must know if it was destroyed," the pilot said.

"What's your name?" Dillon asked, Azi translating his question.

"83719264," the pilot answered, gesturing to the designs on his inner forearm.

"Good God," Dillon said, swallowing as he turned to look out the viewport again. "He doesn't even have a proper name...?"

Sherisza rose and turned to face their guest. "I have destroyed the device," she said, pausing every so often to let Azi catch up. "It was not easy to take you at your word, but as you could not explain before fatigue took you, we erred on the side of caution. Now, though, you owe me an explanation of who you are, where you come from, and why my device was dangerous enough to warrant trying to kill us."

He nodded and leaned against the wall, his breathing troubled for a minute. When he got his wind back, he tried to straighten out again. "Slave Airman 83719264," he said. "Be patient. Must try remember all was told. Device... dangerous.

Open doorway to other place, other time. Different time. Time of Kwaagi Imperium, enslave half galaxy."

"No wonder you are afraid of me," Azi said, still using the Kwaagi tongue. "We are not like that here. Captain Sherisza and your people are our friends. She has saved our emperor from a terrible fate, in fact."

"Device opens doors. Doors cannot be shut. Evil come through, warp Kwaagi like time this one from. Must destroy device, never use."

"What kind of evil?" Azi asked.

"Master race. Control Kwaagi. Control galaxy. Make slaves all."

"Terrific," Dillon said. "Well, that ought to make anyone reseriously consider opening doors into other dimensions. Sherisza, maybe it's best if you put the files under a deep encryption on the off chance anyone ever accesses them."

"I will," she agreed. "But how has he been getting here then?"

"Have similar device, prototypes. You destroy one. One remaining. Will come," he said when Azi translated Sherisza's question.

"What do you mean?"

Azi prompted the pilot. "This one stole ship. Was caught. Other ship come see what this one tried do. Can feel approach," he said, tapping the spot where Dillon assumed his ID chip had been installed.

"Daevol?" Sherisza prompted.

<Captain, there is a warship approaching at high speed within the time stream. I recommend you all prepare for battle.>

"*Maqua*," Sherisza muttered as she slipped into her seat again. "Get him situated and find something to hold onto, Azi.

We must destroy this warship to keep anyone else from coming across from this other dimension if he is right."

"A warship, though?" Dillon asked.

"Pray, Dillon," Sherisza sighed.

He didn't have to be asked twice.

CHAPTER 25

NO SURRENDER

THE TERM *WARSHIP* was certainly concerning, but as Daevol's scans revealed more data, it became slightly less so. It wasn't a cruiser or carrier like they had fought when MacNault was sending assassins and mercenaries to kill them. This was akin to the Kwaagi warships in size and armament. As more data came in, it was apparent that was because it *was* a Kwaagi warship, just one from another time and, apparently, another dimension. Its speed left little mystery to its intentions, though.

"Armaments?" Sherisza prompted her AI.

<Enemy ship carries standard Kwaagi firepower, Captain. It has quad disruptors, missile ports, point-defense lasers, standard high-power blasters, and mines. I am aligning our shields to the frequency of our own disruptors. I do not know if it will be sufficient.>

Sherisza pulled up a holodisplay while she kept on course, waiting for the warship to catch up. She began making changes to something in the shield settings, if Dillon understood what he was looking at. It occurred to him after a few moments that they had worked extensively on the Kwaagi fighter wings and she knew how their shields were programmed. With just a little touch to the *Malshekt*'s settings, she could align their shields to properly disperse disruptor fire. In theory, anyway, and then only for a time.

<Shields realigned. Warship approaching quickly at its maximum speed. Captain, we could outrun them if we use the Chrono Drive to its maximum capacity.>

"We cannot run from this, Daevol," she said. "We must destroy this ship if what our guest has said is true. Is it possible we can change the settings of our own disruptors to bypass their shields?"

<We can try, Captain.>

"Be ready to do so if our attacks prove ineffective," Sherisza ordered. "Dillon, I will handle piloting if you would handle gunnery. Try to land as many shots as you can, glancing or otherwise, so we can determine if our weaponry can even hurt them. I think we will be safe from their attacks at first, but no doubt they will try modifying their cannons as well."

"Of course, Captain," he said. He got his holodisplays in place for ease of targeting, and Daevol brought up the combat HUD for him. Dillon saw the red bogey at the very edge of their sensor range, but it was gaining on them.

Azi tried to escort the Kiandarian pilot to quarters where he could strap in, but he wouldn't leave the corridor. He began scratching at the spot where his identification chip apparently was, and Dillon wondered. If he was a slave, it was possible that chip did far more than act as an electronic identifier. It could be used to inflict pain or worse. The thought made him tighten his grip on the combat sticks, his emotions sliding from anxiousness to a cold calm.

"Azi, strap yourself in but keep your door open for quicker communication," Sherisza said, and the Kwaagi woman went and did as ordered. "Be ready, all of you. When that ship draws within short range, I will be bringing us about and attacking it head on. We cannot afford to be chased down as we were by our guest. We must be aggressive as well as defensive."

"Aye, Captain," Dillon said, echoed by Azi a moment later.

<I will divert additional power to forward shielding. Warp drive is primed for short jumps as you have done before, Captain. I am not certain how or if it will function while we are within the time stream.>

"We will find out," she answered, her muzzle tight. Dillon reached over and laid a hand on her forearm, and she took it in hers.

There was a gasp behind them. "You... mates?"

"Yes," Sherisza said, amending it by nodding.

"No humans my time. Kwaagi destroy. Humans no submit."

"Yeah, that sounds like humanity," Dillon said. "We don't take shit from anyone. You want to conquer us, you'll have to kill almost all of us to do it."

"That was the attitude of Kiandar when we fought the Giannaru," Sherisza said. "We had been slaves before and vowed never again."

That brought Sherisza's reactions at the memorials on Earth into better focus, but Dillon didn't have time to think about it. "And nobody threatens our women or children," he added.

"Our cubs," Sherisza said, squeezing his hand again.

The minutes ticked away as they watched the warship draw closer and closer on the HUD. When Sherisza decided she was tired of being a rabbit and wanted to show them the lioness of Kiandar, she brought the *Malshekt* about. The enemy warship slowed as it sensed they were preparing for combat, and then the two ships headed on a collision course. Sherisza's face was set in a stony glare, the eyes of a predator where those loving orbs full of stars usually were.

The ship came in at incredible speed, and Dillon squeezed off a few mostly blind shots as they passed each other. He thought he caught it a couple of times, though it didn't seem to have any effect through the shielding. The enemy ship tried to pummel the *Malshekt*, but likewise only landed a couple of hits. The HUD indicated the shields had held, with no structural damage to the ship yet.

And then Sherisza demonstrated her remarkable familiarity with her craft. She spun the *Malshekt* one hundred and eighty degrees, then used a short burst from the warp drive to reverse its course. Soon, the Chrono Drive took over again, and they began to pursue the enemy ship. Its pilot was clearly astounded at how quickly the *Malshekt* had come about, and he began using evasive maneuvers as Sherisza bore down on him.

The *Malshekt*'s targeting locked on, and Dillon saw the reticle turn green and begin to spin in his peripheral vision. He hardly glanced up, reaching to touch it out of instinct though he didn't have to at this point. He squeezed off several shots with the disruptors, and though the enemy shields dispersed the blasts, Dillon knew Daevol was modifying them after each burst. It was only a matter of time before they penetrated the enemy shields, assuming it could be done.

"Daevol, can you show me where their point-defense lasers are?" Dillon asked. A diagram of the enemy ship came up on the right side of the HUD, showing the PDL ports on the ship's dorsal ridge. "Perfect. Let's see if we can take those out. Some missile fire may give their pilot more turbulence than he's used to dealing with, but we have to destroy their laser system first."

<Acknowledged. Continuing to modify the Kwaagi disruptors.>

"Don't worry, I'll keep firing," Dillon said, waiting for the targeting reticle to turn green again. It was nice to be the pursuer for a change, but the enemy pilot was no slouch. While he either couldn't or didn't know how to bring their ship about the way Sherisza had the *Malshekt*, he knew how to evade fire. This was a trained Kwaagi combat pilot, and a good one.

There was a grunt behind him, and Dillon looked over his shoulder. The slave pilot was on his knees, clutching desperately at his head and scratching behind his ear. "You all right?" Dillon asked, but he couldn't wait for an answer, turning back to what he was doing. The pilot couldn't understand him anyway.

Sherisza anticipated one of their enemy's evasive maneuvers and Dillon raked the port side of the warship with disruptor fire. Still, none of the shots penetrated, but they were taking their toll on enemy power supplies. They'd either find a modulation that got through the shields, or the enemy ship would eventually run out of power. If they didn't get out of Sherisza's predatory gaze or Dillon's line of fire, they were finished.

In a stunning move, the enemy ship came to an almost complete stop, and Sherisza barely turned the *Malshekt* to avoid a full collision. Nevertheless, the two ships hit, and the *Malshekt* spun away briefly before Sherisza got it back under control. The enemy ship came right at them, having recovered faster, and landed a full flurry of disruptor fire on the *Malshekt*'s dorsal ridge. The shields held, but alarms began going off, and the point-defense lasers had to destroy an entire salvo of missiles that still rocked the ship at close range.

"*Maqua*," Sherisza spat, getting the *Malshekt* moving again. She spun the ship a second time, but in such a way that they were flying backwards, lining up a shot with the ion cannon.

The targeting reticle turned green as the enemy ship came after them again, and Dillon took the combat control lightly in hand and squeezed the trigger. The ion cannon discharged, and that blast of energy leapt forward in a blinding flash like cosmic lightning. It struck the enemy ship right on the nose, and Dillon smiled.

But nothing happened.

"Fuck me!" he yelled in frustration.

"Language, Dillon," Sherisza grumbled.

<Language, Dillon.>

"Shut up, you," he grunted at the AI. "Sorry, Sherisza."

She didn't respond, beginning evasive maneuvers as the enemy ship came for another pass, its disruptors and blasters lighting up space as it fired again and again. Sherisza got them out of the way of most, but they did take a few hits from the disruptors. Daevol kept them informed via the HUD. The shields held, the disruptors causing considerable power drain, but the blasters adding some to the reserves. The *Malshekt* was further able to divert some of the disruptor power to the ion cannon, but not all of it.

And apparently, to little effect.

"How did the ion cannon not work?" Dillon protested.

"They have some impressive shielding," Sherisza said. "We are lucky they did not fire upon us during that brief moment our power shut off."

Both ships came about again, and Sherisza put them on a collision course. "Daevol, aid me if you must. We need to get right on top of that ship, even if it means we strike it."

<Acknowledged, Captain.>

Dillon wasn't sure what she was up to, but he took a moment to see how their "guest" was doing. He wasn't in the corridor anymore. Dillon figured he'd gone to a cabin to strap in or lie down, whatever pain his implant was causing too much to bear. So long as he was safe and they couldn't kill him through the implant, that was enough for Dillon for now.

Dillon wanted to grip the armrests of his copilot's seat but held tight to the combat controls instead. The ships approached at speeds his eyes were hardly able to track, but he squeezed off some disruptor fire and a salvo of missiles just in case. He wasn't sure if he'd even hit anything, but Sherisza showed a savage grin as she executed a short warp jump to get them away from the near miss. Dillon glanced at the rear holodisplay as he saw the other ship partially turn but begin to fly erratically.

"What... what did you do?" he asked.

"Engaged the warp drive while they were within its field of grasp," she said. "Daevol, how much structural damage did we cause?"

<The enemy ship is heavily damaged but still operable. Proceed with caution, Captain.>

"We have you now," Sherisza growled, bringing the *Malshekt* around to begin pursuit again.

"You all right in there, Azi?" Dillon called.

"I am fine, Commander. Do not worry about me," she answered.

Sherisza brought them in on their enemy, zigzagging and using other evasive maneuvers to render their desperate rear shots ineffective. Dillon could see the warship was, appropriately enough, warped in several places by what Sherisza had done. It couldn't fly straight, and though its pilot was talented, there was only so much he could do to evade the *Malshekt*'s pursuit. They were all but finished, and frankly, Dillon didn't feel sorry for them at all.

He looked down when he felt something at his hip. He only realized his blaster had been taken from its holster a second before its butt slammed him in the side of the head. He saw stars, but they weren't the ones out the viewport. A moment later, he heard a shot fired and Sherisza cried out before her head hit the console and the *Malshekt* swerved off course.

"Azi!" Dillon called before he was even cognizant of getting to his feet. He swept his arms before him and knocked the blaster aside before he could get stunned by a real shot. His vision came back piece by piece, and he grabbed at the hands of the Kiandarian slave pilot before the man could do any more damage.

The Kwaagi woman came out of her cabin and gasped when she saw what had happened. She kicked the Kiandarian in the sweet spot, and Dillon had the presence of mind to wonder at a reptilian knowing to do that. Nevertheless, there was little reaction but a minor grunt from their assailant. He was stronger than Dillon, full of compact muscle just like Sherisza, but Dillon had a bit of a size advantage and he also had an ally.

Azi swiped at the pilot's face, then grabbed him before she jumped up and raked his torso with those oversized inner talons on her feet. That finally drew a cry of pain from him despite all those scars, and she began to batter him with her fists. Soon enough, she got the blaster out of his hand and turned it on him, stunning him in the side of the head at point blank range.

Dillon didn't have time to wonder if the shot was fatal. He rushed to Sherisza and eased her back in her seat, still unconscious after the stun. He took his own seat again and got the *Malshekt* under control, then set her back in pursuit of their enemy. He wasn't the pilot Sherisza was, but like in his fight with the Kiandarian slave, he had the advantage of an ally.

"Daevol, take over evasive maneuvers and get us close enough to disable that ship," Dillon said, glancing around his seat. Azi was dragging the unconscious pilot up the corridor, likely to put him in the escape pod and lock him there. Dillon left her to it.

<Acknowledged, Commander.>

Daevol evaded nearly all of the enemy's rear-arc shots, and even those that hit the *Malshekt* were sufficiently deflected or absorbed. Dillon grasped the combat controls but hesitated with his finger over the ion cannon's trigger. If he pulled it when a shot was about to catch the *Malshekt*, it could spell disaster when the ship's systems shut off momentarily. Instead, he took aim at the enemy ship's point-defense laser nodule and began peppering their shields with shots of his own.

<Their shields are about to fail, Commander.>

"Good. As soon as they're down, we're going to take out their weapons systems and then nail them with the ion cannon, got it?"

<Aye, Commander.>

The enemy pilot tried evasive maneuvers again, but Daevol had no problem keeping up with the other ship in its damaged state. Dillon hit their shields again and again with the disruptors, then fired another salvo of missiles for good measure. Their point-defense lasers took out the missiles, but every shot they fired meant that much less power going to their shields. Slamming them with a few more groupings of disruptor blasts, Dillon brought down their shields at last.

He didn't hesitate, taking aim at their point-defense laser turret and destroying it, then following up with shots to their disruptors and cannons. Safe from their energy weapons, Dillon had Daevol bring them in line to take out the missile ports as well, and then he did so. The enemy ship, so far as Dillon could tell, was completely helpless. But he had only to look at his wife's unconscious form in her seat to steel his heart.

"Back us off and line me up to hit them with the ion cannon," Dillon said.

<One moment, Commander. They have dumped their complement of mines. Give me a moment to get us beyond them and... Commander, they are hailing us.>

Dillon sighed. "Put it through."

"Unidentified vessel, you have made your point," came the hissing voice in the Kwaagi tongue. "We came only for the slave. Surrender him to us and we will trouble you no further."

"Get fucked," Dillon said, though he spared a glance at Sherisza before he turned back forward. "I've seen what you've done to him, there's no way in hell you're getting him back, I don't care what you made him do to my wife."

There was a silent pause, then, "He is of no concern to you. Return him and we will leave your space permanently. You have our word."

"Oh, I have your word, huh? Well, here's my counteroffer," Dillon said, and he squeezed the trigger of the ion cannon. The *Malshekt* went dark for a few moments as it discharged its crippling lightning and powered down the enemy ship. There was a scream from deeper in the *Malshekt*, Dillon suspected from the escape pod.

Azi came running up the corridor. "What happened? We lost power for a moment there."

"Just fired the ion cannon," Dillon said.

"Ah, yes, of course. Thank the Scale Father. Are they disabled?" she asked, and Dillon nodded. "I fear our guest has either passed out from the pain or is dead. I did not wish to open the door to find out which."

"Daevol?"

<Our passenger appears to be deceased, Commander. There was a surge of power in his chip when the enemy ship went dark.>

"Shit," Dillon blurted, but he only gave it a moment of thought before he unstrapped himself and went to Sherisza. He patted her muzzle lightly. "Come on, girl. Time to wake up."

Sherisza came to, but it was a few minutes before she seemed to really see and feel anything and sat upright again. Dillon held her while she got her bearings, and Azi kept watch over the HUD and the enemy ship. Sherisza took stock of herself, then Dillon, then looked out the front viewport to behold the enemy ship drifting powerless before them.

"What happened?" she finally asked.

"Our guest took my blaster and shot you after he cracked me in the head," Dillon said.

"Your scalp is bleeding," Sherisza said, reaching clawed fingers toward it.

Dillon kept her hands at bay. "I'm fine. I think they were able to force him to harm us with that chip he has installed. We got him into the escape pod and locked him there. Whatever it was controlling him, though, it killed him when I disabled their ship. I'm sorry, Sherisza."

She hugged Dillon tightly. "It is probably better this way. The poor soul never even had a name, but he will have one now in the Goddess' bosom."

"Amen to that," he said. "Azi helped save all of us. Thanks, Azilija."

"Just doing my duty, Commander," she returned.

<Captain, good to have you back. The enemy ship is attempting to restore power.>

"Back us off a safe distance and then detonate their Chrono Drive," Sherisza ordered.

<Captain...>

"Do it," she said with a tone that would brook no argument.

The *Malshekt* slowed enough to put a safe distance between them, and then Daevol fired the disruptors in three short bursts. The third burst, with nothing in its way, compromised the Chrono Drive. The effects were immediate and incredible, as the ship exploded in a ball of light before imploding into nothingness, leaving no trace. More than that, the entire time stream around where it had happened seemed to shimmer like hot pavement in the summer, but only for a few moments before all went back to normal.

"What was that?" Dillon asked.

"Their atoms are now scattered not just across distance, but time," Sherisza said. "We must pray that our late guest was correct, and that the two ships we have destroyed housed the only prototypes of the phasing device. I will keep my schematics of how to build one solely to counter any invasion from those in the other dimensions. However, I hope to never see them in any way, shape, or form, if they were able to subjugate the Kwaagi and the galaxy."

"You and me both," Dillon said.

"Daevol, get us back on course to our intended time and place at Kiandar," Sherisza ordered. "Dillon, let us check on our guest and see if he truly has died."

"Yes, ma'am," he said, his jaw tight.

"If it is all right to sit in the commander's seat, I will keep watch here for now," Azi said.

Sherisza simply nodded her agreement, then led Dillon up the corridor toward the escape pod. They opened the door and, as expected, found the dead slave pilot on the floor, curled in a fetal position as though he'd died wracked with pain. Sherisza knelt beside him and her mouth tightened. He may have stunned her with a blaster, but she held no apparent ill will toward the unfortunate soul. She was mourning his death instead.

"Get me a laser torch, please," she said quietly.

Dillon wasn't even tempted to snicker about his mother's old fears. He went to engineering and got a torch as requested. He put it in Sherisza's hand when he returned, and he understood what she was doing immediately when she turned the body's forearms over. She burned away the brands that had numbered the slave, then handed the torch back to Dillon.

Sherisza laid a hand on the body. "You are a slave no longer, my brother. Now you rest in the All-Mother's arms. May the All-Father reward you justly for the lives you have saved this day. Go with our eternal thanks, and my love."

"That was beautiful," Dillon whispered, laying a hand on her shoulder.

"We will bury him on Kiandar while there," she said. "In the past, no one will question who he was or where he came from. In our present time, I will mark the site as the grave of a hero."

"Rightly so," Dillon said.

THEY ARRIVED on Kiandar in the past and made their pickups as usual. Dillon still couldn't go down and speak with the people, but Sherisza assured him that he'd be able to eventually. Like those before them, these Kiandarians were surprised to find a Kwaagi and especially a human on board, but there were no rude words said. They weren't made privy to the fact that Dillon and Sherisza were mated, but Dillon didn't read anything into it. The refugees would find out eventually when they got to present-day Kiandar.

While on her home world in the past, Sherisza buried the body of the slave pilot. Dillon didn't recognize the spot she had chosen, but he accompanied her while she performed what was an unusual funeral for her people. Most of them were committed to the pyre; normally, burials were reserved for figures of great importance. It wasn't hard to see how Sherisza felt about her dead kinsman from another dimension, and once again it made Dillon think of how she'd acted at the war memorials back on Earth. He thought he'd seen so much in her at the time, but he was seeing more and more as her past and that of her people came into sharper focus.

Much like the Tomb of the Unknowns, this grave site would never bear the man's name, but it bore his body and his memory. Dillon figured Sherisza would mark it in some fashion when they returned to present-day Kiandar. It was a fitting tribute to a man who'd done the right thing in the end, tortured and misguided though he'd been. There was no telling how things might've turned out had he not stopped Sherisza from opening that "door" he spoke of.

Once the funeral was taken care of, Sherisza and Dillon returned to the *Malshekt*. They had all three groups they'd planned to rescue, and Sherisza closed the hatch behind her and sat on the flight deck. She was pensive as she went through the preparations to take her ship off-world, and Dillon laid his hand on her arm. She turned a smile on him, but she didn't kiss him or say anything just yet.

They took flight and she got them into orbit quickly, avoiding any more attention than their overlong stay may have already gotten. Soon, they were a safe distance from Kiandar, and she engaged the Chrono Drive. There was no missing the intake of breath or the fact that she held it once they were in the time stream. Nothing came to bother them, and she finally let out a long sigh and reached to return Dillon's touch.

He checked the corridor for any of their passengers, then leaned over to meet her halfway for a kiss. They stayed in their seats, vigilant for any more surprise attacks in the time stream, but all remained quiet after nearly twenty minutes. Satisfied for now, they left the scanning to Daevol and made their way to the galley to share a first meal with their guests.

It was cramped with so many there, but everyone was in good spirits. It was always odd to Dillon to consider all these people were buying Sherisza's story at face value. If someone had shown up on Earth claiming to be from the future and requesting to take him there to repopulate the human race, he'd have thought they were a kook. Whatever Sherisza was saying to them, though, they all seemed to come without argument or suspicion. And even with Kiandarians from four different years all together in the galley with a Kwaagi and a human, they were thankful and curious.

The days passed quietly and peacefully, Dillon studying where he could and letting Azi handle their guests as she liked to do. Sherisza had begun work on a standard cloaking device of her own design, something that wouldn't cross dimensions or risk opening any sorts of rifts or doors. It kept her mind busy and focused on engineering, letting her get back to the simple joys of her work. Dillon enjoyed studying beside her so he could see her mind at work, this amazing woman who had chosen him as a mate despite all their differences.

Because despite all those differences, we have so much in common, he thought. *Foremost the content of our character...*

She caught him looking at her from the corner of her eye, and she turned a little smile on him. All those leonine features didn't make her different to him; they made her exotic, and just accentuated so much of what he believed about the "human" spirit.

<Commander, there is something you had asked me to research.>

"I did?" Dillon blurted, his thoughts scattered as the AI ruined yet another moment.

<You had discovered something referred to as the "Doorstep of the Goddess" in Daevol Rousilarru's notes.>

"Oh, right," he said, turning to see Sherisza gazing curiously at him. "It was something he'd mentioned in the notebooks I scanned. I was curious if it was an actual place."

"I know, he spoke of it from time to time," Sherisza said. "It was something he said he had seen through his telescope, though no one was ever able to find it again or confirm it, Daevol himself included."

<That is the conclusion I reached as well, though the data core recovered from the house does have the approximate location marked. When we are on Kiandar, I will create coordinates for the location based on where he was looking.>

"That'll be something to look into in the future," Dillon said, and Sherisza nodded. "Did he ever describe it to you?"

"Not so much a description as a concept. He was never sure just what it was he saw, Dillon. And the fact that he could never find it again and neither could any of our scientists led him to believe perhaps he had imagined or dreamt it. That was a frequent occurrence with him at times."

<There is a drawing in the data core.>

A holodisplay came up, and Dillon and Sherisza both marveled at her late brother's artwork. Sure enough, it depicted what looked like heavenly cloud and a gateway out in space. For him to have been able to see it through a telescope, though, it had to have been huge. It certainly did lend credence to him having imagined or dreamt of it.

"Most curious," Sherisza said. "I will be curious to see where this leads us, but even should this be real, we have not been invited. I should like to finish our work before we go chasing one of my brother's dreams."

"Agreed," Dillon said.

<I will do the calculations and star mapping for future use, Captain.>

"Thank you, Daevol," she said with a content little smile as she said her brother's name.

Dillon took one last look at the drawing and then dismissed it. He couldn't help but chuckle at the thought that Saint Peter might ask if they had a reservation.

———

They arrived at Kiandar in the present day after taking their customary detour to throw off anyone trying to track where they were finding the settlers. Sherisza sent greetings to Outer Dock Seventeen and was cleared to land on Kiandar, so she wasted little time. She set the *Malshekt* down in that little cul-de-sac near her old home, and the ship was soon surrounded by most of the settlers already on Kiandar.

There were many happy greetings, the new arrivals welcomed and escorted with little delay to houses that had been cleaned out and prepared for them. Sherisza was hugged and muzzle-rubbed and thanked so many times before they all left, but she didn't go with them. She stood at the base of the steps to the *Malshekt*, a content smile on her face, and she leaned into Dillon once everyone had departed.

"How bad is the winter here?" Dillon asked.

"Oh, it is hardly even a winter," she said. "We are not in the tropics, but it stays pleasant and sunny here most of the year. They will have plenty of time to grow their food and harvest it before the weather turns even slightly sour."

"Oh, good. I know you said you go into season in the autumn, so I wasn't sure what that meant for the settlers."

"I expect it may mean there will be a number of cubs in the spring, if our women's bodies catch up to the season in this time," Sherisza said. "This is going better than I could have ever hoped, Dillon, and I have you and your parents, among many other people, to thank for it."

"I'm happy to have helped, our relationship aside," he said, giving her a peck at the corner of her mouth. "I would've helped you do this even if we hadn't fallen in love."

"I know. You are a good man. Come, I want to show you something."

She led him toward her house, where Emperor Malshii and his family were out enjoying the yard. Dillon wasn't sure how she was going to react to seeing the children on the rope swing, but it brought a huge smile to her face. She approached the imperial family, and their reactions were similar if a bit subdued on their reptilian countenances. But there were the bobbing feathers and other cues that said they were happy to see their benefactors, even from the normally formal empress.

"Welcome back," Malshii said, shaking hands with Sherisza and Dillon.

"I am glad to see you are enjoying my home world," Sherisza said. "Do not get too attached to it, though. Your people will want you back at some point, and I cannot win a fight against them to try to keep you."

The Kwaagi laughed, but the emperor turned serious after a moment. "I need to speak with you about something, but not in front of the children."

"Can you wait half an hour?" Sherisza asked.

"Of course," Malshii said with a gracious bow of his head. His wife seemed bemused by his behavior before Sherisza, but she, too, bowed her head to Dillon and the Kiandarian.

Sherisza led Dillon down a trail into the woods behind her home. He wasn't sure where they were going at first, but after a few minutes, they arrived at a clearing with a rocky hill in its center. He recognized it immediately, and when they approached the marker at the hill's top, he marveled at the way time travel worked. For here, on this rocky hill, sat the grave of the slave pilot, now Kiandar's equivalent of the Tomb of the Unknown Soldier.

"This is... amazing," Dillon said. "We just laid him to rest a few days ago."

"Incredible, is it not?" Sherisza agreed, crouching by the side of the grave. She picked out some weeds that threatened to overgrow the marker, then set some flowers on its surface. She laid a hand on the marker and just squatted there for a few minutes, and Dillon left her to her thoughts.

Was this what she'd felt when he'd taken her to Earth's war memorials? There were so many back home, and he wondered if she'd want to see some of the ones in Europe, Africa, and other parts of the world. It was something a lot of people found macabre, but he liked to remember history, even the sad and bad bits, to keep it close to his heart and learn from it. It was part of what had made him stop Sherisza from killing the man whose grave they stood beside outright, and that had led to quite a blessing.

At last, she rose again and gave Dillon a quick kiss and a long, tight hug under the strong afternoon sun. She took his hand and led him back to her old home, the Kwaagi imperial family still out enjoying the sunny yard. It occurred to Dillon that Kiandar might feel cold to them, so they enjoyed the sun as much as possible.

After saying hello to the family again, Sherisza walked with Dillon and the emperor out toward the street, away from any nearby ears. "Something is wrong?" she preempted him.

"I hate to impose upon you, but now that the invaders have been destroyed, it's time I go back home," Malshii said. "They are not done with my empire, I fear, and I need to be at the heart of it to lead it going forward. If you can, I'd ask you to continue your work upgrading our fighter wings, but at your leisure. I don't wish to pressure you with how important the work you are doing here is."

"We will be happy and honored to take you back to Kwaa-ganarr," Sherisza said. "How bad are things for the empire?"

"Right now, there's no direct hostility, but they're coming, Captain Rousilarru. The first strike was to test us; now they're coming in force to destroy us. I must get home and begin calling for aid from our allies in the Joint Senates. This is a war that will involve everyone, even you and Dillon, I'm afraid."

"We'll help any way we can," Dillon said, leaving off the honorific for his sake.

"Thank you both. My house is in disarray after the attack upon it. I'll have my work cut out for me when I get back," the emperor said.

"I hate to ask, but considering soldiers attacked us in the escape tunnels, was your first administrator killed defending you?" Dillon asked.

"Yes, she was," Malshii said, letting forth a mournful scent. "I will miss her. She was an asset to me, my household, and the empire as a whole. She will be difficult to replace."

"We might be able to help with that," Dillon said, glancing at Sherisza, and her golden eyes went wide before she smiled.

"Oh?" the emperor prompted.

"Come, let us introduce you to someone," Sherisza said, leading him toward the *Malshekt*.

———

"Just tell me it is not because you are tired of me," Azilija said.

<Actually...>

"Shut up, Daevol," Dillon laughed.

"Not at all," Sherisza said. "This is a great opportunity for you to help your emperor and your people. I am most appreciative of all you have done in helping me bring my people here to settle in this time, and for keeping my secrets. I would make you a permanent part of my crew if it were the best option for you, but it is not. Becoming first administrator to the emperor will open many more doors for a woman of your talents."

"Thank you, Captain, it means a lot to me. And your compliments are an honor. I am glad to have helped foster friendship between Kwaaganarr and Kiandar, and I look forward to seeing you and Dillon in the future."

"That may happen quite a bit if war really is coming," Dillon said. "We don't fly a fighter ship, but the *Malshekt* does pretty well for herself, I think."

"She does. As do you and the captain," Azi agreed.

"Well, we will be delivering you and the imperial family home, so we have a few more meals we may share before you go," Sherisza said. "Emperor Malshii and his family should be joining us soon, and then we may depart. We cannot stay; there is too much at stake."

"And you have more of your people to rescue. It is as it should be. Thank you," the Kwaagi woman said. She bowed to Dillon and Sherisza, then went into her cabin and shut the door. Dillon expected she was getting ready to meet the imperial family for the first time.

"I'm gonna miss her," he said.

"As am I. And poor Daevol... he may have to go back to heckling *you*, Dillon."

"He'd better not. I've got a whole bag of new insults to try."

<That sounds suspiciously like a challenge.>

"Game on, *Winston*."

<Why you...>

Sherisza laughed and sat at her console, laying in a course to be prepared in advance.

<Video message coming in from Earth.>

"Feed it through on the main HUD," Dillon said, sitting beside Sherisza.

"Hi baby," Sasha said, smiling at her son. "So good to see you again, Sherisza."

"Hello, Sasha," the Kiandarian returned.

"How is everything?" Dillon's mother asked, and Dillon and Sherisza exchanged a glance. "Oh, that good as usual, huh?"

"Let's just say you should be hearing from the Kwaagi soon," Dillon answered, leaving out all the troubles the *Malshekt* had faced on its own. "But that can wait. What's up?"

"That's what we're wondering. Are you two planning to come back to Earth soon?"

Dillon looked at Sherisza again. She smiled and said, "Whenever you would like us to. As your sister said, I *do* have the fastest ship in the known galaxy."

"Then let's set the date for eleven days from today. It'll be a Saturday, and I should be able to get the whole family here for the wedding. Even Uncle Amos, I think! I'll let Reverend Warner know, and we already have most of the decorations and other things on hand. Sherisza, would you like to come early and get fitted for a dress?"

"A dress?" she echoed.

"Oh, here, look," Sasha said, adding some wedding dresses to the video feed. "Traditional style human wedding dresses. There are plenty of options from different regions around the world, but it's totally up to you. You can always get married in your work clothes if you really want to. Lord knows Dillon would like that."

"Thanks, Mom," he chuckled with a playful eyeroll.

"This does not suit me," Sherisza said, her mouth tightened as though afraid to be offensive. "However, I will come a couple of days early so we can find something appropriate."

"Good luck finding something on Earth with a hole for your tail on short notice," Dillon teased. "Wear whatever you like, I'm not going to complain."

"I did not think you would, but I would like to look as nice as you will in that suit of yours."

The sound of people coming up the steps preceded the emperor and his family arriving on the *Malshekt*, and Malshii studied Sasha on the holodisplay.

"Mom, may I introduce you to Emperor Malshii Denexxtu of the Kwaagi," Dillon said with a gesture toward him. "Emperor, this is my mother, Sasha Mackey."

"Oh my goodness," Sasha said, bowing her head a bit. "It's an honor, Your Majesty."

"The honor is mine, madam," he said cordially in Terran English. His grasp of the language was amazing, and Dillon wondered when and where he'd learned and practiced it. "Your son is one of the finest humans I have ever heard of, much less had the pleasure of meeting, and he stands as evidence of the honor of his parents and his people."

Dillon tried not to look as chuffed as he felt at that compliment, but his mother couldn't help blinking a few times. "Thank you, sir," Sasha said.

"I expect I may be coming to Terra Prime personally to meet with the Joint Senates in the near future. I look forward to meeting you and your spouse."

"And we look forward to hosting you," she returned.

Dillon smiled. "We've got to get the emperor and his family home, so we're gonna have to cut this call short, Mom. But we'll be home in eight or nine days to get everything ready."

"All right, baby, we'll see you then. Lots of love to you, and to you, too, Sherisza."

"Farewell, Sasha," Sherisza said. Once the holodisplay was dismissed, she turned in her seat to look up at Malshii. "Are you ready to head home, Your Majesty?"

"No," he answered, glancing at his wife and children. "But it is where we must be. Take us there at your leisure, Captain."

"Get comfortable in your cabin and I will soon have us underway. Once we are at cruising speed, I will bring out Azilija to meet you."

The Kwaagi emperor and his wife bowed their heads and then led their children to the guest cabins. Sherisza gave them a few minutes to get settled, staring out the viewport at a brilliant golden-orange sunset. The light danced in her eyes in a way Dillon found mesmerizing, and he realized he wasn't even seeing her as a Kiandarian anymore. She had leonine features, but she wasn't a lioness to him. She was his wife-to-be, his mate, the mother of his children, and the person he loved the most in the universe.

When Sherisza turned to him and saw the way he was looking at her, she dipped her head a bit in that blushing pose, but she smiled broadly. "What are you thinking?" she asked quietly.

"That I'm looking at the most beautiful woman in the galaxy," he said, no longer caring if it sounded corny out loud.

She took a deep breath in through her nose and turned to look out the viewport again. She let forth a wistful sigh, and Dillon knew why. No matter how much he loved her and how much he said and showed it, returns to Kiandar were always going to be bittersweet. She'd had to suffer to come to this place in her life, but she was accepting that what she had lost was still a part of her, and what she had gained would always be, too. And somehow, she had her goddess or his God–whatever the truth was–to thank for it all.

Something caught her eyes, then, and Dillon looked out the viewport with her. The Kiandarian children were all gathered on the front lawn of the nearest house, waving goodbye. Sherisza waved back, and Dillon flashed the *Malshekt*'s lights in farewell. That got the attention of the adults, and soon, many of them gathered to wave farewell, too. But as Sherisza often said, it wasn't goodbye or farewell.

It was *Until we meet again.*

"Like my father said, this is what we fight for. What the emperor is going to fight for. What the Joint Senates will hopefully agree to fight for," Dillon said, and she smiled again.

And then Sherisza got them airborne, on their way to two new beginnings.

The start of a war...

...and the start of their life as husband and wife.

———

THE STORY CONTINUES IN BOOK 3,
A Clash of Empires

THANK YOU FOR READING A GLIMPSE BEYOND

WE HOPE you enjoyed it as much as we enjoyed bringing it to you. We just wanted to take a moment to encourage you to review the book. Follow this link: A Glimpse Beyond to be directed to the book's Amazon product page to leave your review.

Every review helps further the author's reach and, ultimately, helps them continue writing fantastic books for us all to enjoy.

———

ALSO IN SERIES
Escaping Gravity
A Glimpse Beyond
A Clash of Empires

———

You can also join our non-spam mailing list by visiting www.subscribepage.com/AethonReadersGroup and never miss out on future releases. You'll also receive three full books completely Free as our thanks to you.

Facebook | Instagram | Twitter | Website

Want to discuss our books with other readers and even the authors? Join our Discord server today and be a part of the Aethon community.

They've plundered their way across the galaxy and just found the score of a lifetime. All they have to do is steal from the most ruthless crime lord in the galaxy. What could possibly go wrong? Yan and his band of rogues are intent on plundering their way to fame and fortune. When they stumble across the score of a lifetime, they quickly go all in for one last job. With everything on the line, there's no way they can fail. At least that's what they're hoping. In the end, they just might have gotten into something bigger than they ever imagined possible.

Get Most Wanted Now!

———

Holding a galaxy together ain't easy, especially when that galaxy is out to kill you. Doug Lancer is on the run. When the peace-keeping military known as the Federation and the law-enforcing Galactic Rangers join forces, forming the Galactic Empire, things quickly go south, especially for anyone not on-board. Hunted by his former brothers, Lancer is reduced to bounty-hunting to survive. When his path crosses with an ex-imperial fighter pilot fleeing the Empire, things get even worse. Can he stick to his convictions and oath as a Ranger, or will he fold under the pressure? And how can he and the band of outlaws he teams with hope to stand up to a galaxy-spanning empire without getting blown to space debris?

Get Hyperspace Outlaws Now!

———

In the West, there are worse things to fear than bandits and outlaws. Demons. Monsters. Witches. James Crowley's sacred duty as a Black Badge is to hunt them down and send them packing, banish them from the mortal realm for good. He didn't choose this life. No. He didn't choose life at all. Shot dead in a gunfight many years ago, now he's stuck in purgatory, serving the whims of the White Throne to avoid falling to hell. Not quite undead, though not alive either, the best he can hope for is to work off his penance and fade away. This time, the White Throne has sent him investigate a strange bank robbery in Lonely Hill. An outlaw with the ability to conjure ice has frozen and shattered open the bank vault and is now on a spree, robbing the region for all it's worth. In his quest to track down the ice-wielder and suss out which demon is behind granting a mortal such power, Crowley finds himself face-to-face with hellish beasts, shapeshifters, and, worse … temptation. But the truth behind the attacks is worse than he ever imagined … *The Witcher* meets *The Dresden Files* in **this weird Western series by the Audible number-one bestselling duo behind** *Dead Acre.*

GET COLD AS HELL NOW AND EXPERIENCE WHAT
PUBLISHER'S WEEKLY CALLED PERFECT FOR FANS
OF JIM BUTCHER AND MIKE CAREY.

Also available on audio, voiced by Red Dead Redemption 2's
Roger Clark (Arthur Morgan)

For all our Sci-Fi books, visit our website.

9 798882 032484